THE CASE BOOK OF IRENE ADLER

The Irene Adler Trilogy

San Cassimally

Green Okapi Press
Liverpool & Edinburgh
Copyright © 2014 San Cassimally
All rights reserved.
ISBN-13: 9781497301573
ISBN-10: 1497301572
Library of Congress Control Number: 2014905252
CreateSpace Independent Publishing Platform
North Charleston, South Carolina

For
Hakim, Karim and Katrina

CONTENTS

Prologue

Whilst cleaning Mr Holmes' study, I stumbled on the piece below, reproduced here in full, and got the idea to write my own casebook. Mr Reynolds had often suggested that I do so. The money would be more than welcome, as I have responsibilities. The fact that Dr Watson, in his misguided loyalty to Sherlock Holmes, chose to withhold certain facts from his reading public was an added incentive. Sadly he also sometimes ever so slightly filtered away anything he thought likely to diminish his hero. Unless I have been remiss in my reading of the Holmes canon, the words below have never appeared in the chronicler's account. In my admiration for the great detective, I am third to none - I do bow to the good doctor though. This was written on one single sheet of quarto in his characteristic scrawl:

I have often worried about his pallid complexion and, after a lot of preaching, I managed to persuade Holmes to take some exercise. For a while we got into the habit of catching the tram to Westminster once a week, and there we would walk briskly for just over an hour. One day as we were engaged in this fruitful occupation in the Victoria Embankment Gardens, only recently completed by my friend Mr Bazalgette, we saw a handsome well-dressed lady accompanied by a boy who might have been nine or ten walking towards us. The boy had the most unusual limp. He put his left foot forward in the normal manner but when it came to his right foot, he raised it slightly, moved it in an arc of a circle before putting it down again, dipping to his right as if this foot had gone down a cavity, before dragging it up again. Following what my friend and mentor had taught me over the years, I watched the movement more closely until I discovered that the sole of the boy's foot did not point forward but sideways to the right, which was what made him move in this peculiar manner. I gave Holmes a nudge and asked him in a whisper if he had perceived this.

'Yes, Watson, I have. And although I have never seen the boy, I can tell you that he celebrated his birthday last week, on the eleventh to be more precise.'

'My dear fellow, how can anybody deduce that from a limp.'

'I daresay I can tell you even more. He is called David, his father is a draper, the lady with him, his mother, was born in Pennsylvania and they were married in York Minster Cathedral.'

I stared at my companion, unsure as to whether he was not playing a joke on me.

'And to put you out of your misery, my dear fellow, I will tell you how I know. We can check with the little chap himself: As you know, I have made an extensive study of physical defects, as they help in my detective work. For this purpose, I attended a lecture at the Royal College of Surgeons only last year, where the eminent orthopedic surgeon Mr Archibald McLeod was expounding on a unique case which he treated a few years ago. The boy David was born with his right foot pointing the opposite way, which would have made it impossible for the little blighter to walk at all. McLeod was forced to carry out a landmark operation on the young patient, and succeeded in readjusting the foot, but fixing it at right angles to its normal position was the best that he could achieve, which at least permitted the boy to walk, albeit with the bad limp that we have just witnessed. The doctor however, decided that the risk involved was too high and resolved that he would not carry out another such an operation until some fresh techniques were developed. At that lecture I was able to meet and talk to the parents of David who happily recounted to me their history.'

As usual his explanations made everything seem pretty hackneyed, but as we were drawing level with mother and child, we stopped and bowed, indicating that we wished to speak if the lady was agreeable. She must have recognised Holmes and she stopped.

'Tell me, my young fellow, I just told my friend here that you celebrated your birthday last week, that you are called David and that your mother here was born in Pennsylvania. Can you confirm this for my friend here?' The little boy looked at him, then at me, on whom he finally settled his gaze.

'That's absolutely correct, Dr Watson,' at which, my esteemed friend gave him a baffled look.

'It's quite elementary, Mr Holmes.

***

Holmes had written below, in his firm writing: Doctor, I assure you that I have no objection whatsoever to your using this piece. I do not feel in the least threatened because the youngster put me in the shade.

CHAPTER ONE
Mrs Hudson Moves In
(1889)

Dr Watson may be a lovely man, but in his accounts of Mr Holmes' exploits, he has not always been scrupulous about details. I must first dispel the notion that I was their landlady. I was nothing of the sort. I came in as housekeeper, replacing Mrs Turner when she left for a position outside of London. I had my reasons for wanting to work for Mr Holmes and nobody else, and set about preparing to make myself acceptable to him. I knew that he would not want a woman of my age, so I decided that I would make myself up to appear older, more subdued and therefore more dependable. By dint of some rags wrapped round my girth, and putting on a dress and a fur coat that Armande's sister Catherine, who must have been twice my size, left with her when she moved to Senegal after she remarried, I managed to make myself appear buxom and dowdy. With the help of my stage kit, I added a few wrinkles artificially to my face, and practised walking with a waddle and speaking in the manner of a middle-aged semiliterate woman. I experimented with two pebbles in my mouth to puff my cheeks up a tad, but gave up on the idea suspecting that to an observant eye such as, my prospective employer's, this was too risky; besides when I spoke they clattered. I knew that in the exercise of his profession, no detail, however trivial, would escape him. But as is well-known, Mr Holmes is rather in awe of women and, in the guise of someone applying for a position, I had surmised that he would not look directly at me. Was I right or wrong in making that assumption? The events of the next few minutes justified my expectation.

I was, however, quite sanguine about my chances of passing muster and confidently directed my steps towards Baker Street to solicit for the position in person. I had no intention of keeping up my stout appearance in the knowledge that once I was settled in my post in Baker Street, Mr Holmes, who by all accounts is so full of self-belief, not to say dogmatic, would never question his original judgment, enabling me to gradually 'lose' some weight and wrinkles without him being any the wiser, but I would be in no hurry to alter my frumpish appearance. I had the testimonials all ready so when I rang the bell at Number 221B, all things considered, I did so boldly.

To my surprise, Mr Sherlock Holmes himself opened the door and ushered me in. I was struck by his gaunt face; I remembered it otherwise. 'Yes ma'am, you've come to the right place, and I am at your service to solve your difficulties, whatsoever they may be.' But always the cynic, I heard: '*Yes ma'am, the great, the unique Sherlock Holmes at your service, ready once again to dazzle you by my genius.*' He offered me a seat, sat down opposite me behind his desk and, before I could open my mouth, he was already talking.

'You will be amused to hear that I have already discovered a few things about you. But I daresay that should not surprise you, since you have taken the trouble to come seek my help. It must obviously be because you have heard of my powers of deduction. I own to not yet having worked out the purpose of your visit, but am confident of doing so shortly.' I admit to being dazzled by his approach, but did my best not to appear abashed.

'You have only recently arrived from across the Atlantic.' I was on the point of disabusing him, but he shook his head and wagged his finger imperiously, indicating that I should not interrupt his flow.

'You have clearly been under a lot of stress lately, which has caused you sleeplessness and loss of appetite. Ah yes, I see, you've only recently been widowed ... and he left you with a poor fatherless mite ... a boy, for certain.'

He said nothing but the stern look on his face spoke volumes and clearly said, '*Don't interrupt! Genius thinking!*'

'You see Mrs...I don't think you mentioned your name...' (*'Of course not, when did you give me the opportunity.'*)

'Mrs Hudson, Martha Hudson.'

'As I was saying, Mrs Hudson, if you keep your eyes and ears open,' he said wagging a finger, 'and make use of your sense of smell ... capital that ... the mysteries of the world will open up for you like a rosebud whose time has come.' He smiled, or rather twitched his lips in a quick movement, and stretching his hands forward, approached his fingers but not quite allowing them to touch for a while. I was speechless and he looked at me with his steely blue eyes, in a not unfriendly manner, and asked in a whisper: 'Am I not right?'

'Yes and no,' I said.

'And I'll tell you, dear Mrs Hudson, I don't indulge in magic. How did I know that you only recently came from America? Elementary, dear lady. The fur collar on your coat is of the pine squirrel - and I happen to have written a monograph on furs of different types of American squirrels. The pine squirrel, though widespread in America, has not yet crossed over to our shores.'

'But-'

Mr Holmes raised an imperious finger ordering silence. I made up my mind to just listen and enjoy the moment.

'Your recent widowhood is writ large in the contrast between your expensive coat and your very modest shoes. Only a well-to-do husband could afford to buy his wife an expensive coat like yours, but when I notice your footwear, it must be apparent even to a nincompoop' (*which he obviously was not, he didn't need to say*) 'that the well-to-do husband is no longer able to provide. So you must be a widow.' (*Couldn't the husband have gone bankrupt, or run away with another woman?*)

'How do I know that you have had a loss of appetite? I'll tell you forthwith. To an observant eye' (*and none are more so than mine*) 'the very handsome dress you are wearing, is ... if you pardon my lack of gallantry ... floating around your frame in a manner suggesting that it is at least one size too large, possibly two-

'But Mr 'Olmes, how do you know about...'

'Which I hasten to add, does not detract in the least from your elegance.' (*Who said he had no way with the fair sex?*)

He can't have missed my put-on look of awe and incredulity.

'Your loss of weight is a clear indication of stress caused by lack of appetite and sleeplessness, which condition, I might swiftly add, is confirmed by those rings under your eyes. Am I not right?' I was glad he had not spotted my carbon markings. I thought I should have my say now, but before I was able to open my mouth, he had again instructed me in no uncertain manner that he expected no contribution from me, just acquiescence. So, I...eh...just acquiesced.

'And now, I will reveal,' and I could almost hear the roll of drum, 'how I discovered that you are the mother of a little boy.'

' 'Ow?' I managed to blurt out.

'It has not escaped me that the right collar of your upper garment is ever-so-slightly crumpled, indicating a small child has been pulling at it.' I can swear that there wasn't the slightest mark on the collar, but pretended awe at his powers of observation.

'But Mr 'Olmes, you must allow that girls also tug at their mother's clothing.'

'Indeed I do, Mrs Hudson, indeed I do, but boys always pull the right collar and girls the left.' (*Poppycock!*) I hope I was only thinking this and had not blurted it out aloud.

'Now, Mrs Hudson, I don't want you to tell me that I am ninety per cent right, or even ninety-nine, but one hundred percent!' I said nothing, in an attempt to find a tactful way of contradicting him.

'No sir, you are not ninety percent right.'

'Ha! I knew it.' (*Bye bye post.*)

'Mr 'Olmes sir, you are one hundred per cent...eh...wrong.' On hearing this he fairly bobbed up like a jack-in-the-box.

'But that's impossible, Mrs Hudson, it must indeed be as I told you.'

He had become as pale as a ghost, his eyes suddenly appeared sunken and cruel and I noticed that his hands were shaking like a poplar.

'It is as you say, Mr 'Olmes,' I blurted out. (*Had the horse already bolted from the stable?*) He stared at me, frowning darkly, no doubt formulating a salvo at me for not making up my mind.

'It is?' He said, vindicated. Had I managed to square that circle?

'Everything you said is true, Mr 'Olmes, but true of my sister Catherine, whose garments I had inherited. She only recently came back from California, as you rightly said, when her husband passed away.' To avoid too many explanations I turned Catherine into *my* sister.

'And she is much stouter than you, Mrs Hudson, is that right?' His smile showed that he bore me no resentment. (*Is my job saved though?*)

'Yes, and I was wearing those clothes to come for the interview.' The look of anguish had completely disappeared by now, and his face was glowing like rosé wine.

'And to what do I owe the unexpected pleasure of your visit? Did I hear you use the word interview? Am I to deduce that you have come applying for the position made vacant by Mrs Turner's completely unreasonable decision to move to the country? The good opinion people have of country air is much exaggerated, Mrs Hudson, take it from me.'

'One hundred percent right as usual,' I said, and he looked at me with gratitude and I discovered that he had no ear for irony.

Dr Watson chose that very moment to come in, and Holmes greeted him with great good humour and bonhomie.

'Mrs Hudson, pray tell Dr Watson how the moment you ...' He did not however let me, but himself went on with the account of how I had no sooner walked in that he told me the full history of my sister. Watson looked at him with what later I thought of as his, "What else does the world expect of the great Sherlock Holmes?" look.

'One hundred percent accurate too!' he said. And I nodded politely. I did not even have to show him the fake testimonial from "Monsieur Le Marquis de Traverson" that I had so much difficulty persuading Artémise to counterfeit, and the position was mine.

It is not my intention here to deny that the man has one of the most brilliant minds, if not *the* most brilliant, that I have ever encountered. When Dr Watson began publishing his accounts of the cases, I read them avidly.

***

With my curious disposition I have always kept my ears to the ground, or more accurately to the door and walls, and my eyes behind winking curtains. So I was usually aware of whatever case was under scrutiny. Neither of the two men thought of discussing it with me. Why should they? But sometimes when the doctor was busy building up his practice, and when the detective had a big conundrum to solve, he would ask me to make him a cup of tea.

'And bring two cups, Mrs H, oh, and those scones only you know how to bake...' It was only when we were alone that he ever referred to me as Mrs H, creating an imperceptible feeling of intimacy between us. I would sit myself in the armchair opposite his desk, and he would even pour me a cup. He did not need me to speak, but he would talk about the current case. All he wanted was a listener. I knew better than to open my mouth except when I desired to put a morsel of pastry in it.

'Now listen to this hypothesis, Mrs H-'

'And, pray sir, what is a hypopo... what you said?' I thought it was politic to pretend simplicity and ignorance.

'Hypotheses are dangerous toys to play with because you blink and they harden into half-truth and this itself ends up as a conviction. You see what I mean?' (*Genius detective yes, but pedagogue, never!*)

'We don't want the wrong people convicted, eh! Dangerous! But I will advance two of them... hypotheses... one hypothesis, two hy-po-the- ses... and I would like to hear which one your instinct tells you is the correct one. I don't want to put you under any pressure, I won't demand your reasons, just your gut feeling, if you will Mrs H.' Then he'd put his ideas to me and if I felt able to make a comment I would do so, otherwise I'd clam up, demur and shake my head. Whenever I did support an hypothesis, he would nod and invariably say that his instincts and mine were concurrent, adding, 'Not that one must always listen to the little voice if it is unsupported by logic, but it offers a good start.'

For someone who prides himself on his powers of observation, although I made special effort to show how tired my legs were, and how badly my back was hurting, he never asked about my ailments, confirming my suspicions that he is not really interested in people as such. I have not once caught him looking directly at me which, in view of my impersonation, is reassuring. The doctor is nothing but courteous to me, but he is distant and formal, never showing any interest in my health either. When he was around, Mr Holmes naturally never shared an hypothesis with me.

The two gentlemen never showed anything but courtesy to me at all times, so I am not going to start spreading insinuations. I will maintain to the death that Dr Watson does not tell untruths in his account —hardly ever— but he's not above embellishing facts and committing sins of omissions. And of course Mr Holmes, who does have a big ego, says nothing because these discrepancies always show him in a flattering light. Oh, another thing there have been rumours about the nature of their relationship given that for some time they were both bachelors and shared the same roof. Even after the arrival of Mrs Watson on the scene they were always together. Don't expect me to dish the dirt on them as there is none. I never caught them exchanging the sort of glances I have witnessed between some of Lord Clarihoe's friends. What's more, Mr Holmes and the doctor never once came within touching distance of one another. It was the great man himself who taught me to sharpen my powers of observation. Mrs Hudson, he has said more than once, the good Lord gave you eyes and ears, the power of smell and a brain. Use them and the world will contain fewer mysteries. All I am saying is that I have sometimes caught an expression in the doctor's eyes when he looks at Mr Sherlock, reminiscent of a look on dear Michael, who was besotted with me, when we were rehearsing *The Maid of 'Ackney*.

I admit to feeling frustrated when a case was ongoing and I was unable to be part of the team. Often I might even have an hypothesis, but it would have been injudicious of me to pass on my ideas to the detective unsolicited. Fortunately, I discovered that when he comes out of his cocaine torpor, although this might strike some as contradictory, he is befuddled and at the same time acutely aware. His antennae seem to be working overtime then. The moment I come into the room, even when I walk on tiptoes, he signifies that my presence has been detected. He would incline his head in my direction, and without opening his eyes, he would invariabl says, 'Oh, it's you Irene...' before giving in to gibberish.

I did not immediately register this the first time, thinking that he might have been saying, "I dream..." I was mightily surprised when I caught the syllables Irene again. I had never appreciated the impact that the much maligned Irene Adler had made upon him. He would mumble something which I took to mean, 'Come and sit near me.' I would comply and talk to him. He would respond but when he came out of his torpor, he would show no recollection of what had gone on. I was speechless the first time I suggested to him, in his drugged state, that in my opinion the confession signed by the butler of Lord Hopewell, the prime suspect in the case of the theft of a Holman Hunt painting, had been beaten out of him by the police, and heard him offer this hypothesis to Dr Watson the same afternoon. Later it transpired that his lordship was indeed trying to make a fraudulent insurance claim. After that, I have, on a number of occasions, offered my ha'penny worth, which helped him get better insight into a case. Neither he nor Dr Watson seemed aware of my contribution, nor was it acknowledged in the chronicles and I was not disquieted. It is not my intention to dwell upon those instances. However, when my contribution was offered openly or has been central to the resolution of a case, I feel I ought to put the record straight. I will use the well-known case of the Red-Headed League to illustrate my point. I shall not say that the case would not have been solved without my help, only that the villain might have gotten away with the loot first.

Oh, an afterthought: Although Mr Holmes never once referred to it, I am sure he discovered my true identity at an early stage in our acquaintanceship, but it suited both of us to pretend neither of us knew the other knew that I was Irene Adler.

CHAPTER TWO

How The Club des As Began

(1882)

The name Irene Adler inspires awe in people. So much nonsense has been written about me that I am going to keep a truthful account of my life and adventures, although it would be injudicious of me to have them made public at the moment.

I was not born in New Jersey as has been said. A self-respecting woman never reveals her date of birth, but I am a true Englishwoman, albeit born to an Austrian father, the wonderful bass baritone Wilhelm Adler, who never had the opportunity of showing the world to what heights he could rise as he was cut down at an early age by a mysterious ailment. My mother was a devout Catholic Glaswegian nurse.

Although I had a reasonable voice and aimed to follow in my dear father's footsteps and become an opera singer, I was not lucky in my chosen career. Admittedly, I might not have had the voice. I drifted onto the London stage instead, where under the name of Lily Constantine, I was a patchy if unspectacular success in plays by Aphra Behn, Mary Russell Mitford, Douglas Jerrold and Richard Brinsley Sheridan. Sadly I was not able to realise my full potential either. For a number of years I kept rooms in the house of a widowed French music hall actress, not much older than myself. Her elderly husband had left her a handsome property on Water Lane, Brixton. As she disliked her married name of Mrs Lowchin, she chose to be called by her maiden name of *Mademoiselle* Armande Le Solliec. Although I was not averse to the pleasures of the flesh, I absolutely refused to trade my favours for parts when impresarios and theatre owners indicated that the road to the planks passed through their alcoves. Even if my strict Mam had not inculcated some of her values into me, pride alone would have dictated to me to starve rather than take that unsavoury path.

I never starved. There were minor parts for the taking and I was not choosy. I worked with many excellent people in the theatre world, who would remain my lifelong friends and we had many good times together. I have believed myself to be in love on a few occasions but none of these *amours* ended unhappily or even in tears. I may have a sensual and passionate nature, but a romantic I am not.

I never contemplated crime as a profession or as a hobby. That evolved quite naturally. One night after a show, a dashing young gentleman came backstage to offer me an orchid and bonbons, swearing he had fallen heads over heels in love with me. I knew what he was after and as Mademoiselle Armande had no objection to what she called '*un peu de gaîté dans sa vie*', and understanding very clearly what Mr Jasper Coleville-Mountdown's intentions were, I accepted his invitation to champagne and supper at The Ritz. Naturally we ended up in my bed in Water Lane.

Mam had taught us to always call a spade a spade, so I will own up to a very enjoyable night of love, after which we slept in each other's arms. My poor father had inherited a family heirloom, a moderately valuable ruby-encrusted brooch, which he gave to Mam on their wedding day. This was passed on to me on her demise, and has been my most treasured possession. As I have always thought that beautiful things are made to be displayed and admired and not locked in strong boxes, I wear it on my blouse whenever I can. It was worth a small fortune. Armande estimated it at about fifty sovereigns. In the middle of the night, Jasper went to use the facilities and woke me up by knocking against a chair. Not wanting to make him feel guilty about the disturbance, I pretended to snore, mumbled something and turned over. I was puzzled when I saw that he was in no hurry to come back to bed. Discreetly opening my eyes so I might see the reason, I watched him in the moonlight coming in through the lace curtains, lingering and furtively moving around across the bedroom, picking little statuettes and trifles I displayed to decorate my room. To my amazement he bent down to pick up the blouse with the brooch still attached to it, which I had carelessly dropped on the floor last night in a frenzy of libidinous passion. Good man, I thought, he likes order. Then to my utter disbelief, he detached the jewel from it, dropped the garment where he had found it and walk on tiptoes towards the chair, on whose backrest he had tidily arranged his jacket, carefully slipping it in a pocket. He then sneaked back into bed with me, taking great care not to touch me. He promptly fell asleep. I was flabbergasted and unable to sleep for the rest of the night. There was this rich heir stealing from a near pauper. How depraved can that be! It was when I realised how profoundly asleep he was that an idea occurred to me. I got up noiselessly and, moonlight abetting felony once more, I was able to extract his bulging wallet from his inside pocket. I had espied where it was at The Ritz. I removed the notes and replaced them by some folded sheets of paper I had on my desk, took possession of my heirloom and climbed back into bed. I convinced myself that my Catholic mother would not have entirely disapproved of the manner in which I had dealt with the thieving aristocrat.

Next morning, when Jasper woke up, he was in a frantic hurry to leave Water Lane and rather inelegantly refused Mademoiselle's offer of 'A leetel somsing to put under your tith before affronting zee day.' I saw him feel the wallet inside his jacket, smile to himself and before Armande could shower him with more greetings he was gone.

I wasted no time in narrating the events of the night to my land-lady, and we rolled with laughter. Armande, however, stopped suddenly, all hilarity drained from her face, anxiety taking over. When I asked her what the matter was, she expressed apprehension about the possibility of Coleville-Mountdown going to the police to report the theft of his money.

'Ma chère,' she said with great authority, 'you are so naive, these pipple have a lot of poweur, 'e'll get you arrested and sent to the toweur of London. You're an actress, you're supposed to have no morals, they'll lock you eup and throw away ze key.' I found myself redoubling with laughter at her fears. I was very sanguine about my position.

'Going to the police to admit that he had stolen from a lady ... alright an actress ... and then afterwards become a victim of theft himself, is the last thing a young puppy like him is going to do, *Mademoiselle*. The fellow may be a worthless cad, but his pride is very important to him. No, he will never admit to being bested by a mere woman. What's fifty guineas to him?' When it became clear later that Coleville-Mountdown was not going to take any action, Armande's admiration for me grew and grew. Every time our paths crossed, she would laugh, shake her head and repeat, '*Le voleur volé, hein! Ah, sacrée* Irene, *va!*'

Although she had always treated me with great kindness, she had never invited me to her *soirées* where she received her circle of special friends. After the incident she asked me to join them the next time they came over. She thought that it would amuse them to hear the story of the aristocratic thief from my own lips. That was to be the start of my life of crime.

Armande had told me that her Bohemian friends held interesting views about the idle rich, people who acquired wealth by the sweat of others. Since they would come to play important roles in my life, I need to introduce them properly to my readers (said my editor, Mr Reynolds). I was greatly impressed by every single one of her friends: the Bishop, Lord Clarihoe, Bartola de Acestis, Anatole Frunk, Hugh Probert, Ivan Vissarionovich Chekhonte and Artémise Traverson. Later the group would be expanded by Coleridge, an erstwhile lover of mine whom I met when we were working together on stage. Although most of them would not be received in polite society, I found them to be people of sterling qualities. Were I to be shipwrecked on an island, I would blindly choose any one of them as a companion in the certainty that they would be as dependable as the tides.

The Bishop had been a Catholic priest who ran his modest parish near Epping Forest without attracting overdue attention to himself until one day his brother who lectured in Natural Sciences at Caius College gave him a copy of Darwin's *Origin of Species*. The book shook the very foundation of his deeply entrenched beliefs, which made him repudiate creationism and embrace evolution with a vengeance. Obviously he could not continue officiating after that. He now made a precarious living by teaching Latin in a grammar school in Putney.

I met Algernon Edward Norton, or Lord Clarihoe, for the first time one morning when he called on Armande to offer advice on some banking business ('I 'ave no 'ead for figueurs'). I found myself terribly attracted to him, his bearing, his cheerfulness. He noticed this and, in the most casual manner, gave me to understand that his romantic inclinations tilted towards people of his own sex. Then I hope we'll become great platonic friends, I averred. He is the least pompous man that I have ever come across. Peer of the realm though he be, he held unconventional views for someone who came from the privileged class. He advocated the end of the monarchy and the abolition of titles, which he said were an anachronism. Maybe it was because, as a man who had strong preferences for own sex, his mind had been concentrated on issues his class usually brushed under the carpet. Unimpeded by the presence of any sexual component in our relationship, we soon became the closest of friends. We often share a bed fondling each other's naked bodies and massaging each other's sore backs.

Bartola de Acestis was a woman of a certain notoriety, a *chanteuse*, who, after being acquitted of poisoning her husband, was forced to give up her career. She now earned her living by giving tuition to businessmen who needed foreign languages when travelling abroad.

Anatole Frunk, an accountant from Switzerland, readily admitted to us that he had been to prison for defrauding some clients, insisting that he was only guilty of being found out. If he could start again, he said unabashedly, he would be much more careful and not get caught. His credo? Stealing from anybody who could not honestly account for his wealth, far from being a sin, was a commandment - the eleventh. He was now making a living using a system that he had elaborated, which enabled him to win modest amounts on horse racing.

The history of the thespian Hugh Probert was probably the most extraordinary. He was born in the Valleys but had had a meteoric rise on the London stage. His Lear was said by the *cognoscenti* to be as near perfection as can be imagined. However, he had made theatrical history by unwittingly sabotaging a production of the play attended by the Prince of Wales. Had one of our authors of popular melodrama invented such a plot, his publisher would have gone bankrupt. The actress playing Goneril, who in the play was plotting her father's downfall, whilst waiting backstage for her cue, was so moved by the poignancy of his delivery that she broke down in tears and could not get into the skin of the treacherous daughter. This made a mess of the performance, whereupon the tragic Cordelia started giggling and the Fool had a breakdown on stage. Probert was now fighting alcoholism and depression, both fairly successfully, crediting the support of his friends at Water Lane for this.

Ivan Vissarionovitch Chekhonte was related to the Romanovs. Although his family owned over a thousand serfs and huge swathes of land in Muscovy, he hated the aristocracy and called them parasites. He had made London his temporary home, swearing that he would only ever go back to his homeland if the same fate happened to his cousins as befell the French monarchy in the last century. I was always a bit in awe of him and his size but he was a gentle giant.

I first heard of Artémise Guilleret Traverson when I saw his painting *Les Lavandières de l'Oise* at the *Salon des Réfusés*, when I was visiting Paris with Mam in my teens. He was an amazing painter and the art critics compared his work very favourably with Manet's *Déjeuner Sur l'Herbe*, which was displayed by its side. However, his fame had been short-lived and he had come to London in an attempt to link up with the Pre-Raphaelites. So far this had not happened.

I consider Armande as my mentor as well as my friend. She had been a Fan dancer once, but after marrying her rich (and older) husband, she had abandoned the cabaret. Now widowed, she made a comfortable living by renting out rooms in the large house Mr Lowchin had left her. Although some had done so in the past, none of her hand-picked friends lived at Water Lane any longer, but as there were any number of spare bedrooms at their disposal whenever the fancy took them, they were invited to stay overnight.

That first night, the visitors had brought *petits fours* and éclairs, *pâtés*, caviar, *marrons glâcés*, cognac and champagne and a lot more besides, but it was the conversation which I found the most sparkling. Anatole Frunk, speaking in his delightful staccato voice and enchanting accent, averred that theft was not always reprehensible. I was heartened to discover that this was a view unanimously held by the assembly. Not only is it not a sin to steal from those degenerate '*fils à papa*' with more money than sense, said Armande to immediate applause, but it is something that should be encouraged by everybody who had a heart. The Bishop solemnly said 'Amen!' The good-hearted Bartola suggested that such pickings be distributed to good causes, a sentiment greeted by unanimity. These ideas were to recur frequently, and from them sprouted the *Club des As*, a name Armande had chosen. We proudly dubbed ourselves "equalisers". Informally we agreed on a number of principles which will reveal themselves to our readers in due course.

This distinguished assembly immediately took to me, and, as the youngest, I soon became their mascot. None of them would hurt a fly, nor would refuse a hungry man his or her last piece of bread. I was as surprised as much as I was heartened (and flattered) when I discovered that my opinion on any topic was always sought, and when given, was much valued by this distinguished panel. Did this mean that there was more to this jobbing actress than met the eye?

In less than three weeks, we were earnestly discussing schemes designed to deviate money and items of jewellery, paintings or *objets d'art* from those people we had named "the Parasites." Oh, incidentally, in the company of this mixed band, I soon discovered that I had a great propensity for languages, and Bartola was more than happy to help me with my studies.

I never understood how or why I emerged as the driving force behind the *Club*, but when I mentioned this to Armande, she said, 'But *ma chérie*, it did not take long for everybodie to be amaized at the poweur, clarté and logique of your ideas.' Moi!

Anatole, who knew where to look, began by drawing a list of possible targets. In no time at all we were brimming with ideas and these were very soon being successfully carried out with astonishing ease. I have kept a record of all the details of our schemes and will use them in future articles for Mr Reynolds. The revenues from our ventures exceeded even our most optimistic expectations. As I said, they went to good causes, including our own. '*Charité bien ordonnée commence par soi-même,*' Armande proposed.

Lord Clarihoe, Uranian though he was, loved to parade me in the fashionable places, and regularly took me out to dinner at The Ritz, tea at The Palm Court and to Covent Garden and Sadler's Wells to attend operas and ballets.

Our exploits, or crimes if you will, have been well-chronicled in the press. Although the accounts were based on conjectures and were full of inaccuracies, they did not give an altogether unfair account of our activities. The reporters guessed the existence of an association but, of the eight or nine names associated with it, only mine seemed to have leaked out. Was I careless? Although they referred to us as villains and our actions as "their nefarious ventures" or "their daring felonies," no one could fail to detect ill-disguised admiration for them. Articles even suggested that we carried out our scams not for lucre, but for fun. I would like to point out, however, that we donated over ninety percent of our takings anonymously to charities which I shall not name to save them any stigma that would otherwise be accrued to them.

CHAPTER THREE
Red-haired Jabez
(1889)

Shortly after having been installed at Number 221B, I was cleaning house one morning when the doorbell rang. I opened it to reddest man I have ever met - I mean his hair. His face was rather sallow and pasty. Dr Watson is rather derogatory in his description of Jabez Wilson, calling him portly and obese, but in my opinion, he was no more so than the good doctor himself. A trivial point, perhaps.

I knew Jabez from his pawnbroker shop in Saxe-Coburgh Street, which I have been driven to visit by necessity on at least two occasions in the past. I found that as pawnbrokers went, Mr Wilson was professional and fair.

If there's one thing Mr Holmes cannot resist, it is playing his guessing games. Of course I know that they are logical deductions. He has worked this art to perfection and is usually right on, even if (exceptionally)? he was wrong in my case. But I have watched and listened to him and have seen how he does it. He has elaborated his technique for delivering his findings in the most dramatic manner possible, seemingly stating them negligently as afterthoughts. However, I know my man, and there is nothing casual about his pronouncement. It is disguised grandiloquence, with every word, every gesture, calculated to deliver the biggest possible effect and cause maximum amazement. I call this subdued self-aggrandisement. He nurtures his reputation as a top-notch detective by this two-pronged attack, his genuine genius for deduction on one flank and a bit of refined drama on the other.

'Observe Watson,' he said in characteristic Holmesian style, 'that Mr Wilson started life as a manual worker. He takes snuff, is a Freemason, and has spent time in China. He does a considerable amount of writing. Can *you* deduce anything else?'

He knows very well that poor Dr Watson had not seen beyond the visitors's portliness. Mr Jabez seemed stunned by these fairground she-nanigans, as if he was in the presence of Our Lord walking across the Galilee. The great man then explained to the pawnbroker how his right hand, being a size larger than the left, had indicated the manual nature of his labours. The wide-eyed Wilson readily revealed that he had been a ship's carpenter for a number of year.

'Holmes,' said the still bemused Watson, 'yes, we can see that, but how the devil did you know about the snuff ... or the Freemasonry?'

The consummate performer said nothing but, bending forward, picked a tiny speck, presumably a particle of tobacco, from Mr Wilson's coat and flicked it in the direction of his friend.

'As for the Freemasonry, I have observed that no one ever wore an Arc and Compass breast-pin who did not belong to that fraternity.'

'And 'ow did you know that I spend much time writing, Mr 'Olmes?' asked the dazzled Jabez.

'Mr Wilson, I will let my colleague Dr Watson answer that for you.'

I thought that was a bit cruel, for the poor man began to stammer and bluster, obviously having not the faintest clue. Through a chink in the door that I had craftily pushed open just wide enough to permit me to follow proceedings undetected, I immediately noticed the right cuff of Jabez's coat was shiny and the left one had a smooth patch near the elbow where one normally rests it, indicating that he indeed was often crouched upon his desk, doing damage to his clothing. Holmes seemed to have read my thoughts when he explained. At this, Watson shook his head in wonder and Wilson nodded gravely.

'Well, but 'ow did you figure China, sir?' That was the cue that my employer needed to propel himself into his "aren't I clever mode."

'My dear Mr Wilson, I'll gladly tell you how. I have had the honour of making a modest contribution to the literature of certain areas of interest to those of us fighting crime, among others, a study of tattoo marks. As a result I can confidently tell you that the trick of staining the fishes' scales with delicate pink - as is visible on the marking you're sporting above your wrist, is quite peculiar to China. When, in addition, I see a Kuang Hsu 5 Cash coin hanging from your watch chain, the proof becomes much more evident.'

Watson said, he never, and Wilson nodded in agreement.

Having been duly impressed by Holmes' wizardry, the client looked at the detective in obvious awe and began to relate the events leading to his being appointed a member of the Red-headed League by virtue of his flaming red follicles. A position which entitled him to a splendid stipend of four pounds a week. He explained that the League had benefited from the bequest of an American benefactor.

'What does membership of this League entail? For doing what?' asked my employer.

The League only demands a token presence, Mr Jabez explained, at which the doctor became quite excited.

'My good man, four pounds a week for doing what?'

'Something purely nominal.'

'What do you call purely nominal?'

'I had to undertake to be in the office of the League, or at least in the building, for a set period of time, four times a week. I'd forfeit my whole position forever if I didn't comply to these conditions, but it were only four hours a day.' And he elaborated: Mr Duncan Ross, the League's secretary, had insisted that neither sickness, nor business, nor anything else would be of any avail. He had to conform one hundred percent or lose his billet.

'And what the blazes were you supposed to do in those four hours,' asked the doctor impatiently.

'Copy out the Encyclopedia Britannica, sir.' Watson looked at him in amazement.

'Yes, sir, word for word.'

If Mr Holmes realised that this was an extraordinary activity, nothing in his expression revealed this, but my antennae began to vibrate alarmingly on hearing this.

'What about your work at the shop?' asked Mr Holmes. Mr Wilson was so flushed with pleasure when asked that his face became nearly as red as his head. And with obvious fondness, he explained how no man was better served than he, by his young devoted assistant, Vincent Spaulding.

'Mr Spaulding?'

'Ah, yes. My assistant.' Spaulding was the one who brought the League to Wilson's attention, and indeed encouraged him to apply for the position.

'If my head was as red as yours. Mr Wilson,' Spaulding had told him, 'I'd go like a shot myself.'

'I could use four pounds a week,' Jabez admitted. 'The lad is a treasure, gentlemen. A model worker, arrives early, leaves late. Knowledgeable too. He knows at a glance the value of rings and things people brought to be pawned. Why he chose to work for me I'll never know.'

I knew instantly.

'If I were Mr 'Enery 'Arrod himself,' the redheaded man continued, 'I'd have snapped him up, he'd be an asset to any big shop.'

'And how long have you benefited from the services of this paragon?' asked Mr Holmes. I think he too had finally seen the light.

Mr Jabez nodded happily, obviously basking in his fond memories of the young man. Only two months, he said, and needed no prompting to give a full account.

'By a happy coincidence, one afternoon Spaulding walked into me shop with something to pawn and we got talking. I was deeply impressed by the young fellow's manners and his knowledge of baubles and forgeries and expressed surprise that a man such as he could be short of money. Simple sir, he said, he didn't have a job. I'd give you one if I could, I says, but with our turnover and over'eads, the shop couldn't afford someone of your obvious worth. Ah, but I ain't greedy, Mr Wilson, Spaulding said.'

The long and short of it, Mr Holmes, the red-haired man said, there and then we agreed on terms which were highly advantageous to me. One thing though, Spaulding said, he had an 'obby. Could he use the basement to prepare his photographic solutions and develop his films? I said but of course, dear boy, of course, photography is an admirable 'obby.'

One did not have to be a genius to understand that all was not as it seemed, but the world is full of innocents like Mr Jabez Wilson, I'll be bound. And Dr Watson.

'It would seem that this happy state of affairs did not last.'

This took Wilson by surprise. 'How did you work that out, Mr Holmes?'

'Well, why else would you come here and ask for my help,' Holmes tut tutted.

'That's right,' conceded Wilson once he had stopped marvelling at the detective's uncanny powers. 'After four weeks, one morning when I went to Pope's Court in Fleet Street ...'

'That's where the League's office is, did you say?' Dr Watson intervened. Wilson nodded.

'As I was saying, that morning there was a notice on the door.'

'The Red-headed League has moved,' said Holmes.

Jabez opened his eyes wide in admiration, but his smile showed he had struck on the means of putting one past the master as he added, 'Oh there was something else ... mind you, just the day's date ... October 8.1890.' Holmes was unable to hide his irritation at this childishness.

'It's clear as daylight to me,' guffawed Dr Watson. 'Spaulding has bolted with all your possessions. Wanted you out of the way, the villain. I guessed from the beginning.'

'Oh no, no,' Wilson shook his head, obviously hurt by this baseless attack on the integrity of his peerless assistant, 'Vincent's a good boy. He was in shock when he heard about the shabby treatment I had received. He's still with me and is holding the fort right now as we speak. What would I do without him?'

At that moment, Mr Holmes had a call of nature. Begging the pardon of his visitor, he nearly crushed my nose as he pushed the door open in my face. Yes I was eavesdropping. I have already admitted to this weakness. Mr Holmes tut tutted merrily, wagging a finger at me playfully. I knew that he did not disapprove of the practice.

'Mr 'Olmes,' I said as I followed him, 'it is clear as daylight to me that Spaulding is up to something.'

'No, Martha,' he said. He rarely uses my first name. He isn't even sure what it is. Sometimes he says Martha, sometimes Mary. He has even called me Mrs Turner. When he is drugged, he calls me Irene.

'Anyway,' he said, 'I was also minded to give credence to that theory, Mrs Hudson, until Mr Wilson said that Spaulding was still working at the pawnshop. Remember, we must not jump to conclusions on insufficient grounds.' I did not much care for his wagging finger.

'I see,' I said, but I could not dismiss my hypothesis. There must be an explanation even if we aren't aware of it, I surmised. By the time Mr Holmes had done his business, I had put some order into my thoughts. I cornered him again as he was going back to the front room. He looked at me with his great piercing eyes. I thought he was going to order me to mind my kitchen and cutlery, or say something harsh to me, but instead he smiled, nodded, and allowed me to air my views. He excused himself and rejoined his visitor and the doctor. I immediately regained my position behind the door and pressed an ear against it.

'Tell me, what is he like, this Vincent Spaulding?' I heard Sherlock ask. I was happy that my words seemed to have produced an effect upon him. Mr Wilson was happy to oblige. Small, stout-built, very quick in his ways, no hair on his face though he's not short of thirty. Has a white splash of acid upon his forehead. I saw my employer sit up in his chair in considerable excitement on hearing this.

'Ah!' he said, seemingly suddenly enlightened, 'have you ever observed that his ears are pierced for earrings?'

'Yes, sir,' said Mr Jabez, 'he told me that a Gypsy had done it for him at a fair when he was a lad.'

'Hum!' said the detective sinking back in his chair, deep in thought. 'And he attended to your business in your absence?'

'With great devotion, Mr 'Olmes. I have nothing to complain of, sir. Young Vincent is as dependable as clients the day after the races.'

For a whole minute nobody said a word. I watched Holmes, his eyes closed, his two hands raised under his chin, fingertips touching, lost in thought.

'I shall be happy to give you an opinion upon the subject in due course,' he said finally breaking the silence. 'Today is Saturday and I hope that by Monday we may come to a conclusion.'

'Well, Watson,' he said when our visitor had left, 'what do you make of it all?'

'I make nothing of it,' said the good doctor. 'It is a damned mysterious business.'

For my part I was now convinced that Spaulding was up to his neck in this affair, and I had indeed told my employer what I suspected was at the root of it. He never confided in me as to what his own thoughts might have been.

On the morrow he disappeared for a whole day with the doctor. I know they went to a concert. He needs music to help him think, either to listen to, or to produce it himself on his violin. I was relieved that he did not open the cabinet where he keeps the white powder. When they regained Baker Street late that night, I served them a reheated leg of lamb, but they never noticed. I overheard them talking and gathered that they had taken a short walk to Saxe-Coburg Square, where Mr Wilson's pawnshop is. I remembered it as a poky little place with three gilt balls and a brown board with "Jabez Wilson" in white letters in front.

'My dear Holmes,' said Dr Watson, who I had rarely seen in such good spirits before. 'I meant to ask, when we walked up and down the square studying the location and the houses. Why did you thump vigorously on the pavement three times with your stick?'

'So you noticed?' said Holmes. 'Nothing escapes you, does it?' The doctor beamed with pleasure. I am surprised that he does not pick on his friend's sarcasm.

Mr Holmes has this habit which drives me mad sometimes. Often he chooses to ignore what you ask him as if he never heard your question. He clearly had no intention of enlightening the poor doctor.

I had to do my own detective work to untangle relevant information from their irritatingly mixed-up ramblings, as they jumped from one topic to the next in a seemingly random nature. It became clear to me that they ended up knocking on the door of the esteemed Mr Wilson's shop, when a bright-looking, clean-chinned young fellow, opened the door and asked them to please step inside.

'Capital, my dear fellow, capital, your asking him for the way to the Strand,' guffawed Doctor Watson, 'when all the time what you wanted was ... eh, I mean it was so obvious that you pretended to inquire your way merely so you might take a good look at Spaulding. It was he, wasn't it?' Dr Watson glowed with triumph and his eyes sparkled merrily as he had worked that out, or so he thought.

'Not him, my dear fellow,' said the detective with a sneer, never too keen to spare his companion's feelings.

'W-what then?'

'The knees of his trousers, Watson,' was the curt answer.

'What the blazes did you want to see the knees of his trousers for? All trouser knees look alike, don't they?' After a bemused pause he asked, 'And pray, what did you see?'

'What I expected to see,' was the perverse reply.

'And why did you beat the pavement, Holmes?' The doctor asked again, without the slightest hint of irritation. It was clear to me that Holmes had not the least intention of vouchsafing an explanation.

'My dear Watson,' the detective answered in his superior manner which makes me wonder how the doctor puts up with his discourtesy. 'You have all the ingredients for a delicious meal of the mind in your possession. I shall not insult your intelligence by telling you how to light a stove to cook it. You give the matter some thought and the truth will appear in front of you.'

'But, but...' spluttered the good doctor. He was even more confused now than he was before.

'If you will be so good as to indulge me and give me a couple of hours of your time, we will be able to stop London's fourth smartest criminal from doing his worst.'

'How do we know that?' asked the doctor in despair.

'Did you notice his earring? The acid mark? The frayed knee of his trousers? There were a total of eleven clues, dear doctor. Shall I name them all?' He treated the doctor very much like an experienced hair-dresser his twelve-year-old apprentice, except that I have never seen him clip the medical man on the ear. Doctor Watson blinked like someone was shining a light in his eyes.

'You r-r-reckon Jabez Wilson's been planning a big coup?' The doctor asked. Then alarmingly, he burst out laughing in a knowing manner. 'I see quite clearly now, it's a case of insurance fraud, I never trusted that red-haired fellow.'

'When we were in Saxe-Coburg Square, did you not notice what was next to Mortimer's the tobacconist?' Holmes asked, ignoring his friend's words completely.

'I did,' exclaimed the doctor happily, 'the little newspaper shop. No it did not escape my attention, Holmes. Oh no, my dear fellow, I've learnt a thing or two since I met you.'

'Then you can't have missed the Coburg branch of the City and Suburban Bank?' The doctor seemed taken aback. I noticed that Holmes stated this as if he knew every street in London inside out. He then added, with a pointed look in my direction, 'Even Mrs Hudson knows this.'

'The b-b-ank? Did you say the bank? Can't say that I noticed. Is that relevant, Holmes?'

'We are going to stop a considerable crime being committed tonight, you and I, my dear Watson ... eh, but there will be some danger to this, so bring your army revolver with you when we meet later.'

'My revolver? Did you say there will be shooting?' A delighted Watson opened his eyes wide with excitement. He had completely regained his composure. I reflected on Wordsworth's notion that the child was the father of the man. Boys love playing soldiers and war games. Mr Holmes knew it and Dr Watson ... eh no, perhaps he didn't. Spaulding was too clever for that. He needed no guns, his brains were stronger than guns. He didn't go to all this planning, setting up a fake League for Red-headed gentlemen, dig tunnels, to then risk a shoot-out with the London coppers. You have to admire the fellow. He thought that he'd dig his tunnel after getting the poor Mr Jabez out of the way. After four weeks, when the work was done, all he needed to do was to enter the bank on Saturday night without so much as a by your leave, with his accomplice Mr Duncan Ross, serve themselves and then disappear with the loot. They needed no gun.

Mr Holmes had gotten in touch with Scotland Yard and the police agents were waiting for the two blackguards who walked straight into the trap that was waiting for them. I am not sure where my sympathy lay, between Mr Spaulding and the Bank.

It was exactly as the doctor described it in his narrative, but omitting my contribution. He was probably unaware of what transpired between Mr Holmes and me when the latter came out of the facilities?

'Mr Holmes,' I had said to him after he had flushed the toilet, 'when I went to Mr Jabez's shop, I couldn't fail to espy the City and Suburban Bank in Saxe-Coburg Square. From what I heard today, I bet that all these red-headed tomfooleries lead to what's inside there by means of a tunnel.'

'You mean from what you've eavesdropped today.' No, he was never one to give credit to others.

CHAPTER FOUR
The Millais Forgery
(1882)

The press usually goes wild with its conjectures about our multifarious activities. They print all manners of outlandish scenarios and, admittedly, it happens that every so often some of them hit target, but in the affair of the Millais forgery, they could not have been further from the truth. The public deserves to be presented with our version of the events, so they can determine for themselves what was fact and what was fiction in the many acres of print that they have been submitted to over the years. The art theft was a fairly typical case and I am about to put in writing all the facts associated with it but I might, one day, time permitting, write a complete history of our, shall I call them "misdemeanours"?

At one of our *soirées*, Ivan Vissarionovich, in a maudlin state after having imbibed too much vodka started talking about the great Russian artists. With tears in his eyes, he began extolling the personal as well as artistic virtues of his great hero Alexey Gavrilovich Venetsianov, regaling us with stories of how this descendent of Greek aristocracy had bought a small village and started his own school of painting by inviting common people from poor backgrounds and even serfs to join. He provided them with canvas and paint from his own pocket. One topic leading to another, we found ourselves talking about the possibility of stealing a work by a well-known Pre-Raphaelite. This idea took firm root in our minds and we began our preparations by visiting Baker's the auctioneers in Bond Street, combining pleasure with work, learning not only the finer points of the medium, but also the lie of the land in preparation for our action. In those days our notoriety was just burgeoning, and so, in spite of our extravagant appearances — for we loved exotic colours, silk scarves, beads and hats - our presence in those hallowed chambers went largely unnoticed.

The recently knighted Sir John Millais was considered the greatest artist of the age. When one night Traverson mentioned that Millais was engaged in painting *Miranda Watching the Tempest Brewing on her Island*, we looked at each other and chorused: Yes, that's our target! His last masterpiece had fetched five hundred guineas. We reckoned that we would earn ourselves upwards of six this time. A new crop of American millionaires was emerging and many wanted to buy respectability. Frunk had the contacts.

It was four in the morning when we suddenly took the daring decision to carry out our robbery under the very nose of all the good burghers come to bid for the painting at the gallery. Frunk had gathered that, after a recent clumsy attempt had been made to hold up the cab taking an exhibit which had just been sold to its new owner, Mr Baker had become apprehensive of similar mishaps and had hired Sherlock Holmes to ensure the safety of future exhibits. This news was greeted with gloom and despondency, but I told my friends to leave him to me, with no idea about how I would deal with the problem.

The first thing that had to be done was to steal a peek at the picture. One night Artémise and I made our way to Palace Gate in Kensington where Millais had his studio. While I kept guard outside, the Frenchman went in with the utmost ease, He had a good look at the work, making a *croquis* and notes of the colours used. The very next day he set to work. In very little time, he had produced his copy. A reflective Miranda in an ochre robe sitting on a rock with a little lamb by her side, watching dark clouds brewing up in the sky. The *Club* expressed its collective admiration of the piece, and wondered whether it might not well be better than the original.

We knew that Holmes was not going to circulate among the prospective buyers with "SHERLOCK HOLMES" writ large on his forehead. None of us knew what he looked like apart from Algernon, who had seen him once or twice before. I asked him to describe the man to us but however much he tried, I could not visualise him. Unfortunately Algie is not an artist, but I had an inspiration.

We sent word to Traverson to come to Water Lane to meet Algie and me. I sat with him in Armande's airy front room around a table where we had provided paper, pens and ink and asked him to draw likenesses according to Clarihoe's description. He began by producing a large number of aquiline noses. Algie picked two which he pronounced satisfactory. Artémise next worked on the eyes, producing a good few, none of which satisfied the expert. It was only after another hour that an eye passed muster. Lips were much easier, as was the subject's jutting jaw. The gaunt face and the cheekbones were quite elusive. It was after lunch that Algie finally pronounced them "astounding." Putting together these various parts was an arduous task. Only two hours later did Lord Clarihoe espress satisfaction. 'Artémise,' he exclaimed, 'I don't think a daguerreotype could have produced a better likeness. Quite astounding!'

We had learnt that besides Holmes, there would be vigilant eyes in every room on the day of the auction. It was clear that once an item had been deviated, there remained the bigger hurdle of removing it from the premises.

'So it's difficult, so we work on it, so zere!' thundered Armande. When we parted after a merry evening, we promised that we would each of us bring an idea next time we met. In the meantime we continued attending Baker's auctions regularly. However, we were now dressing ourselves less conspicuously, taking care to avoid being seen together. We usually went in pairs and met afterwards at Fernandez and Hammerstein's for lunch. We had seen with our own eyes how on an auction day, the exhibits were displayed across three or four halls, depending on the number of items in the program. Each room was about thirty feet long and twenty feet wide and were patrolled by two hawk-eyed guards. It was also a tradition at Baker's that potential bidders were served with champagne as they came in. Bartola, who could flutter eyelids with Madame de Pompadour was going to engage the attention of one Cerberus by offering him her champagne. This, we hoped, would halve the security, discarding Holmes, that is. Over three weeks she had lavished her seductive smiles on the guards, who now gave her polite nods every time they saw her. It was Coleridge - I will introduce him to you properly in due course - who said that we could do better and suggested a powerful laxative. It is tasteless and dissolves in water leaving no trace, he assured us. He knew a place in Tottenham Court Road where he could get it. The original plan kept being refined until we thought that although not all the possible dangers had been eliminated, it was now as good as it would ever get. We might be thought perverse, but in all our undertakings we relished the element of risk.

On the appointed day, we made our way to Bond Street, arriving separately at the auction house. Although no one had spread any rumour about Coleridge to this effect, we heard whispers that the Baganda of Buganda himself was interested in the bidding. We, bunch of iconoclasts that we were, punctuated this assembly of snobs and *cognoscenti* like commas and semicolons on the page, all the time sipping our champagne. The Millais was in one corner, leaning against the backrest of a velvet chair opposite a window admitting ample sunlight.

I was convinced that although Sherlock Holmes was aware of my notoriety, he had no idea of what I looked like. I had dressed myself in unspectacular clothes in order not to attract attention. In contrast, Armande was wearing a stupendous outfit. We had rehearsed every step meticulously. Arm in arm, we circulated around the gallery, conspicuously commenting on the various exhibits. Traverson's strategy enabled us to spot Holmes easily although the resourceful fellow had attached a moustache to his appearance. I sensed that he was on his guard and knew that the two of us were up to something. When we saw him stealthily winding his way through the crowd towards us, we made no effort to move away, pretending that we were unaware of him.

When we were close enough to him, I turned to Armande, and spoke to her in a stage whisper. 'You know Irene, I don't think you should spend your money on this painting, it's very dull if you ask me.'

We felt that Holmes was hooked. When Armande announced that she needed to go to the facilities, our stalker discreetly followed her, leaving me alone. Armande later told me that the hawk-eyed sleuth was waiting outside the powder room when she emerged from it and never once let her out of his sight for the duration.

For her part, as planned, Bartola had approached her guard target to engage him in conversation.

'You poor man,' she said, fluttering those eyelids, 'your poor feet must be killing you after standing guard for so long.'

'I ain't complaining none your ladyship,' the game fellow responded.

'I bet Mr Baker did not think of sending you a glass of water let alone some champagne,' she continued.

'We knows our place, yer ladyship.'

'Here, my good man, no one's looking, have this.' She forced her glass on the bemused man who stared at it open-mouthed.

'Drink it, my good man, it's not for holding.' In a flash, he had tipped the whole contents of the glass in his mouth, returning it to her like it was a live charcoal. The powder which the Baganda of Buganda had provided was a quick action laxative. Our friend opened her mouth wide as the man brushed past her and rushed out of the room. The others, on cue, moved with studied randomness and surrounded the second Cerberus, barring his view entirely. It then took no more than ten- seconds for me to extract Traverson's fake from under my garments with one hand, and seize the genuine Millais with the other. I deftly committed it into the knitted pocket under my skirt, simultaneously positioning the fake on the chair. Not a single member of the worshipful would-be buyers in the room was any the wiser to our prestidigitation. I had spent hours rehearsing this operation in preparation and it was therefore not surprising that it went so well. Admittedly, I was endowed with light fingers at birth.

To avoid arousing any suspicions, we had decided to brazen it out, and stay for the auction. It took a whole hour before the fake *Miranda* was moved to the gallery where the bidding was taking place. The auction master knocked his hammer on the lectern and demanded attention.

'Ladies and gentlemen, Oyez! Oyez! Recently the good name of Baker's the Auctioneers could have been damaged by a dastardly spate of forgeries which, in all innocence, we had the misfortune to handle. I do not need to tell you that Mr Samuel Baker and our team were completely unaware of this, relying a bit too readily on the goodwill of our artists and agents. We have however, resolved to tighten our operations, and are inaugurating a new feature to our proceedings. In front of your very eyes, we will have not one but two men of the highest integrity and expertise carry out their analysis, and confirm to you the authenticity of every item Graded A on our list. And of course few items are more deserving of this grade than Sir John's *Miranda*. Thank you. Herr Doctor Wertheimer and Professor Worthingdon de la Clairfontaine...'

At this point, two distinguished-looking worthies, both monocled and moustachioed, appeared, the lean one towering by a whole head over his orotund companion. They bowed to the audience and entreated each other to begin. Then each taking out a magnifying glass, they proceeded to examine Traverson's fake. We dared not look at each other. They tapped gently at the canvas, looked at each other gloomily several times, demurring and shrugging. We watched apprehensively in silence. The assembly followed the proceedings with bated breath until they finally seemed to have completed their assessment. With studied movements, they moved away from the painting with their backs to us. They made a right angle turn to face each other. They bowed, took a step back, and approached the auction master. Each whispered in one ear of the latter, who being much shorter than the one and much taller than the other, had to contort his frame and wriggle his head energetically to receive the messages being simultaneously delivered. He began by pinching his lips and demurring but then beamed a happy smile at the assembled crowd.

'Ladies and gentlemen, Herr Doctor Wertheimer and Professor Worthingdon de la Clairfontaine have been kind enough to confirm the one hundred percent authenticity of Mr Millais' latest masterpiece, I am delighted to inform you. We shall now begin procedures.' It took no more than eight minutes for the price of eight hundred and fifty guineas to be reached, when the hammer was struck and the delighted buyer of the fake opened his wallet.

Frunk's contact was also an internationally known art expert, a Swiss connoisseur who went around Europe buying masterpieces, no questions asked, for his reclusive millionaire American patron who bought paintings as an investment for his heirs, Frunk was told.

The genuine Millais was taken to Water Lane and kept in the cellar until the Swiss expert was able to come see it, which he did a week later.

'I neet to hev a look at it, bevore making an offer,' he said. Armande went down to collect *Miranda*, and when she came up with it, she placed it opposite the bay window where a good light was streaming in. Herr Dr Steinauer's face lit up as he approached it. He took out a small magnifying glass and more or less repeated what the pair at Baker's had done. He tapped it gently all over and we noticed that his face had changed expression. He turned round to face us, pursed his lips and shook his head gloomily.

'I cannot put be buzzled py this biece... a vurthy biece no toubt... I to not know its brovenance, it's not wisout merit, laties and chentlemen, put it is certainly no Millais. I am tisappointed that you hev mate me looce so much faluable time. *Wieder sehen, meine damen und herren.*'

If our faith in critics was badly shaken at Baker's, it now toppled over like a thunderstruck oak. We were dumbfounded, but once the thought of restituting it to Mr Millais occurred to me, the idea became irresistible to us, showing that, above everything else, we were artists of crime. We made up our minds to take it back to the eminent artist's studio in Kensington that very night. He, at least, would recognise it for what it was. How he reacted when he saw the painting, which was supposed to have been sold for a small fortune, back in his possession, we will of course never know. He changed one or two things, turned the lamb in to a rabbit, painted the dark clouds blue, modified the apprehension on the girl's face into one of serenity and renamed it *Miranda Looking at Sunrise*. It was the first Pre-Raphaelite painting to fetch over one thousand guineas.

Sherlock Holmes was said to have been congratulated for stopping anything untoward happening on the day of the auction. After the return of the genuine article to Millais, the latter invited him to Palace Gate, confided the truth to him and offered to immortalise him in paint if the great detective could fathom out the mystery of the theft in reverse. To this day, no painting of the detective has been found.

We had hoped that Traverson might have been able to break into that lucrative art market now that his work had been acknowledged by world experts as pure marble, albeit unbeknownst to them, but it took no more than a glimpse of anything he produced for the *cognoscenti* to shake their collective heads wearily, pinch their nose, demur and ... say nothing.

CHAPTER FIVE
The Mycroft Veto
(1884)

The events I shall recount forthwith took place before my time at Baker Street but I am taking the liberty of including the story here, because it has not seen the light of the day. Besides, I would be involved with some of the events connected to it later. I am doing this with Dr Watson's, admittedly grudging, consent. I learnt much later that Mr Holmes' brother Mycroft, who considered himself a guardian of the establishment, saw fit to demand that the story be quashed, but I owe him no fealty.

Having an enquiring mind, and being of an inquisitive bent, when Mr Holmes is away and I have complete liberty of the apartment, I take the opportunity of what my employer himself calls 'broadening my outlook.'

'Look around yourself, Mrs Hudson, seeing is not enough, *observe*! Do not just hear, *listen* actively, not just to the words, but how they are uttered, the pauses between them, smelling isn't enough my dear Mrs Hudson, *sniff*, feel with your fingertips, the surface and the chinks. Eavesdrop if you must, sneak glances through winking curtains, holes in the wall.' Clearly I did not need Mr Holmes to tell me to do things that I have done all my life anyway.

As is well known (at least to those who have followed Dr Watson's accounts of his cases), Holmes has files on a wide range of topics. These are methodically arranged, in a manner clearly commensurate with his orderly and clear thinking. I find few occupations more opportune to the 'broadening' of one's outlook than poring over them. Recently I came across a file bearing the name of Edward Hardstone. He is described as a wealthy *chevalier de l'industrie*, owner of the *Medea* and the *Unicorn*, a man of numerous affairs with a finger in many pies when it is not poking the eye of a rival. In other words, a crime genius. According to the notes, some in the hand of Mr Holmes, others in Dr Watson's, the man is a villain of the first order. He seems to have been accused of countless felonies, including more than one murder but he has always come out of the court unscathed. If anything, his reputation among the criminal fraternity was enhanced, making him more feared, therefore more powerful. He has a lawyer, a Mr Francis Waverick QC, who seems to work exclusively for him.

Edward, son of an innkeeper, was born in Wiltshire but ended in St Albans where he lives in an opulent mansion he facetiously calls *The Hut*, with his pack of hounds and a large retinue of ill-defined servants, many of them old recidivists with stained teeth and evil-looking eyes. He has never been married, but is always in the company of women, not all of them visibly disreputable. He is well-known as smuggler, gambler, huntsman, opium eater, drinker and lecher. There are suggestions in the reports that his shipping activities, on the surface conveying legitimate goods on which duty has been paid, is a front for his more lucrative if less legal pursuits, including gun running to rebel groups in southern Italy and the Balkans. According to one testimony, before docking at the Liverpool port, his ship would usually touch a small creek near Southport, where it is said that he possesses warehouses. Often, having signed papers for a trip to Brest, he would end up near the wine regions of Bordeaux. He was known to pay his crew over the odds. When hired, their capacity to keep mum and obey *any* order was valued above their seamanship. As a result, their loyalty to him was absolute. There have been reports of sailors falling overboard on the *Unicorn*, but these and similar unconscionable stories of his smuggling activities have attracted but scant attention from the police. Enquiries initiated on these rumours were systematically dropped "for lack of reasonable grounds," as Holmes comments sardonically in the margins.

As a gambler, he cannot abide losing. He has been known to stop people leaving his table when they were ahead. There is a suspicion that a man found on Watling Street about a year ago, with his throat slit, had won two thousand guineas at *The Hut* the previous night. Not one farthing was found on him. His carriage was found nearby, with his horse wandering the Hertfordshire wilds. After a cursory enquiry, the police announced that the dead man had been attacked by highwaymen who still operated on the Roman Road. No one interviewed Hardstone. The police seemed as much in awe of the man known in the whole of the County as Hardstone Ted, as was everyone else.

There is a daguerreotype of the scoundrel in the files. He is a solid giant of a man with clean shaven cheeks, a horseshoe moustache and sleepy eyes which gave him a lugubrious and sinister appearance. I covered the follicular growth to see whether this modified his look. It diminished the mournful but emphasised the sinister in the man. His baleful veiled eyes gave a distinct impression of pitilessness. Impeccably dressed in the photo, he has a horsewhip between his hands. Elsewhere in Holmes' notes there is an allusion to the fact that he is rarely seen without that implement, which the detective wryly calls his third hand. Further, he comments on his readiness to use it on the back of his servants. He boasts of being worth over one million pounds and maintains that all his activities are within the bounds of the law.

"*Is T.H. more evil than Moriarty himself?*" my employer had commented at the bottom of an article. There were also reports in Holmes' characteristic scrawl, apparently testimonies by various individuals about Hardstone and his friends participating in orgies at *The Hut*, with young women who were not all there voluntarily. There is a written statement, although it is not clear to whom it was given, by a certain Madge Durie, a milkmaid. She recounts how, as she was walking home from the farm where she worked, late at sundown, some young men in a carriage stopped by her side and began exchanging banter with her. They invited her to jump in for a ride, and she unwisely accepted the drink that they offered her. She did not remember how she got to this big opulent mansion which looked like a castle. Once there she was urged to wash and was given a nice frock and shoes to wear. When she had sobered up, she demanded to be taken back home, for she was scared, with no idea where she was. A man fitting the description of Hardstone spoke to her nicely and promised that if only she would have a little fun first, have a few nice things to eat, some more to drink, listen to a little of music and dance a jig or two, he would be happy to take her home himself in his hansom cab. She knew that she had no choice, for although the man was speaking softly and kindly, she could see that his cold and cruel eyes were full of menace. She understood that if she did not do as he was saying, something very bad would happen to her. There were many men, friends of Hardstone and they forced her to drink and made her dance. One taste was enough to convince her that the drinks were spiked, but she was too scared of being thrashed to refuse. She could not remember much, but was able to describe how first the master of the house, then his guests took advantage of her, with her being able to do nothing because of the drink and drug in her. When the party ended at dawn, a coachman took her in the cab and dropped her five miles from home, telling her to keep the dress. When the neighbours urged her to go the police, Mum was dubious, fearing that they would get into more trouble. Finally she allowed them to talk her into it. The upshot was that poor Madge was locked up in the cell for two nights for vagrancy. 'I will never fight the masters again,' she said, 'the police are always on their side.'

There was little doubt in my mind that the methodical investigator was collecting material and testimonies with a view to apprehending the villain once there was enough evidence. He knew that his hands were tied, owing to the influence and power of the ship owner, for he was reputed to be a staunch backer of the Marquess of Salisbury and his party.

Another daguerreotype of a man with a dirty cap, a pipe in his mouth and a bandana tied round his neck, attracted my attention. He had laughing eyes, and the name "Maggles, alias Crowbar Bob" was written on the other side. Holmes had further commented that Maggles seemed to have been a childhood friend of Hardstone and that they had been inseparable companions to this day. He has been taken to court a few times, but has never been sent to prison. He earned his nickname of Crowbar

Bob after being taken to court on the charge of beating a nightwatchman to death with a crowbar, but was acquitted. There is an uncredited quote here: "Mister Bob will put hissel in the path of a bullet to save the master."

There was another file bearing the name of Mr Francis Aloysius Waverick QC. Of course I had a look at it. His photograph from a newspaper cutting shows a man with an impeccably trimmed bearded face, kindly eyes and regal bearing. He is from a family of rich Huguenot clothiers who came over from Lyon after the Bartholomew's Day Massacre, and changed their names from De Vouvric to Waverick. He finished brilliant law studies at Lincoln's Inn and took silk, only the third man ever to do that before reaching thirty. His career seems to consist of two contrasting halves. The first ten years he was a champion of lost causes, defending, often for next to nothing, people accused of serious offences on the flimsiest of evidence, or trumped-up charges. He did not win all his cases, but he was noted for his relentless passion in the defence of the weak. His most famous victory, as recounted in the cuttings from the *Pall Mall Gazette* was in the case of Regina versus Albert Mullion, when he persuaded the jury to pronounce a verdict of not guilty, saving the man from the gallows. At the last minute he had called the Vicar of St George's in Doncaster to testify. The man of the cloth had confirmed that the accused man had worshipped in his church on the Sunday morning of the killing. It became manifest to one and all that no method of transportation existed that could have conveyed the accused to Bethnal Green to commit murder at noon on the same day.

Then Waverick seems to have suddenly opted for lucre, working exclusively for the disreputable Hardstone in the last five years. In a paper to the Law Society, he expounds his credo:

'... *First of all I need to dispel the notion that any man, howsoever damning the indictment, is undeserving of having his case defended in a court of justice. We do not condemn people and send them to jail or worse because the public or police is inclined to believe in their guilt. A man comes to me accused of murder. I abhor the taking of human life as much as the next man, so what is to be my position? I am well aware of the fact that witnesses tell lies and give false testimony, often causing an innocent man to be sent to the gallows. I would be failing in my professional duty if I did not do my best to nail the lie and highlight any extenuating circumstance. It is also my belief that there are degrees of guilt. No two men who commit murder are responsible or guilty to the same extent. A man who after an altercation angrily pushes his companion, who falls down, knocks his head against something hard and breathes his last, is not as culpable as the fellow who has planned the elimination of his enemy and carries it out in cold blood. It is my duty to convince the jury of this when it occurs. In France, a man who kills his wife's lover is often considered a victim, is just given a rap on his fingers and told by the judge to behave himself in future. Or make sure his next wife is the faithful type.*

If a client confesses to me that he did commit the felony he is accused of, I tell him to plead guilty, and then I try to persuade judge and jury that he deserves a more lenient sentence for some attenuating circumstances. In my view there usually are.

My purport in presenting this paper is to state my conviction that every man deserves to be heard and that the guiding star of the English Legal System is the tenet that every man is deemed to be innocent until proven guilty.

***

I was surprised to find a short account of a case among Mr Holmes' papers, bearing a date of three years previously. It did not involve him though. It was written in Dr Watson's hand. When I questioned the latter, he explained that he was reluctant to have the story printed in the *Clarion*, as he sometimes does, under a pseudonym, because its contents might have been deemed libelous. Now I have his permission to use it as I like. Watson declared that, in his opinion, no other story shows how clearly that the law is an ass.

***

When the fancy took him, Hardstone the shipowner, gambler and businessman and his shadow Crowbar Bob sometimes jumped on the *Unicorn* just as it was preparing to set sail and travel to Portugal or Spain or wherever it was going. He said that the sea air did him a power of good. In any case he had his own berth on board, and Crowbar his.

One-eyed Captain Bale, former pirate that he was, did not look favourably on this. The two men interfered too much, and this made the running of the ship more difficult, especially in view of the contraband concealed in recesses in the hull. It was an open secret that when a Hardstone ship landed at a regular port with twenty tons of import on which duty was paid, prior to this, another twenty tons had already been inveigled away at some unofficial port en route. When Hardstone did not show up at departure, Bale would breathe a sigh of relief. His crew of reprobates and he understood each other perfectly and the relationship between them, uneasy though it was, never got out of hand.

Bale had often reminded the proprietor that on board the captain only came after God, but Hardstone thought that he was God! So what happened on the ship on a stormy day in November last year was inevitable. Captain Bale was pushed overboard and I daresay, with the catalogue of crimes and misdemeanours attributed to him, met with a fitting end.

The moment the *Unicorn* cast anchor in Liverpool, Hardstone asked to consult with his lawyer, Francis Waverick, summoned by telegram. After a short consultation, he requested to be seen by the police, and to everybody's surprise made a signed confession of guilt. It seemed that it all started with a theft. The captain had investigated the matter and found the second baker innocent, but Hardstone had ordered the man to be given twenty lashes anyway, *pour l'exemple*. This had angered the reformed pirate captain, who shouted that he was going to get Hardstone, proprietor though he was, arrested and put in chains if he continued to interfere. The confrontation had ended in a scuffle. The quick-tempered Hardstone had grabbed the slighter Bale by the neck and pushed him overboard. An offering to the sharks. That would have made for an open and shut case, but Robert Maggles, otherwise known as Crowbar Bob, made a similar confession. It was he, he claimed, and not Hardstone, who had ordered a sailor to give twenty lashes to a young assistant pantryman against the express order of the captain. After Bale had threatened to have *him* put in chains, Crowbar Bob had lashed out with *his* third arm, the crowbar he seemed to be always carrying. Grabbing the smaller man, he had thrown him overboard. The crew, to a man claimed to have been below deck when the incident happened, except for the ship's cook and the second steward. The former swore to the truth of Hardstone's account and the latter claimed that he saw Crowbar carry out the deed as he had said.

Francis Waverick was appointed to defend Hardstone, and Roger Feverell, a man no less formidable than the QC, represented Maggles. However, because of the confusion arising from the bizarre multiple confessions, neither case reached the Assizes Court. The judge put the case in abeyance, instructing the police to start their enquiries from scratch and come back when they had a watertight case. However, before they could reignite their enquiry, the two eyewitnesses, the cook and the steward, seemed to have migrated to the Carolinas. No more action was taken. This type of defence bore the typical Waverick trademark and the judge knew it. As did the jury and the public. Still, the law operates within fixed parameters and thus does justice become a victim of the statutes, dare it be said?

CHAPTER SIX

An Abduction

(1884)

The reader has not yet been properly introduced to my erstwhile lover Coleridge. (*"Coleridge, reader; reader, Coleridge."*) He was born in North Dakota to an ex-slave father and a Nez Percé mother. At an early age, his teacher, Miss Morag Falworth, who played the piano on Sundays at church, recognised his voice as unique and said it was a pity that he was both black and red. He could so easily have made it in the operatic world, which then, was dominated by the Italians. His voice went on to develop and mature, and far exceeded her expectations. When he was eighteen, he moved to New York, where he was told that he might be able to train as a tenor and sing on stage. A Jewish impresario befriended him, paid for his lessons, promising that he would help him break into the world of the opera. He had secured the rights to Verdi's opera *Otello*, and offered young Coleridge this dream part. Mr Grossman had urged his entire team to keep Coleridge's colour secret, telling the press that he had an excellent make-up team who could work miracles. There was little doubt that the production was a triumph and was going to make much money for the company. However, Enzo Pinelli, who ironically was singing the part of the jealous Iago, enraged by the rave reviews the black man had received, spilled the beans. Thus it was that folks who had applauded the performance of Coleridge to the rafters only the night before, threatened to burn the opera house down "if that cannibal dared show his ugly black face anywhere near it." He was forced to escape from New York dressed as a woman.

After many tribulations, he decided to seek his fortune in England, a haven for racial harmony and justice, people had assured him. When this proved not to be entirely the case, he mentally shrugged and philosophically made up his mind to find the means of keeping the wolf from the door.

He was able to find manual work in the theatre, lifting and carrying, doing some carpentry. On very rare occasions he was given small parts, playing monsters, villains and cutthroats in popular melodramas. The high point of his career was when he was given the part of Caliban to Irving's Prospero. He sometimes made a living as a docker and admittedly he had had recourse to pickpocketing in his time when faced with starvation. I had met him whilst singing "Beep-Bo" in *The Mikado,* where he was working as a scene shifter. I was first impressed by his sheer physical beauty and we became friends, then lovers. Later I invited him to Water Lane to meet Armande, as I had discovered that he had a truly lovely soul that was every bit as beautiful as his appearance. We were never in love with each other, but our bodies were. (Feel free to remove this Mr Reynolds, in case you think it's a bit risqué.). It was only natural for me to put forward his name to the *Club,* who welcomed him enthusiastically. Coleridge is the sort of man who is only happy if he can exercise his loins at least once a night, preferably twice. When I am in the mood I am an equally sensual beast, but I often feel disinclined to give myself to the pleasures of the flesh. I disclose this to explain why he was entirely at liberty to do as he pleased with nothing to answer for, as far as I was concerned. This understanding naturally gave me leave to choose other bed companions if the fancy took me. There is, however, an unwritten law, that neither of us flaunts a new lover flagrantly in front of the other.

Cole is friends with a Somali man, Abdi, an ex-sailor who is married to an English woman, Nell. They lived no more that a mile away from Water Lane, in Camberwell. Although he had not intimated this to me, I suspected that there is something going on between him and Nell's younger unmarried sister Alice who lived round the corner from them. His friend and his wife have a nine year old son Ishaq. Abdi and his family have often been subjected to abuse and mockery by the neigh-bours. The little boy has often heard things like:

'Quick, hide the children or they might disappear into some pot!'

'You've got it wrong dearie, they eat them raw.'

'Hey there, nigger, you've no place in Camberwell, go to Africa.'

'Go to Liverpool, this 'ere is white man country.'

'Go to Whitechapel, nigger.'

'Brixton is for whites only.'

Sometimes Ishaq was waylaid on the way home, when two or three lads would surround him and take turns to push him around like a play-thing. Until now no one had actually hit him, although they purposely walked on his toes. The abuse addressed to the couple had never been more than verbal, but things were beginning to change. On a few occa-sions stones had been thrown at their windows, and matters had come to a head when excrement had been daubed on their door and the walls of their house.

Nell was becoming increasingly alarmed and was sleeping badly. She was subject to palpitations. Abdi decided to go to the Police Station in Stockwell to complain. Coleridge's friend did not believe it would help but he went anyway, for his wife's sake. The moment he knocked on the door and entered, the two constables, Sylvester Boneheath and Ebenezer Deepship burst out laughing, exchanging the following thoughts aloud:

'Have you heard, some big ape has escaped from the circus.'

'Two little children have gone missing.'

'Did you see the order, shoot on sight?'

'Hoo, hoo, hoo hoo!'

'Get the Fire Brigade to come over.'

'Yeah, I'll tell them to bring their net along.'

'Don't forget to tell them to bring bananas.'

Abdi was greatly alarmed by this outburst. He was a slightly built fel-low, unassertive and shy. This treatment left him speechless for a while, but after the men had calmed down and wiped the tears of mirth from their eyes, he managed to open his mouth.

'Good morning sirs, I have come to make a complaint.'

' 'Es come to make a complaint did y' hear that, Sylvester?'

'I've got a complaint an all, Ebenezer, I can't breathe.'

'Why's that Sylvester? Is it the stench?'

'Absolutely, in the jungle there's no bathroom.'

Abdi was no coward and even as the two men continued abusing him, he managed to give them an account of the tribulations he and his family were having to endure.

'Then, man, get the hell outa here. Take the hint, you don't belong.'

'Them folks is right. South London is for people.'

'Not apes.'

'Is there nothing the police can do for us then?'

'Now 'es getting on my wick,' said Ebenezer. 'We told yer, go to Africa, go to Whitechapel or Liverpool.'

'Do you not understand when you're not wanted.'

'Give him thirty-seconds, Ebenezer, if he's not outa here, lock him up.'

Finally, with a heavy heart and an aching throat, poor Abdi left and walked home, making a superhuman effort not to cry tears of frustration in public.

When Cole told the *Club* the tale of his poor friend and his family, we resolved to look into the matter and find a solution. Clearly there was no legal route, for this presented the eternal conundrum: who polices the police? This was a tailor-made situation for action by the *Club des As* if ever there was one. We convened a special meeting to discuss Abdi's case, and it took us less than half an hour to elaborate a plan.

On the appointed day, we all made our way to the Stockwell Police Station. It happens to be on a side street off Vassal Street, with little or no traffic after sunset. Lord Clarihoe, the Bishop, Ivan, Armande and myself were chosen to lead the first assault. We pushed open the door and entered the station. We found Sylvester Boneheath and Ebenezer Deepship with their feet on their desk drinking ale and eating beef sandwiches. They immediately stood to attention and the following conversation took place:

'Your ladyships, gentlemen, the London Constabulary at your service.'

'We apologise to be caught like this, but it's our tea time.'

'We ain't breaking no rules, your ... eh ... worships.'

'No, of course not, my good men,' Lord Clarihoe said in a very urbane manner.

'What can we do for your ... worships then?'

'How very civil of you, gentlemen,' said Ivan Vissarionovitch. 'We were told wrong. We were warned not to expect civility here.' Upon hearing this the two constables laughed, but it was an uneasy chortle.

'What can you mean, your ... lordships? We in the force pride ourselves on our efficiency and our civility.'

'Oh! You do?' the Bishop butted in.

At this juncture, on cue, Coleridge came in, adopting a very meek attitude.

'What 'ave we 'ere?' said Boneheath.

'I think another big ape has escaped from the Zoo,' said Deepship.

'We had one of them last week,' Boneheath told us, ignoring the black man. The two coppers started laughing at the memory of the great time they had at the expense of the Somali, exchanging snippets with each other, but generously trying to include us in their merriment. Then, changing tone suddenly, they turned on the new arrival.

'Can you not see, nigger, than we 'ave some 'igh class visitors 'ere. You can't just butt in like this. Not in a civilised society.'

'The trouble wiv the country now is that people don't know their places,' said Deepship, apostrophising us. We pretended to smile as Coleridge took a few steps towards the back of the room. This caused a real eruption on the part of the law enforcers.

'Out, man! Out does not mean go to the back of the room, it means OUT, O-U-T, did you not understand? Get lost! *Jao! Imshi*!'

'You don't call that very civil, do you?' the Bishop asked softly.

'But he's a nigger,' said Boneheath surprised. 'Do we have to be civil to *them*?'

At this point the other members of the team walked in, and we all drew as near their desk as possible, looking at the two men in the eyes. The uniformed pair began to sense that we were not on their side, something which was clearly a mystery to them. They began to look uneasy, casting furtive glances at each other, unable to keep still.

'*Messieurs*,' said Artémise, 'I am a Frenshman, am I entiteuled to the protection of the lo?'

'Everybody is entitled to our protection,' chorused the two. Suddenly Coleridge who had been standing quietly at the back surged forward.

'But not black people!' he boomed in his bass tenor voice which took the two men by surprise.

'B....bu....b...'

'We... w... we...'

At this point, as we had planned, Armande and Bartola handed over the phials that each had in their bags to the two heftiest of our group, Cole and Ivan. They crossed over to the other side of the counter, where each grabbed one policeman in a deathly grip. This will not hurt, they said as they applied a cloth soaked in ether to the nose of the two reprobates. They became instantly limp. They were dragged outside, where Frunk was sitting in a cab we had recently purchased, with Probert by his side.

We put blindfolds round their eyes, gagged them, and made our way to Water Lane, by a circuitous route. They were then unceremoniously forced out of the cab, frogmarched towards the house and pushed none too gently towards the cellar which had been prepared for the occasion. They swore and kicked, to no avail. We tied them securely to chairs facing each other after which the gags and blindfolds were removed. They blinked comically. We were greatly amused. They were still groggy, and obviously had no understanding of what was happening. Nor had they the slightest idea where they were. Suddenly they both seemed to come to life and began demanding with great vehemence to be freed immediately or face the consequences, something which redoubled our hilarity. When we had dried our tears (of laughter), I approached them, and standing between them, looking at each alternately, I assumed my most dulcet voice. The others got chairs from the back and sat themselves in an arc. They would act as jury.

'The pair of you, Sylvester Boneheath and Ebenezer Deepship, have been accused of aggravated abuse of power, causing great mental distress to a family who had approached you for help. I will not spell out the details, as you are not complete morons and will remember them clearly. How do you plead?' They stared at me defiantly. At this point Ivan Vissarionovitch came forward and demanded the floor.

'This is the plan: we will give you a fair trial and then pass judgement. Until you answer our questions, you will remain fixed to you chairs with only water. You can shout as much as you like but no one will hear you.'

'Will you answer our question now?'

Silence and defiance. We gave them blankets and left. Next morning we went downstairs and found our prisoners in a pitiful state, smelling of urine. We untied them, allowed them to use the toilet facilities. We gave them a change of clothes, after which we led them back to the cellar in a more subdued state. They indicated that they were willing to talk.

'But not before you eat something' said Armande kindly. She had thought of making the men a proper breakfast with tea, eggs and bacon, but I had a brainwave.

'Unfortunately we have run out of eggs and bacon, so we can only offer you champagne and caviar. Will that do?' My friends smiled their admiration for my idea but the two pair stared at each other in confusion. I went upstairs with Bartola to collect the special breakfast. The Bishop and Ivan tied the men back to their chairs, leaving their hands free to eat. We then came down with a platter each in which we had made room for a small Murano flower vase with freshly cut rosebuds, with the food. There was a bottle of *Cliquot Ponsardin*, two crystal glasses from Bohemia, a bowl of caviar and bread lovingly toasted golden brown, all served in appropriate silver. The *Club* applauded merrily. The pair looked at this offering as if it were poison, refusing to touch it. However, after a short wait, they made tentative attempts, resisting the urge to spit the caviare out, but soon began to eat and drink with more gusto. We had asked Coleridge to sit halfway between the two men in a way to make his presence felt, and we resumed our hearing.

'I repeat my question,' I said. 'Do you plead guilty to-' It was Boneheath who intervened.

'Your honour,' he said, 'we are always civil to people but the man wot came into our station was a nigger.' Cole cleared his throat menacingly.

'Are we really meant to be civil to niggers and kaffirs?' added Deepship defiantly.

'So you plead not guilty to the charge?' I asked.

'Yeah,' the pair chorused, one of them adding, 'it ain't as if we woz rude to our own.'

'We'd never dream of that.'

'So what you're saying,' said Ivan Vissarionovitch, 'is that given another opportunity, you'd act in the same manner?' The accused did not have to think too hard before nodding. You had to admire them for their bravery and honesty even if we despised their attitude.

'Members of the jury,' I said, addressing the arc, 'consult among yourselves and please advise on a course of action.' I went upstairs because I did not want to impose my ideas.

'Have you reached a decision?' I asked when I rejoined them. They nodded, and Lord Clarihoe stood up and spoke solemnly.

'Yes, ma'am.'

'And was that decision unanimous?'

'Yes, ma'am, it was,' Lord Clarihoe said.

'Will you tell the court what that decision is.

'That the accused be detained for a period, initially of three days, to give them time to reflect on their conduct, on the meaning of what is a human being and on what the rights of that aforesaid human being might be. If at the end of that period, we establish that the accused have learnt nothing, we will prescribe an extension of another three days, *ad nauseam*. They will only be released into society, unharmed, after they have proved beyond reasonable doubt that they will henceforth treat everybody, irrespective of all other considerations, with absolute fairness, in the exercise of their onerous duty.'

'And all the time fed on caviar and champagne?' I asked, whereupon Algernon replied, 'Yes, ma'am.'

Without further ado, we left them there, making sure that they were allowed a little exercise and the use of bathroom facilities. We heard them discuss their plight, but made no effort to listen to what they were saying.

After three days, the men indicated that they had given the matter much thought and had arrived at a verdict on themselves. Boneheath was chosen as spokesman.

'After giving the matter in question much thought and due consideration, we have arrived at the concloosion and realised the enormity and grossness of our action. The n... sorry, man of negro persuasion came to us as officers of 'er Majesty law for safety and protection, and we woz unable to look beyond the colour of his skin. We failed in our dooty as law enforcers in not only withholding the aforesaid protection, but to add to our guilt, we treated the nigger, oh, a thousand pardons, the ... the man, with scorn and with rudeness, incivility and discourtesy.' I looked at the arc, and we nodded to each other.

'Please proceed, Mr Representative, and inform the jury how you plan to remedy this failing and atone for your sin.' Deepship now took over.

'Henceforth and subsequent to this, my esteemed colleague and accomplice will treat all indivijules with courtesy and politeness, civility and recti... rectal... rec-'

'Rectitude,' whispered Boneheath.

'Wot Boneheath just said. And on hearing a complaint from any member of society, we will take appropriate, necessary and sufficient action to bring succour, relief and assuagement to the plaintiff.'

'Oh, and we will do nothing to put your lordships and ladyships in any sort of danger.' We felt no danger whatsoever from our prisoners. They knew that we were not to be trifled with, we knew where they worked whilst they neither knew who we were, nor where *we* lived. Still, at midnight, we blindfolded them again and delivered them back to Vassal Crescent, still shaken, but no worse for wear and tear.

CHAPTER SEVEN

Hardstone

(1889)

I was putting the Hardstone file away, to be finished some other day, as I had some chores pending. At that very moment, the *Evening News* came in through the door. It was with shock that I saw the banner headline: WARRANT FOR TED HARDSTONE'S ARREST. Since I had just been reading about the man, I could not resist the temptation of postponing the ironing that I had planned on finishing before Mr Holmes arrived. I sat down in the great armchair opposite his desk instead, and began reading the account.

On the previous Thursday night the warehouse of Boone & Verneuil, the famous Huddersfield textile manufacturers, had been broken into with a consignment of new quality Dormeuil fabric worth ten thousand pounds stolen. I collected the article:

It was clear that the watchdogs had been poisoned and of the two armed guards, one was shot at point blank range and died on the spot, whilst the other has severe head wound, with doctors giving him no more than a fifty-fifty chance of survival. The bulk of the material being taken away with such despatch suggested that the heist was the work of a well-organised gang. There have been similar outrages in the recent past. Three months ago a factory in Bradford was broken into and an exact working model of a new loom being developed at the factory was taken away, fortunately without any loss of lives. The indications are that this would find its way to

Germany, where our competitors have been trying their hardest to steal our technology. The police have little doubt that there is a connection between the two outrages.

The police have received intelligence to the effect that there was some unusual activity in a Whitechapel warehouse on Sunday night and, a warrant having been sought, they went to the address, forced their way in and as they expected, discovered the whole consignment there. The proprietor of the aforesaid godown, a Hebraic gentleman, Mr Abraham Fleischmann, was apprehended but he denied any involvement in either the theft or the murder, explaining that with his bad back he could hardly leave Whitechapel, let alone London, to go commit murders hundreds of miles to the north. Fleischmann explained that he had rented out the premises to Mr Hardstone in all good faith, seeing that the gentleman had a legitimate shipping business, the plying of which not being incompatible with the use of warehouse space. Fleischmann was released on bail and fresh warrants issued for the apprehension of the aforesaid Ted Hardstone and Robert Maggles. When the police went to apprehend them, they learnt, to their chagrin, that the suspects had left the country on the Medea bound for the port of Tangiers only the day before. The police accepted the harsh reality that nothing could be done at the moment, but have promised that they will devote the time between now and the return of the fugitives to build up a watertight case against them. They are pursuing no other line of enquiry.

I am now writing this after the case had been resolved. Although I was not an eyewitness, I questioned people who were closely connected to the affair, including Dr Watson.

The Attorney General's Office was delighted with the thoroughness of their case. The moment the *Medea* dropped anchor at Tilbury, Hardstone and Maggles were greeted by Scotland Yard's best, taken to Brixton Prison and indicted on a count of premeditated murder and the willful inflicting of grievous bodily harm and aggravated theft. Waverick, with his gift for pulling many a spectacular rabbits out of a hat, managed to get the trial moved from the Harrogate Assizes to the Old Bailey, on the grounds that although the theft had occurred in Huddersfield, the stolen goods had been found in Whitechapel. He even wangled a joint trial for the two accused.

Standing at the box, neither man seemed unduly perturbed by his plight. They both exuded to court and jury a confidence bordering on arrogance, reflecting their certainty of being acquitted. This was based on either their innocence or their absolute faith in their defence counsel. Waverick had been ruthless in the past in ripping apart the prosecution in all the seven actions in which one or both of the accused had figured. However, this time the evidence against the two men seemed overwhelming and watertight.

The court gathered round Chief Justice Boblington-Fuzzle, with the formidable Erasmus Faversby prosecuting. The accused had the charges against them read, and they duly pleaded not guilty on all counts. Faversby then told the jury that he had a watertight case based on the testimony of Gabriel Marbell, the guard who had survived the attack, and of Abraham Fleischmann, the owner of the Whitechapel warehouse. Waverick stood up and mocked his opponent for his temerity in taking on such a case. Never in his entire career, he exclaimed, had he seen such a massive action being brought in front of a jury on such flimsy evidence. He suggested that his learned colleague might be well-advised to light a candle to Saint Jude.

'Members of the jury,' he went on, 'please note that a crime was obviously committed in Huddersfield. A heinous crime indeed, make no mistake about that. A man has been killed in the execution of his duty, another grievously wounded and two dogs brutally shot. Ten thousand pounds worth of goods were expropriated. However, my learned friend bases his case on the testimony of a London warehouse owner who was two hundred miles away. And let us not forget a man so badly wounded that he is reported to have lost both his sight and his mental faculties.' Boblington-Fuzzle stopped the counsel peremptorily, warning him not to make unsubstantiated judgement on the quality of a putative witness he has not yet even encountered.

'I unreservedly withdraw the imputation, my lord.'

When Abraham Fleischmann was sworn in and questioned by Faversby, he corroborated that story the police had presented to the office of the Attorney General: that in all innocence he had rented out his premises to the accused, Hardstone, as he had often done in the past. No, he had not enquired as to the nature of the goods to be stored therein, he had not thought it was an intelligence he needed to possess. Yes, he had often done business with Hardstone and Maggles and had never had any problems with them.

'Naturally you have submitted all documents relating to your transactions with my client to the appropriate authorities, namely the police and the office of the Attorney General?' Waverick asked softly. Fleischmann blanched on hearing this question, unable to open his mouth.

'Surely you must have!' thundered the lawyer breathing incredulity from every pore. Blinking and stammering incoherently, the warehouse owner conceded that he had not done so. There were no paper documents.

'None whatsoever?'

'No, your honour.' He explained that as his clients usually required the use of his space for short and irregular periods, all negotiations were on a basis of gentlemen's agreement.

'So you do have not one solitary sheet of paper, even the size of a postage stamp, relating to your supposed transaction with my clients?' asked the counsel opening his eyes wide in disbelief. The question had to be repeated before Fleischmann mumbled an answer in the affirmative.

'Do you expect the jury to believe that?'

'We are a small company and we try to avoid extra costs.'

'Ah! You are a small company bent,' Waverick laid significant emphasis on the word "bent", paused and repeated it. 'Bent on expanding, Mr Ab-ra-ham Moi-se-vitch Fleisch-mann.' The jury did not fail to note how he dwelled on each syllable of the name, 'Bent ... on expanding by any means, straight or crooked.' Faversby sprang to his feet, shaking his fist at his opposite number, demanding that he withdrew the malicious insinuation, whereupon Waverick bowed slightly and smiled.

'I intended no malice, your honour, but if your lordship so directs, I shall be happy to withdraw the statement.' His lordship frowned, nodded, and instructed the clerk to strike the sentence from the record. The complicit jury, to a man, smiled knowingly.

'Mr A-bra-ham Moi-se-vitch Fleisch-mann, I have evidence here to the effect that on the 27th February 1883, you were sent down for two weeks for receiving stolen goods, is that a fact?' The witness began spluttering and shaking on his legs but could say nothing until prompted by his lordship.

'I b-bought the stuff in g-g-good faith sir, I p-p-paid cash for it.'

'But the court did not believe you?'

'No sir.'

'Tut tut!'

Fleischmann came out of the cross-interrogation in tatters. The prosecution had another trump card, an eyewitness. Gabriel Marbell. Next day, the guard came into the box limping, his face bearing the scars from the attack in the warehouse. He answered Faversby's questions, confirming that on the night of the burglary, he and his fellow guard had heard two shots followed by the dogs howling in agony as they died. Then the accused wearing masks burst inside the warehouse and shot Joe in the neck, after which he, Gabriel, tried to confront them. They shot him in the face.

'You said they, Mr Marbell, did they both shoot you?'

'No, sir, only one of them.'

'Are you positive about that? You did say, and I quote,' he ruffled some papers before continuing, "I tried to confront them..." you said them ... "and they shot me in the face". Are you sure you're in a fit state to testify in this court?' He was obviously trying to instill in jury and judge the notion that in view of the trauma the witness had experienced, his testimony was not reliable. Marbell took a deep breath, said nothing for a while, but managed a response.

'You're right, I said they shot me. I meant one of them shot me. I am not used to courts of law. I get confused, but I have clear memory of what happened.'

'Which one? Mr Hardstone here or Mr Maggles?' Waverick asked. Marbell hesitated.

'I will point at one of them first and ask you.' Marbell nodded, and Waverick pointed a finger at Maggles.

'Yes, sir, that were 'im.'

'Mr Marbell, it can't have escaped the jury that you hesitated before answering. Why?'

'I am a simple man sir, words don't come easily out of my mouth.'

'Mr Marbell, you surprise me, you said the men were wearing masks, how can you be so sure?'

'They have different shapes sir, this man is shorter and...'

'And?'

'Fatter, sir.'

'Will learned counsel instruct the witness not to use derogatory terms in his description of the physical characteristics of individuals here present, whatever his feelings might be about their appearances. He could, for example say stouter,' intervened his portly lordship.

'Mr Marbell, how good are your eyes?'

'I had perfect vision, but after the shooting...'

'Ah! So you lost your sight?'

'Only in one eye.'

'So you are half-blind! The jury and I naturally sympathise with you on your great loss, and offer you our unbounded admiration for your heroism in the exercise of your profession. But you understand that two men are standing trial for their lives here. Are you sure this was the man you saw brandishing the gun at you?'

'It 'appened very quickly, sir.'

'So you are saying that you aren't sure.'

'It 'appened very quickly, is not the same thing as I ain't sure.'

'Will the witness just answer the question and save any other observations for himself,' admonished his lordship.

'Mr Marbell, did the two aggressors exchange any words?'

'And will the witness say the exact words.' Boblington-Fuzzle instructed.

'Aye, I heard one say, "Jimmy, are you sure the other bastard's dead." '

'Jimmy? Is that what you heard? But there is no Jimmy here. One man fighting to establish his innocence is baptised Edward and the other is Robert. Ed and Bob, if you like.' Then addressing the jury solemnly he shook his head.

'There is no Jimmy here. Mr Marbell, did you not know that? Address the jury'

'Sirs, that's what I heard sir, burglars are not going to use their real names in the presence of a third party. It's like wearing a mask for their names.'

'Just restrict yourself to facts, and avoid embellishments in the future,' instructed his lordship.

'You heard anything else?'

'The exact words?' queried Marbell.

'The exact words,' repeated his lordship.

'Aye. The other one then replied, "when I have a" ,' he paused before adding, "when I have a fooking gun in my hand, I sure know how to fooking use it, Roger." '

'Will the witness refrain from using profanities in my court,' said the judge angrily.

'The learned counsel asked if I heard anything, your honour, and I repeated the exact words.'

'Next time you feel the urge to use obscene words, just use the initial.' Marbell opened his eyes wide and nodded.

'Right. He said, when I have a f–ing gun–' The judge stopped him by raising his hand, signifying that there was no need to go over grounds already covered.

'How good is your hearing, Mr Marbell,' asked Waverick 'I 'ave perfect 'earing, sir.'

'Now Mr Marbell, with his lordship's permission I will ask you to turn round and I will instruct one of the accused to read a sentence. I will then ask you to identify who it is.' Marbell duly turned round, and Waverick assuming Maggles' accent spoke out the words: "If the 'orses don't let us down Jimmy, we will be in f–ing Leeds before dawn."

Then in his own voice he asked, 'Mr Marbell, can you identify the voice?'

'I can, sir.'

'Good, whose voice was it?'

'Yours, sir.' Marbell replied confidently.

'Mr Marbell, let's hope your sight is as good as your hearing. How many fingers am I holding out?' Waverick held out four fingers keeping his index and middle finger together and the other two separate so that they looked like two normal fingers and a thick one.

'Three,' said Marbell, whereupon the attorney took three steps towards the jury maintaining his hand in the same position and displaying the configuration.

The case lasted three days. On the third day, Waverick summed up his defence by suggesting that Abraham Fleischmann was part of a wider conspiracy, possibly with two as yet unidentified men named Jimmy and Roger. 'He is a convicted felon, and having learnt that my clients were on the point of setting sail for North Africa, he and his gang thought out the wicked plan to incriminate two innocent men. The prosecution has not one jot or tittle of evidence to link my clients with the warehouse.'

He then dwelled upon the half blindness of the guard, his voice full of compassion as he extolled the valour of the man who had braved his attackers with utter contempt for his own life, losing his sight in the heroic execution of his duty, which is why the police must not do their level best to catch the real culprits.

'The Real Culprits! Members of the jury. Or poor Mr Marbell would have risked his life in vain!' The jury returned a verdict of not guilty, and the two men were duly discharged.

CHAPTER EIGHT

A Love Story

(1885)

Lord Clarihoe soon became my best friend in the *Club*. Together we went to the Café Royal once a week, attended races at Ascot, saw art exhibitions, went to concerts or to the theatre. We even took trips to the Continent, but we had yet to realise our dream of going tiger shooting in Bengal. This may appear surprising, seeing that he is not attracted to the fair sex and I display all the marks of normality in that respect, but I rate friendship above romance. I liked his jokes and he admired what he called my healthy irreverence for received wisdom. We enjoyed each other's company and complemented each other's personalities. As a Uranian, he has greater understanding of the female psyche and is an ideal companion to go shopping with. I greatly admire his aesthetic tastes. We often sleep in the same bed, our arms round each other.

We were sipping Assam tea with a plate of *petits fours* and *amuse-gueules*, seated under the faux palm tree, at the Café Royal, whilst the resident violinist Jacopo Sacerdoti was entertaining afternoon aesthetes with pieces of *Boccherini* or *Pergolesi*, when I saw Algernon blanch. A thin effeminate young man, impeccably dressed in a cream suit, carrying a silk parasol on a bamboo frame had just tottered in. He was accompanied by two rather loud and scruffy individuals. The waiter made a fuss of the new arrivals and deferentially showed them to a corner three or four tables away, opposite us. With a bow he pocketed the sovereign I saw change hands. All the wit of my companion, who until now had been charming and voluble, froze up like the taps of fountains in public squares in Florence in winter. The newcomer stared at him with an ironical smile on his lips. I noticed that the hands of the usually self-assured aristocrat were trembling as he lifted his Minton cup.

'That fop seems to have discomfited you, Algie,' I observed.

'Douglas Mill de La Marelle,' whispered Algernon. 'Once the love of my life, now the bane of my existence.'

'The artist?'

'Also known as Lassie. I'll tell you about him later. Let's be off now, dear heart.' It was a shame to leave half-finished plates of those *délices* but I was happy to oblige my good friend, especially considering how upset he was.

That evening at Water Lane he explained how he had met Lassie four years ago. He had been dazzled by his beauty as well as by his talent. He wrote beautiful poetry and produced brilliant drawings. I happened to know the reputation of the man as an artist, and had admired his line drawings when they were exhibited at the Francis Salisbury Gallery in Oxford Circus, but I had not yet come across his verse. Algernon laughed and said that he only wrote homoerotic poems which were hand printed and distributed to members of the *Patroclus Club*, of which he, Algernon, had been an assiduous member for a number of years. He had, however, allowed his membership to lapse because Lassie's behaviour was becoming erratic, bordering on dangerous. Unfortunately the latter knew where to find him, and regularly did.

'You mean he is persecuting you?' I asked in shock.

'If blackmail is persecution then, yes, my dear Irene, he is.'

My good friend had tears in his eyes when he told me that whilst the fellow should have been producing masterpieces, he wasted his time whoring, gambling, drinking, brawling and eating opium. Yes, he still had feelings for him, he supposed, but he could not put up with his demands.

'What demands?'

'He has decided that I must finance his debauchery, dear heart.'

'Tell him to go to blazes, Algie,' I cried in horror.

He kept silent for a whole minute. I knew that I should not interrupt. Finally he turned to me and took my hand. 'I paid him one hundred pounds for each letter I sent him, eh ... I must have spent three thousand pounds. He said he'd go to the police and ruin me if I don't pay up.'

'You mean ... but assuredly he will go down with you.'

'He is the sort of fellow who never thinks out the consequences. He seems convinced that he will get away with it by suggesting that I, the older man, had corrupted him.'

'Did you?' Clarihoe laughed. 'It does not work like that, we were in love you see.' Suddenly an idea hit me.

'But Algie, you said you paid him off for the letters-'

'He kept three of them. He wants ten thousand pounds for them now. Even if I had that sort of money...' he left the rest unsaid. 'Something's got to be done then,' I said with great conviction although I hadn't the faintest idea where to begin. Algernon shook his head wistfully. 'Easier said than done,' he said.

I thought that we needed to consult our friends, and we all met two nights later.

'Let's invite him for dinner,' said Armande. 'Get Bartola to feed him her famous concoctions.' This made our *chanteuse* indignant although she knew that she was just being teased.

'I have told you that poison ees my o-o-o bee, you do not expect stamp collectors to spend the whole day writing letters? Or people who collect guns to go about shooting their enemies, do you? The guns are for their collection. I aim to learn all there ees to know about poisons and not to keel no-o-bo-dy.'

Coleridge suggested that he cornered the painter in a dark alley and convince him that something bad was going to happen to him if he did not stop this nonsense. We all agreed that threats were of no use to an irresponsible man. Besides he had already been telling everybody that Clarihoe was a pervert and had seduced him. This had already taken its toll on his no longer immaculate reputation. People now looked at him mockingly wherever he went, exchanging whispers. Just shutting him up is not going to be enough then, said the Bishop.

'I am against the taking of human lives, but a man like him deserves the same fate as those decadent Galitzins, Khilkhovs and Romanovs. I could strangle him with my bare hands with fingers to spare,' said Ivan

Vissarionovich. We discussed the situation late into the night and finally I proposed that, having recently honed my skills as a burglar, I could easily break into his mews flat in Cadogan Gardens and steal those letters. That idea was approved unanimously. Nevertheless I was not entirely convinced. Would this alone save Clarihoe?

Perhaps Mill de La Marelle could then be challenged in court to produce the evidence. Would that stop tongues wagging when he could not deliver? Doesn't the blackmailer deserve some sort of retribution? This temporary solution seemed the one most likely to help our friend. A more permanent one might evolve later.

It was decided that the following evening, when Mill de La Marelle was known to be at some gambling table, it would be the ideal time for action. In the night, insomnia and my fevered brain had collided and sparked off a new idea. We were going to involve Sherlock Holmes, who although he was not obviously on our side, was going to act for us, albeit unwittingly.

I am loathe to give the details of how I worked my way inside the Mulberry Mews flat of the young artist, lest it inspires miscreants to burglary. Suffice it to say that it was not toilsome. I was surprised at how meticulously arranged the flat was, seeing what a disorderly life its occupant led. Knowing that there wasn't the remotest risk of being caught, I settled down at his desk and looked at a collection of his *croquis* for future projects. With his obvious talent, the man could have made a name for himself in the art world if he could but discipline himself. I suspected that the letters, probably his most valuable assets, would be in his safe. I had come prepared and opened it with ease. I found all three letters. It needed no more than a cursory glance to establish the explosive nature of the correspondence. Algernon had repeatedly spelled out in lyrical terms what effect the appearance of the artist produced in him, and what his dearest wish was every time he caught a glimpse of the shape of his *derrière*. Worse, were the grovelling letters in which he abjectly swore eternal devotion to the young fop. No judge or jury would have needed much persuasion to arrive at a guilty verdict. I put the three highly incriminating missives in a large envelope, and was on the point of leaving when on an impulse, I seized a small phial of Pelikan Sepia Samt

83 and put it in my bag next to the incriminating evidence. Algernon was waiting for me in Sloane Square in a hansom cab, smoking a cigar with his friend Albert the cabbie. We made straight for Water Lane.

Artémise Traverson to whom we had sent a note by Albert last night, arrived at Water Lane on the dot at nine the next morning. He and I were closeted in Armande's study. Each equipped with a magnifying glass, we pored over the documents, studying all the idiosyncrasies present in his lordship's hand. We noted that his writing leant backwards at a small but noticeable inclination. Graphologists claim that the angle of the slant of the vertical components of letters t, l, h or k for example is peculiar to each individual. This rarely varies and stays with the writer for life. We noticed that he never dotted his i's but placed a little concave squiggle over his j's. We made note of many other interesting peculiarities. Most people leave roughly the same distance between two words, not Algernon. Some words almost touched, other adjacent pairs had large spaces between them. We kept going for about two hours and were satisfied that we had obtained a very good idea of the personality of the handwriting. He was surprised when we presented him with a list of the foibles in his script, assuring us that he had never noticed any of them.

After a short tea-break, we were again closeted in the study. This time, fitted with a set of steel nibs, the Pelikan Sepia samt 83, and paper provided by Clarihoe himself, we set to work. Traverson was given the task of copying the three letters, keeping the *appearance* of the writing as close as possible to the original, but craftily subverting all those hidden characteristics that we had unearthed. Punctuation marks were to be placed exactly in the middle rather than at unequal intervals like Algie did. In our version we kept the writing horizontal and did not slope up as Algie does, albeit almost imperceptibly.

After he had finished, just as daylight was beginning to fade, we compared them with the originals and marvelled at how similar they *appeared* superficially. The sepia colour was different to the black that Algernon had used, but to the casual eye this did not immediately attract attention.

No wonder I love Algernon so much. The dear man is devoid of malice. Although he knew that Mill de La Marelle had already been telling anyone within earshot that he, Algie, was a pervert and a pederast, we had a lot of convincing to do before he consented to part two of the planned action. He hesitated about the necessity of having his erstwhile lover punished. We explained that removing the incriminating evidence alone would not undo the slurs already circulating.

'Algie,' Frunk said finally, 'the man has already sullied your good name, and Irene's plan is the only one that can restore it, so don't be a milksop.' Reluctantly he agreed and the same night I visited Cadogan Gardens once more. However, this time round, it was for the purpose of carrying out a burglary in reverse, replacing the forgeries in Mill de La Marelle's safe.

Shortly after, Lassie sent word to Algernon that he had to see him urgently and they met at the *Patroclus*. Clarihoe expected him to make his demands forcefully and was not disappointed.

'Don't do it, Lassie,' he said. 'I don't want to see you go to jail. And please, don't keep telling our enemies about us.' The younger man was in hysterics. 'Me go to jail. You're joking, Gernie old sweetheart. I told you I am going to swear that you forced yourself upon me, and by my troth they will believe me. It's you who're going to rot in Reading Gaol or wherever, and I'll come to visit you and bring you a bag of orange ... pips.'

'I'll swear that I never wrote those letters.'

'Ha! There are experts who can tell now.'

'That's exactly what I mean,' said Clarihoe in despair. The menace inherent in this sentence was lost on the blackguard.

'What's ten thousand pounds to you, Gernie?'

'I won't give you a penny, you puppy, not if you went on your knees and begged,' Algernon finally snapped. 'And I told you I hate being called Gernie. Go ahead, do your worse, you're all bluster and threats, but you don't have the wherewithal to fight a case in court ... one you will surely lose. And don't say I didn't warn you.' And that was that.

Algernon was expecting Lestrade of The Yard to pay him a visit in the coming week, and he did not disappoint. The men of Scotland Yard went through his papers and assembled a number of documents in his handwriting, put them in a wooden box and invited him to follow them to Scotland Yard.

Douglas did not realise that he had played into our hands, and handed over our fakes to the police. We had read Lestrade's mind perfectly. At the Yard, after Algernon had the indictment read to him he was released on bail.

The trial date was fixed, and all the members of the *Club* turned up to support our friend, but avoiding to be seen together. As rumours about me had trickled into the public consciousness, I took special care to disguise myself, dressing up as an elderly dowager, walking with a stick. Clarihoe had his eminent cousin Sir Arthur Clarke-Norton acting for him, with the formidable Sir Carson Mellowtroe prosecuting.

Algernon had no option but to deny that he had been friends with Douglas. He knew him but only casually. Yes, he admired him for his artistic merit. No, he was a bachelor. Yes, he had a fiancée. No, he had never indulged in pederasty, with Mill de La Marelle or with anybody else. No, he certainly did not approve of unnatural practices between men. No, he hadn't the faintest idea why de La Marelle would make his false accusation against him; perhaps he thought he had a great deal of money. Yes, he remembered giving the artist some money. Because he considered himself to be a patron of the arts.

The prosecution then produced a chambermaid who swore under oath that she had seen the two men in the lounge of the Rutland Hotel where she worked on at least three different occasions. Clarke-Norton asked if she had seen them together, and the young woman admitted that she had not, but -. The judge interrupted her and instructed her to just answer the question. No, she had not. Other witnesses were called, but there were so many contradictions in their statements that no one could be sanguine about what judgement the jury had formed so far.

On the third day, Sir Carson, glowing with anticipated triumph, produced his star witness: Mr Sherlock Holmes of Baker Street, who would demonstrate beyond the shadow of a doubt the authenticity of the letters. The illustrious detective walked in, unsmiling, head high, without looking at gallery, judge or jury and took his stand. He confirmed his name and his place of residence. Yes, he exercised the profession of detective. He declined to confirm that he was the greatest practitioner of his trade. It was not for him to say. He had no intimate knowledge of the working practices of his colleagues. Yes, he had made a number of studies in fields likely to help him in his detective work, and was happy to name them. He had written monographs on, among others, tobacco ash, on the speech patterns of middle England, the sand on English beaches, inks, dyes, furs and stains. His most recent work was a study of handwriting styles, carried out with the specific aim of exposing forger-ies. It's a monograph with the title of *A Study in Graphology*, your lordship.

'Did Inspector Lestrade of Scotland Yard hand over to you some documents enjoining you to make a thorough study of them?'

'If I make a study of anything, it's always thorough, my lord.'

'Will you be so good as to inform us if they were the exhibits marked AB4?'

'Yes, they were.'

'Did Mr Lestrade also hand over to you the exhibit AB5, have a good look.' A clerk of court duly passed the latter to him.

'Yes, I did have a *good* look at exhibit AB5,' said Holmes.

'Mr Holmes, will you describe to the court what your findings were.'

'In your own words,' added his lordship to the detective's irritation, which he made no attempt to hide.

'In my own words? Hmm. I could hardly fail to do so.' At this point, the detective opened a file that he had with him and took out some sheets of paper.

'First, I discovered that the paper was made by Rankin-Holder. Having read the contents of the documents referred to as AB4, I was surprised that it bore a distinct watermark which was obviously incorpo-rated by the Cylinder mould process.'

'And what is the significance of that?' asked Sir Carson. Holmes took a deep breath and addressed the judge.

'Will your lordship who so kindly directed me to use *my own words* just now, allow me the indulgence of answering this question in *my own time*?' said Holmes drily. To my surprise the judge gave a curt nod. Indeed Mr Holmes had such an aura of authority about his person that even a distinguished judge felt obliged to yield to what I thought was an unjusti-fied demand.

'Mr Holmes,' said Sir Carson in a subdued tone. 'Are you able to tell us directly if in your view, the letters were genuine or forgeries?'

'I am able to do so, but again, I will crave the court's indulgence to give my opinion only after I have exposed my reasons.'

'Why is the judge allowing him to get away with that?' I wondered.

'What, may I enquire,' Sir Carson asked making no effort to hide his irritation, 'were those findings?'

For the first time Holmes looked at jury and gallery. I thought for a moment that he had rested his gaze on me. Then he turned away from me and started talking in his monotone voice.

'My task was to verify or otherwise that the documents in AB5 were written by the same person as those in AB4.'

'And were they?' Holmes ignored the question and continued regardless.

'At first glance, it seemed as if the documents in both cases were written by the same person, but I began by studying the patterns in AB5, the documents Inspector Lestrade collected from Lord Clarihoe's desks.

Whilst there is a striking similarity between the writing style in the two exhibits, AB4 and AB5, a close scrutiny revealed a number of marked differences. As an example a study revealed immediately that whereas Lord Clarihoe's letters lean backwards by an average of ten degrees, those in AB4 also lean backwards but by no less than fifteen degrees on average.'

'Mr Holmes, I am lost, can you elucidate?'

'Your honour, if you look at letters t, h, k, capital I for example, the main the parts of those letters that more usually appear vertical. In both cases here they slope leftwards. I worked on a sample of one hundred such letters in each case, measured the slant, and worked out the average. As I said-'

'Yes, I understand, have the members of the jury?' They nodded. 'Thank you Mr Holmes, please proceed.'

'I noticed something even more strange about the letters i and j. Mr Clarihoe does not dot his i's, but places a little concave squiggle over his j's. On the other hand, the author of AB4 does the opposite. He places a little concave squiggle over his i's but dots his j's.'

Holmes then listed seventeen significant discrepancies, dwelling on the difference between the letters v, w, x and y. Lord Clarihoe writes them like newspaper letters, avoiding curvatures, whereas the author of AB4 uses rounded forms more common to ordinary handwriting. Lord Clarihoe crosses his t's with a line sloping upwards, the opposite of the author of AB4. All this, explained Holmes, was in marked contrast with the other letters which he found to be exceptionally identical apart from their angle of inclination.

'So what's your conclusion then?' demanded Sir Arthur hiding his impatience.

'May it please your lordship ... there were a total of nineteen striking differences, which would normally have led me to the conclusion that the letters were not written by Lord Clarihoe.'

On hearing this, Douglas sprang to his feet and began screaming incoherently. The judge instructed Sir Carson to explain to his client that unless he calmed down, he would have no alternative but to have him removed from the court and continue the trial without him, something which would indubitably be prejudicial to his case.

'Mr Holmes, if I heard you right, you said, and I quote... "which would normally have led me to the conclusion"?' said Sir Carson when his client had managed to control himself.

'In my extensive study of handwriting, I have never come across a specimen of writing which was so consistently inconsistent in its style. The writer of the letters seemed to be taking special care to distance his script from Lord Clarihoe's. It is an obvious forgery, but-'

'So your expert opinion is that it was not written by Lord Clarihoe?'

'I am not saying that, my lord.'

'So, you are saying that it is and is not a forgery.'

'An extraordinary conclusion, I'll vouchsafe. It might well have been written by Lord Clarihoe purposely in that style, for some reason I am unable to fathom.'

'You mean Lord Clarihoe's forged his own handwriting?' asked Clarke-Norton springing up like a startled rabbit. 'This is preposterous.' A rumble of stunned murmurs was followed by a period of uneasy silence until his lordship instructed Holmes to continue his testimony.

'There were a few other things which struck me as unusual,' said Holmes. 'The letters all bore a date in May 1881 at the top, but there are two factors which make nonsense of this.'

'I received them in May 1881, there is no doubt about that,' said Douglas jumping on his feet again.

'Mr Holmes, you mentioned two factors,' said his lordship. 'Please inform the court what they were.'

'Concerning the watermark I mentioned earlier, I have obtained confirmation from Rankin-Holder that, until 1883, they were using the Dandy Roll process for the insertion of watermarks in their product and had only replaced the system by the more modern Cylinder Mould process in that year. Besides, the lion rampant mark was only introduced last year.' The attendance gasped in unison on hearing this extraordinary fact.

'And the other factor?'

'I was intrigued by the absence of melanin in the ink, and did some tests on it ... I mean in the letters purportedly written by Lord Clarihoe to Mr de La Marelle ... AB4 ... and discovered it to be a Pelikan Sepia Samt. I have in my possession a letter from the distributors, certifying that the ink was not available in England before 1884.'

'What can all this mean?' asked the judge.

'Your honour, I will read my summary,' and he picked a single sheet of paper and read from it.

'Point: I am unable to rule out that the letter was not written by Lord Clarihoe. Point: None of the three letters were actually written in May 1881 as indicated by the watermark. Point: The ink used in the three letters had not been on sale before last year, as evidenced by a certificate from the sole distributors, Morton & Sons of Regent Street.'

'So you're saying that Mr Mill de La Marelle is bringing a fraudulent case against my client?' Clarke-Norton said jubilantly.

'No sir, I am stopping short of emitting that opinion. Perhaps his lordship could allow the plaintiff to have another look at the letters and tell us what he thinks. The judge agreed to this and exhibit AB4 was passed on to Douglas who took it with trembling fingers and examined them for a good while, the folds on his forehead showing the degree to which he was perplexed.

'The letters look identical to the ones Lord Clarihoe sent me, but I thought they were written in black ink.'

'So you're saying that they are not the same you claim to have received?' asked the judge.

'I am baffled your lordship. It is clear that the police have plotted with Algie to undermine my case... I swear that he sent me those letters... I mean they were in my safe and I gave them to Lestrade ... he changed them. This is a disgrace. That man's a villain, that's the only explanation.' This outburst earned him a strong rebuke from the judge who would not permit the good name of our loyal police force to be sullied by baseless allegations. Lassie was in tears and shaking all over.

The case went on for a while longer. The two sides gave their summing up, after which the jury was sent out to decide upon a verdict. We realised that we had not contended with the perspicacity of Holmes. He had pierced through our stratagems. We held our breaths, not daring to exchange looks with each other. Fortunately we did not have to wait long, for the jury returned and pronounced a verdict of not guilty. The judge told Algernon that he was free to go. As he was making for the door, Lestrade, who was still seething with anger at the slur cast on him, approached Clarihoe.

'If your lordship wishes to bring a case for blackmail and libel against de la Marelle, you would almost certainly win it.'

That night we debated the pros and cons, and in the end Algernon arrived at a decision. Yes, he was going to send the young man to jail. This came as a disappointment to me. I had always thought of Algie as a kind, compassionate and forgiving man. Witnessing how devastated the young villain had been in court, my erstwhile rigid stance towards him had softened.

'Algie,' I said, 'what's the point? Hasn't the poor boy suffered enough? This court action has vindicated your reputation. I didn't expect you to be so unforgiving.' Clarihoe blushed and began stammering.

'You don't understand, Irene. I have never stopped loving the dear boy. I don't want to punish him. S-s-s-sending him to jail... don't you see?... can only do him a power of good. Once inside he won't have those distractions ... you understand? He will be bound to pick up his drawing pens...'

CHAPTER NINE

Hardstone's Death

(1889)

I f Sherlock Holmes had indeed been collecting evidence to confound Hardstone, the events of the following week gave him a severe jolt. The villain had given a lavish party to celebrate his not guilty verdict. During the riotous festivities, he was found battered to death in his card room with a crowbar. It was in all the newspapers. I saw Holmes flinch as he read the headlines, on his face a clear expression of disappointment.

Next day, the intelligence was that a young waiter Arnold Meehan had been taken in for questioning, and like my employer, I lost interest in the case. That is, until the following note arrived at our door:

***

The man now weting for Judge Albemarle D'Arleville Axquist, knone as The Henging Jugde to pronouns the deth sentense on him, Arnold Meehan is innosent. if you dotn want a miskarriage of jusstise, you shoud look closly at Maggles, aka Crobar Bob; he was akwitted of murder with a crobar, but the chief witness comited perjury. The fifty sovereigns is to cover your expenditure for your elping Meehan establish his innicence.

A frend of jusstise.

When I gave the note to Mr Holmes, I mentioned to him that I thought it strange that someone who spelled Albemarle D'Arleville Axquist to perfection would stumble over the easier words. He pursed his lips and said nothing, but my own interest was reawakened. I will relate the facts using notes made by Dr Watson's, presumably for an account of the affair to be composed at a more convenient time:

This note, written on paper from which the heading had been carefully cut off, together with fifty gold sovereigns in a small leather bag were deposited outside number 221B early one morning a few days later. Meehan had only been formally charged by the police the day before. This was written in the most unseemly scrawl and when Holmes passed it on to me, I could not help exclaiming, 'What an illiterate scoundrel!' Whereupon Holmes looked at me and pursed his lips. 'On the contrary doctor, have another look.' He handed a magnifying glass over to me. I seized it, not sure what to do with it.

'Observe how many spelling mistakes there are,' Holmes muttered encouragingly.

'But almost every single word is badly spelled,' I exclaimed. 'I have perfect eyesight, I'll have you know Holmes, eh what!'

'But not D'Arleville Axquist, or sovereigns, you will observe. And expenditure, I see... I just checked in Who's Who... Lord Chief Justice Albemarle D'Arleville Axquist ... one apostrophe, two "l"'s, the "u" com- ing after the "q"...'

'Ah but Holmes, by the law of averages-'

'Now, Watson, use the magnifying glass and focus on the mistakes. Take the "e" in weting for instance, what do you notice?' I noticed nothing, an "e" is an "e", and in this case should have been "a" and "i". I demurred and shook my head.

What about the second "s" in sentence? What about the "k" in mis-karriage, or in akwitted... need I go on? Look closely.' I did not fail to detect a note of irritation in my friend's tone, and the answer suddenly dawned upon me.

'The wrong letters are all a shade darker.' I was unable to hide a self-congratulatory blush as I emitted my opinion.

'Written with greater emphasis. It's called self-consciousness, doctor,' said Holmes full of admiration. 'You are a fast learner, there's hope for you yet.'

Encouraged, I went on. 'This means that the perpetrator was taking extra care to draw attention to the mistakes,' adding as an afterthought, 'subconsciously of course.'

'Capital.'

'So he must in fact be an erudite.'

'Couldn't have put it better myself, doctor.'

'Now, the question is why did he do it? Why did he write with his left hand?' I was lost. I hadn't even noticed that he had done that.

'Why indeed? I haven't the faintest, my dear fellow.'

'Because he doesn't want us to identify him, Watson.' Without stopping he went on. 'And why, have you asked yourself, does he not want us to identify him?' He did not wait for my answer, probably because he must have thought - rightly of course - that I had none to offer. 'I'll tell you. Because he knows more than he wants to let on. He may even know who the true killer is.' He paused for just a few seconds here. 'He may even be the killer.' I was baffled.

'But Holmes, why would the killer put us on the right track?'

'Why indeed? I must own to not having an answer to this conundrum at the moment. Is he playing games with us perhaps?'

'Aye, that must be it,' I said, shaking my head at my friend's unique insight.

'Or he might not like the idea of the waiter Meehan paying for his crime.' I said nothing. I was too stunned by the genius of my companion. For a moment we said nothing. I, because I had nothing to say, and Holmes, no doubt because he was dealing with the hundreds of hypotheses bubbling inside his large brain.

'Ah but Holmes, how are we to find the author of an anonymous letter?'

'There are clues here, Watson. Feel the paper.' I did, it was obviously quality paper. But surely not even Holmes could discover the writer of an anonymous letter by means of the width of the paper it is written on. Or could he?

'Hold it to the light, doctor.' I did, and saw the watermarks, the letters RH. When I recognised a small figure of Lady Justice with the scales, I could contain my delight no longer and must have hooted with delight. Holmes smiled and nodded happily, like a father whose son has brought home good marks from school.

'RH stands for Rankin Holder, the quality paper manufacturers, and the Lady Justice, inserted by the Cylindrical Mould Process, is usually for the purpose of professionals in the legal profession. His mood changed at this point, and he became morose and withdrawn.

***

I remember well that evening. The doctor was to be proved right, but for over an hour Mr Holmes was not able to sit in one place and kept pacing up and down the room, mumbling and muttering to himself. Neither Watson nor I were able to catch his drift.

'Could it have been sent to us by the judge himself?' he suddenly said aloud.

'No, Holmes, you're talking a lot of rot, that doesn't make sense.' Watson did not say. Not because it was *not* rot, but the doctor is convinced that from his friend's mouth only pearls of wisdom ever dropped.

'You could be right my dear fellow,' he said instead, at which, Holmes, presumably not overwhelmed by the less than fullsome approval of his friend, directed a cold stare at him with his steely blue eyes. Then they sat together and ate in silence.

After dinner, as Watson and I hoped, he took out his violin and started playing. The doctor and I exchanged wary looks. As we feared, the moment he put the violin in its case he made for the triangular glass case, perched in the corner of two walls, where he kept the white powder. To our sorrow, he was soon in a drugged state, ensconced in his armchair his legs sprawled in front of him as was his wont. After Watson went to his bedroom, I came to spread a blanket over him. He started mumbling. Key ... is ... lawyer. Must be a lawyer. What lawyer? I asked gently. There's the rub, Irene, there's the rub. Not for the first time, in his drugged state, he was calling me Irene. How about Mr Waverick? I said without thinking. He half opened his eyes for a split second, looked at me strangely and closed them again and went to sleep. Let Dr Watson pick up the baton and continue our story.

***

Next day, Holmes asked me if I wished to accompany him to Pentonville Prison where we wanted to see Meehan. I was greatly gratified to witness the esteem shown to my friend by the men in uniform and the petty officials. They were all in awe of his genius.

Meehan cowered when he was told that Holmes had come for him. Tearfully, he asked if he was being taken to the gallows right away. My friend urged him to calm down, reminding him that he had not even been gone to trial yet. The guards sat him opposite us. Take a deep breath, I instructed him, and tell us what happened.

'Well, Mr Holmes ... Doctor Watson, quite early as I was servin' the master a drink ... Mr Hardstone that is, someone jostled me ... it were well crowded ... and I spilled some on his cravat, which made him very wrathful sir, and he lashed out at me... with the back of his hand, full in the face sir, but I didn't say nothin' excepting sorry sir, and took my leave. Mr Crowbar... Maggles sir, I don't know why, but he was always good to me... Arnold, he says, avoid coming near the master so as not to vex him, jess stick to serving 'em folks as are in the other rooms, I was 'appy to do that. Then after midnight we heard a big scuffle upstairs, followed by screams and the master was found dead, battered by a crowbar, the police was fetched sir, and everybody had a ... now what's it called when someone says you was wi' 'em?'

'Alibi...'

'That's 'im... alibi... everybody had one of them, sir, but I was 'aving a smoke by missel behind the oak like. And the police said I dun it sir, cos Mr Hardstone 'ad slapped me, they said I wanted revenge. If I killed everybody wot had slapped me sir... And the poor fellow burst into tears. 'Now they's gonna 'ang me. I ain't dun it sir, I swear on the 'ead of my never to be born son...'

Holmes tut tutted. 'They aren't going to do anything of the sort, Meehan. Trust me.'

We went directly to Scotland Yard after our visit, and Holmes asked to see Lestrade.

'Lestrade,' he said without any preliminaries the moment the inspector appeared. 'If you ask me where I was when Hardstone was killed, I am

unable to tell you.' The Scotland Yard man and I exchanged glances, neither of us understanding the purport of this gambit. My friend continued.

'And Lestrade, if you ask me if Hardstone has given me cause for wishing him harm, my answer will be a resounding yes!'

'So?' asked Lestrade blinking uneasily.

'So,' said Holmes tending his wrists to the Inspector. 'Arrest us, we have no alibi... the doctor and I.'

'Ah, Mr Holmes,' said Lestrade relieved. 'Always trying to mock me.' After a pause he continued. 'You will be pleased to hear, Mr Holmes, that I was inspired by your own form of reasoning. Are you not always saying that once you have eliminated the impossible, what cannot be eliminated must be fact?' Lestrade's eyes glowed with self-satisfaction and, like a sausage in a hot frying pan, he could not keep still. 'There were sixty-five people at that celebration, and sixty-four of them were able to provide watertight alibis,' he said with an emphatic nod. 'Only Meehan failed so to do. Ergo, Mr Holmes.' Turning to me, he explained, 'Ergo my dear doctor is Latin for therefore. Ergo, Meehan having no alibi must have done the deed.'

'Lestrade,' said Holmes, 'I am glad you have not yet sent your papers to the Attorney General's Office. I know that your enquiries are not yet finished. I am sure you will arrive at the conclusion that you need rather more evidence than you have collected so far in order to indict the poor fellow. Trust me, he didn't do it.' Lestrade appeared reluctant to concede the point, but we both had the certainty that the Scotland Yard man would think again and that Meehan would soon be released.

We did not have to wait long. Next day the newspapers all carried the headlines: MEEHAN RELEASED, SCOTLAND YARD PURSUES NEW LEAD. After breakfast Holmes asked me to accompany him to the Waverick home in Knightsbridge, explaining that the QC was a good friend of the deceased. Since he was invited to the party, he might *provide a clue or two. We were greeted by the elderly housekeeper, who said that Mr Waverick was spending a few days in Cornwall.*

'What's he doing there, Mrs Wendover?' asked Holmes. The lady looked at him suspiciously, unaware of the fact that when we had stopped to enquire about the whereabouts of the house, the tobacconist mentioned her name. Nevertheless, she asked us in.

'At this time of the year he goes sailing, he's got a cottage in Cornwall.'

'By himself?'

'Ay, he used to go with his daughter Miss Cissy. Cecilia. But since she left, he goes by himself.'

'Cissy? She left? For where?'

'She went to Africa, didn't she? To be a missionary ... to save the little 'eathens.'

She offered us some excellent tea and biscuits and Holmes asked more questions about the daughter. Mrs Wendover laughed nervously.

'That was quite a to-do, that was, I mean Miss Cissy leaving. Took us all by surprise ... seeing that ever since she was a toddler Mr Francis had been grooming her to take over his practice. His ambition was to make Cissy the first woman QC.'

'I don't suppose you know what made her change her mind?'

'Course I know, but it ain't my place to tell family secrets to every Tom, Dick and Harry.' Holmes and I were not flattered by these epithets and our disappointment must have shown, making the housekeeper uneasy. Then perhaps keen to atone for the faux-pas, she suddenly seemed gnawed by an indomitable desire to confide.

'Might as well, eh,' she said but kept quiet. We stared at each other, and then at her.

'Might as well, I mean the truth never 'urts nobody does it?' We nodded encouragingly.'

'What an almighty row that were, Mr Holmes. They was so loving, father and daughter. Ever since the missus got gathered ... fell ill and died in a day, she did ... Miss Cissy and Mr Francis were ... how shall I put it? Closer than ... a sandwich and its filling. But you see, she never approved.'

'Approved of what?'

'I was just coming to that... Miss Cissy said Mr Francis no longer made the difference between law and justice.'

' "There is no justice, darling. If there were, why would the Lord take your mother away from us?" I heard him tell her many a time.'

'Until five years ago, before his wife passed away,' Holmes said to me, 'he used to be much preoccupied by the distinction between justice and law, and this was indeed the theme of many a dissertation of his in the Law Journals. "When Law and Justice take opposite routes," he wrote once, "practitioners of the art should weep." After a short pause, she continued, 'It was after his wife died that he sort of had a change of heart.'

'Miss Cissy says that he ... prostitutes ... her word, sirs, not mine, I do beg your pardon ... that he prostitutes hisself by defending guilty criminals.' The lady wiped a tear before speaking again.

'I remember, sirs, I have been with the family for twenty years ... time was when he would only take up cases of the poor, the wrongly accused ... and there's a lot of them sirs, believe me ... and in them days they was always broke ... but I was ever so proud when on my shopping rounds them folks told me, what a gem "your Mr Francis" were. Then *when Mrs Waverick died, he became a changed man. Miss Cissy said that he used to love her … "You loved my mum more than life," she said, "now your new love is Mammon." I've not met that lady yet so I can't say nothing … but he's always loved his little girl … it's like I can hear them now as we speak.' Mrs Wendover went on to relay a conversation that went like this:*

'You must live in the real world, darling,' he told her.

'The world of criminals like Hardstone and Maggles?' she shouted. 'No, Papa, people like them befoul my world.'

'Don't you dare pass judgement on me. You were only too glad to benefit from my ill-gotten gains as you call them.'

'You know very well that they shot those guards in Huddersfield, Papa.'

'Of course I do. It's the job of the prosecution to prove it, and it's my job to stop him doing just that.'

'And when Crowbar Bob defenestrated that beggar's skull because he grabbed his leg and wouldn't let go, you persuaded the jury that the eyewitness was a drunk in the throes of delirium tremens.'

'They did not have to believe me. The counsel was an ass.'

'You're on the side of murderers! Mama would have been so ashamed of you.' He received this like he had been hit by cold lightning … if you see what I mean. He froze, Mr Holmes. It's like what the preacher explained 'appened when Lot's wife turned round and were turned into statue of salt.'

'I wish I had starved!' Miss Cissy said amid tears.

'When you run the chambers, you'll do as you please sweetheart,' he said in a conciliatory tone.

'Who says I want to follow in your footsteps? It's the last thing I want to do!'

'But darling, it's been your lifelong ambition.'

'It isn't anymore, you've trampled upon my ambition, Papa. It's in tatters.

Next, she stormed out. The first time she'd spent the night away from home. He was a complete wreck, wouldn't sleep or eat. He went looking for her everywhere, but she wasn't at any relative's or friend's. At the time he was in court, defending those two very people, Hardstone and Maggles in the Huddersfield case.

'The night he won the case, he came home a beaten man. He had never come home drunk before. Miss Cissy was still gone. "Mrs Wendover, what have I done?" he asked me. "I feel covered in filth ... Cissy is right, I have lost my sense of right and wrong, my direction, everything." That night Miss Cissy came back and told him that she was going to Africa. It was like she had exploded a bomb. He ordered her to drop that crazy notion. You'll die of malaria, you will be torn from limb to limb by lions, the cannibals will eat you. He used every argument, but she just picked up her things and left. Her ship was sailing in the morning, she said ... never a hug nor nothing.'

'Then he calmed down, or so it seemed, but I know my Francis, 'e were 'eart-broken. What did he really care about money or fame? He had lost his little girl ... so I was surprised to find out that he meant to go to the big party those 'orrid men wuz givin' to celebrate their not-guilty verdict. I was sure he was going to do something 'orrible. When I heard that Hardstone had been done in, my first thought was that it were Master Francis, and was so relieved when I heard that it were the waiter.'

Waverick came back from Cornwall a day or two later, and we went to visit him. He saw the expression on Sherlock Holmes' face, and knew that the game was up. He decided that he might as well admit his guilt. Yes, he

82

had betrayed everything and everyone, his vocation, his dead wife, and now he had lost his girl. He had nothing to live for. At least he had had the satisfaction of punishing the main artisan of his downfall. He went even further.

'My plan was to kill Hardstone and make it appear like it was Maggles who had done it, so he'd hang like the cur he is. God knows they both deserved death ten times over for the many horrible things that they have done. I thought I was clever in adopting his chosen method of killing ... the crowbar. I wasn't thinking clearly ... and I had not counted on the lack of imagination of our police force. I don't suppose I could ask you to use your own talent and stick the murder on him. No don't answer that, I was just musing... I am so glad you were able to set Meehan free. Getting the guilty off the hook might be reprehensible, Mr Holmes, but sending an innocent man to the gallows? No sir, I couldn't allow that. I suppose you will arrest me now... No, you aren't empowered to do that ...yes... if there's any money left from the advance I sent you, let the poor fellow have it. And tell Lestrade I shall be waiting for him, my wrists joined together ... good-bye Mr Holmes...'

***

Mr Waverick did not keep his word. When Lestrade came for him next morning, he had disappeared, taking his boat out on a stormy night. Two days later, his body was washed ashore on the beach at St Ives Bay. A tragic accident, said the press.

Mycroft paid a visit to Number 221B, and I heard him urge his brother and Doctor Watson to pass a veil of silence over the affair. It served no purpose to let the public know that respectable members of the judiciary were able to carry out reprehensible acts. Which is why Watson never used the story. I feel under no such obligation.

CHAPTER TEN

An Eye for An Eye

(1886)

When the newspapers reported the story of the disappearance of the *Eye of Golconda*, they gave an account which was unanimously favourable to the Earl and Countess of Balsingham. The Earl was the seventeenth in the line of succession to the British throne. The Countess was the daughter of Jersey-born Sir Maxwell de la Maroulière, probably the richest man in the United Kingdom.

The pair had inherited massive fortunes from their respective families and possessed large swathes of the kingdom where they exploited all manner of commodities including farm workers. In other words, they could mislay one million pounds without becoming aware of it. Suffice it to say that they were not likely to lose track of even a single pound. The Countess had inherited a large number of extremely valuable jewels, diamond necklaces, ruby cameos, beryl bracelets, sapphire rings, gold chains, which she loved to wear at the many *soirées* she hosted or attended, often as the guest of honour, almost every week. She knew exactly how many items there were - one thousand nine hundred and forty-seven. On top of that, the pair also had gems they collected and kept in a securely locked room in Balsingham Court, their Knightsbridge Mansion or in their country seat of Fixton Abbey in Sussex. Among them were eighty-four diamonds each worth at least fifty-thousand pounds, some considerably more, to say nothing of Fabergé eggs, rubies, Swiss mobiles in gold or platinum, music boxes from ancient Persia, miniatures, carpets and rugs from Samarkand and many similar visible manifestations of opulence. According to gossip, the Balsinghams were richer than Queen Victoria herself. What they prized most in the world was a diamond which fell just short of the famous Kohinoor by one carat, at 104 carats: *The Eye of Golconda*, more familiarly known as *The Eye*. The *cognoscenti* agree that it may be marginally smaller than the Kohinoor, but it surpassed the latter in éclat.

One morning, the newspapers carried almost nothing but stories of how thieves had broken into the Knightsbridge Mansion and stolen that eighth marvel of the universe while the noble couple were soundly asleep in their bedroom next door. Nobody had heard anything, nor had the faintest idea of how the theft was carried out. When her Ladyship went into the secured room which was always kept under lock and key, she was horrified to find that the glass case which housed *The Eye* had been carefully opened and its occupant gone. The locks showed no signs of having been tampered with.

The nation went into deep mourning over the disappearance of the gem, estimated at half a million pounds. Anybody would have believed that a member of the beloved royal family itself had gone missing. People were in tears when they met in public as they recounted to each other the latest snippet gleaned from the day's newspaper. The poor Countess has lost her appetite and was now as thin as a rake. The doctor has been called to her bedside. She has gone three whole days without any sustenance. Three sleepless nights. The press declared that her ladyship seemed to be falling prey to the *Curse of The Eye*. This was something dire befalling a custodian who did not take good care of it: The Maharajah of Allahpur who was mauled to death on a tiger shoot had bought it from an English director of the East India Company, who it was claimed, had shot his wife's Indian lover from whom he had purchased the gem. Then the nation breathed a collective sigh of relief when they read that Lloyd's had decided to make good the loss and was paying the noble couple an undisclosed sum, reported by those in the know to be close to half a million.

At the *Club* we regaled each other with dramatic readings of extracts from the newspapers, no one believing a word of what we read. Frunk who had his ears close to the ground told us tales of skulduggery connected with the noble couple. We had found it hard to believe those press stories. Why would people with so much wealth act in such a dishonest manner? wondered Bartola. The Bishop explained that such wealth was indubitably the result of inborn dishonesty which had infected the fabric of their psyche. Folks, he averred, never accepted that they were rich enough and were always trying to find the means of augmenting their possessions. Frunk observed that in his experience, the rich always believed that they did not have enough and that the poor invariably had more than they really needed. We easily convinced ourselves that there had been no theft and that the whole operation was mounted to defraud the insurers by collecting the indemnity whilst at the same time hanging on to their possession. We knew about the unwillingness of insurers to pay out and were surprised that Lloyd's had offered the handsome compensation.

I hate to reveal this, but the Bishop, now freed from Catholic restraint, had developed the habit of picking wenches for a night of lust. He alerted us to an interesting fact. Daisy, who used to be a maid at Balsingham Court, but who had been unfairly dismissed, told our friend that the staff, to a man (and woman), were convinced that there never was any theft. She had also given him a number of leads, which obviously none of us could verify. This confirmed our own instincts. Lord Clarihoe volunteered to talk to Daisy (*"I've always had a strong urge to pick one of 'em fallen angels up"*) who swore that *The Eye* was still in its glass case. The Countess had brazenly claimed that it was its twin. They let out that they had not thought it judicious to reveal this, but shortly after they had acquired *The Eye*, a near identical one had emerged, and they had had the foresight to buy that one too. At a special meeting, the *Club* decided that action needed to be taken, if only because we did not approve of *others* defrauding those venerable insurance companies.

With the help of Artémise, I transformed myself into a frump by padding myself up, wearing specially made clothes and theatre make-up, and made my way to Knightsbridge. The artist had further counterfeited some impressive looking references, to the effect that I had been in service in France and Germany, at the British Embassies there. Knowing that women who are served upon and have servants to do their every bidding invariably suffer from fatigue pains and twinges, I got him to add that I had magical fingertips which have been used on royalty to assuage their superior cramps and aches. Brazenly I set out for Balsinghman Court one morning.

It was a cold crisp spring dawn and as we crossed the many green areas of this lovely city I was so relaxed that I found myself admiring the scattered rainbow embedded in the ground, pretending to be crocuses. Ivan Vissarionovich dropped me in Hyde Park and I walked to the lordly residence. Her ladyship was unsurprisingly still in bed so I was asked to wait in the kitchen. I wasted no time questioning the cooks and kitchen hands, on whom I made an excellent impression when I offered to join them in their chores.

Countess Araminta finally summoned me to the Games Room, where she questioned me at great length about myself and my previous employments. I have to explain that I owe the success of the many enterprises that I have carried out as part of the schemes of the *Club* to my absolute self-belief and our carefully laid-out plans. All the time I felt quite sanguine about the undertaking. The noble lady was completely taken in. She mentioned a wage and I opened my eyes wide in gratitude and said, thank you, your ladyship.

I was surprised that I blended in seamlessly with the maids and page boys, cooks and gardeners. I knew that one sure way of making a good name among them was to insinuate that one was of a rather better class but had fallen on bad times, and then act without the slightest trace of haughtiness. In any case, I have never been condescending or patronising to anybody. Mam taught us that we were all equal before our Maker, servants and lords, black, yellow or white. I have acted haughty when attending balls and *soirées* frequented by so-called ladies of class or breeding with nothing much to recommend themselves, and I know that I can look regal when I choose to. I am slim and tall with the narrowest of waists, a nose which is deemed to be the shapeliest in London and immediately attracts attention, as does my jet black hair. My eyes have been compared to mountain tarns. Indeed I am the envy of many a matronly ladyship of my age. When I do flaunt my natural qualities, it has always been in fun.

I became very fond of Mathilda the talented and hard-working head cook. I daresay that this penchant was fully reciprocated. The stable boys would jump at the sight of me, in the hope of being able to serve me. The steward grew weak at the knees at my approach. In an endearing stammer he asked me if I was spoken for. I replied in the affirmative. I thought that it might be useful to me to have him eat out of the palm of my hands, but I did not want to cause him pain later when I would have to take my leave of him out of necessity. He ate out of my hand anyway so I needn't have worried.

One day after a strenuous morning reclining on a chaise longue in the warm spring sun which had suddenly decided to honour us with a rare visit, the Countess summoned me and declared that she was extremely tired. Her back was killing her. 'It's as if I had spent a whole day working in the salt mines,' she added without irony.

'Oh, poor ma'am, I am so sorry to hear that. Will your ladyship be so kind as to allow me to do what I can to alleviate your ladyship's discomfort?' She beams a grateful smile at me. I follow her into the bedroom and set to work immediately. She lies on her face and exposes her bare back to me. I admit to a little frisson as I begin applying my fingertips to her soft supple skin the colour of ivory. I am here to do a job, I remind myself. I control my urges and continue kneading (Feel free to remove these comments, Mr Reynolds). I seize chunks of flesh by the inner side of each shoulder blade between the thumb and the other fingers of each hand and knead them repeatedly. It does not take long for her to start purring with relief and, dare I say, pleasure? I perform a professional job. After forty minutes, she indicates that I might stop. I do so gratefully as my arms are beginning to ache. *I* have nobody to pamper me at the moment. Often Algernon and I hold each other with our arms round each other squeezing or digging each other's flesh in the regions next to the shoulder blades - an innocent experience we both value.

With the help of my new friends downstairs, I learned the lie of the land. I discover that the so-called secured room is a hall oblong in shape, with the side giving onto the garden bedecked with tasty round glass windows small enough that they might even stop a cat going through them if opened. They were designed both for their beauty and for allowing the right amount of sunlight in. From the opposite wall hanged paintings by the most celebrated artists, English as well as French and Flemish, weavings and *broderies*. Two massive oak carved doors on the opposite two other sides offered the only entry into this unique museum. The Balsinghams only take their most intimate friends there to view the treasures on the wall, the *objets d'art* and the gems in the glass cases. These are made of the strongest glass which apparently cannot be broken even with a massive hammer. They are secured by locks specially made by Mr Yale himself for the noble couple. Unsurprisingly, her astute ladyship kept the locks of the doors and the glass cases in a massive iron box fixed to the underside of her bed, which itself is also locked, with its key kept at all times in a chain round her neck, even when she takes a bath.

I came to Balsingham House ready for a long haul and enjoyed my stay there in the company of the staff, sharing the occasional risqué joke with my new friends and colleagues. We ate well and I found that Mathilda had her foolproof method for deviating the odd bottle of claret or port and we indulged whenever a good occasion arose.

After three weeks, I felt emboldened enough to start considering setting in train the planned-for action. The Earl had gone tiger shooting in India, and when he does (I now knew), his wife received her own friends and they held raucous all-female bacchanalian parties, at which champagne, whisky and cognac flowed more than copiously, to say nothing of a little indulging in the fumes of the poppy.

The party was planned for the last Saturday of April. In the kitchen we had toiled for over twelve hours to prepare the feast. Bartola, who had struck me as a person who would never entertain a mean thought about anybody, and never contemplate harming anyone, human or animal, was, however, ready for any human she saw as an enemy. She had a small stock of mandrake at her disposition. She knew what dosage would be fatal and how much would just induce sleep. She had assiduously instructed me in its use. On top of all the alcohol that the good lady was going to imbibe, the opium she would have inhaled, I hardly needed more than half the dose suggested by the *chanteuse*. Clearly I did not want to endanger lives. We are not murderers. I was not aiming to induce sleep in the whole worshipful company as that would have caused complications. I had to make sure to contaminate her ladyship's sorbet and no one else's. That did not prove too difficult. The set for eating ice-cream was one specially ordered from Delft, each one with a unique theme. Araminta particularly liked the one with a Satyr passing water in a grotesque fashion. That was where I sprinkled no more than a pinch of the powdered sleep-inducer. To make assurance doubly sure, I had sprinkled some of the stuff on her pillow and tapped it all in. According to the expert, mandrake can induce sleep even when minute quantities are inhaled.

'Who made that *glace* today?' the Countess asked. I was shaken, and did not want the finger pointed at the new kitchen help Anne in the event of the subterfuge being discovered.

'I did, your l-ladyship,' it takes a lot to make me stammer.

'That woman,' Araminta laughingly exclaimed to her friends. 'She is an absolute gem. If one day I want to repay a kindness, I'll send her to you so she can give you a neck massage. I swear there is only one thing in the whole wide world that I like rather better.' After a little pause, she looked at the ladies with a saucy smile. 'No, I am not so sure of that.' The ladies cackled raucously and drank a toast to me, but she had not finished.

'And as you can discover for yourselves, she also makes the most delectable ice-cream this side of Italy.' I hoped Anne never gets to hear that I had unwittingly stolen her thunder.

The party ended after midnight when their ladyships were taken to their mansions by their coachmen. Araminta declared that she did not want her maid to put her to bed, but me, so I could massage her with my "cherubic fingertips, and make a flawless night even more perfect."

Sadly for the narration, but fortunately for me, nothing unforeseen happened and I was able to operate freely. Before the sun rose on the Sunday morning, *The Eye* had acquired new owners: the *Club des As*.

I quietly slipped out of Balsingham Court, telling the Cerberus at the gate that I was going for my early morning walk. As the man had always been sweet on me. Besides, as I had, in anticipation of my final escape, inured him to my early morning habit, he nodded knowingly and opened me up. I walked briskly towards the embankment where I caught a hansom and made for Water Lane, asking to be dropped in Effra Road. If an enquiry stumbled on this woman asking to be taken to Water Lane at dawn, it might lead to me. We had watertight plans to dispose of our ill-gotten loot and set them in motion right away.

It is universally acknowledged that last time, the Balsinghams had engineered a fake theft to claim a massive insurance from Lloyd's. They had fooled nobody, but the aristocratic aura surrounding them made them fireproof. Now that there had been a real theft, what was going to stop them filing a similar claim? After receiving Lloyd's cheque, paid out to protect their reputation, they had let it be known that, although they had lost the *Right Eye*, they still had the *Left Eye*. This, they made out, was a gem similar in grandeur to the one stolen. Incredibly it was also of 104 carats. They summoned the press and police to announce that another daring robbery had deprived them of that one too. In keeping with the twinned nature of the gems, they were now claiming a similar compensation to the one Lloyd's had paid out.

The first time round, the insurers had not disbursed gladly. The good grace they manifested was only superficial. Their business acumen had dictated that to contest a claim from such high-born clients might work against them. A very public denial of the claim might undo the good name the firm had built for itself over the years. They did not want potential insurers to think that their readiness to take in premiums was not commensurate with their willingness to pay indemnities. They had therefore paid without too much public fuss. Mr Charles Lloyd, it seems, did not mind who knew what his suspicions were. This time however, they were not going to be so supine.

They consulted Mr Holmes. I knew about this, but I would only be able to work out the details much later when some of Dr Watson's notes came my way.

Holmes arrived at Balsingham Court in the guise of someone sent by the police to help them catch the thief and bring him to book. If he suspected that her ladyship had instigated a fraud, his attitude revealed this not one whit. He treated her with absolute courtesy and manifested his sympathy and admiration for her in no uncertain way. About one thing there was unanimity: the culprit was the woman who had wormed her way into the household as a servant, and had disappeared after the theft. Holmes asked the Countess to describe her.

'Tall and slim,' she had begun. Already Holmes had cast a knowing glance at Watson. 'Coming to think of it now, she had a deportment which belied her assumed status,' she continued. 'But I confess to not having been immediately cognisant of this.' Without irony, she continued. 'But Mr Holmes knows that villains do not have their perfidy writ large on their forehead, am I not right?' Holmes smiled deferentially. 'It is clear that the woman has hypnotic powers,' he said, which caused some alarm in her ladyship.

'You mean–'

'No, I am not suggesting magic or circus trickery, ma'am. What I mean is that she has a personality that one immediately finds captivating. This makes it difficult for people she is dealing with to make full use of all their judgement.'

'There is a medico-technical word for this, charisma,' said Watson, but the Countess brushed him aside and spoke to Holmes.

'I think I know what you mean, people I meet tell me the same thing about myself.'

'I had noticed similarities,' said Holmes, adding with a faint smile. 'I hope, ma'am, that you do not make use of this ... eh ... charisma ... to inveigle others and dispossess them of their property.' Her ladyship laughed this away.

She led the two men to her bedroom and showed them where the box was in which she kept the keys. Araminta was very frank about the drunken stupor she was in, and conceded that she had fallen into the arms of Lethe the moment her head had touched the pillow. 'Which is not in the least surprising, ma'am,' said Holmes picking up a pillow. 'Not trusting that alcohol alone would put you in the helpless state she wanted you in, to enable her to carry out her nefarious intent, she had ... smell this ...' he ordered, handing the pillow over to the lady who did as she was told but shook her head.

'Watson?' said Holmes meaningfully. The medical man picked it up and after inhaling it deeply, he nodded. Holmes looked at him questioningly.

'Finely powdered *mandragora officinarum*.'

'What we ordinary mortals call mandrake, ma'am,' Holmes added.

'My goodness me! She thought of everything, didn't she, the little vixen?' said the Countess, unable to hide her admiration for the perfection of the plan. 'I bet she put some in that ice-cream as well,' mused Araminta aloud, to which Holmes nodded absently.

'Tell me all the details you can remember about the first theft.'

'The first theft?' she asked. Holmes did not fail to detect the first sign of unease on the self-assured lady. 'Oh yes, the first time. I had not partaken of a single drop of alcohol. Eugene ... that's my dear husband ... the Earl and I were in the bedroom all night long ... he being a light sleeper ... how the thief, or thieves carried out their felony, I will never understand. D'you believe in the supernatural, Mr Holmes?'

'My scientifically trained friend here will not allow me the luxury.'

'How else can you explain it then?'

'I have a few theories.' On hearing this her ladyship appeared a little discomfited.

'My friend Dr Watson here, who flatters me by publishing histories of my modest achievements has written about this. You may have read it yourself. When you have eliminated all the impossible solutions to a problem, whatever remains, however improbable must be the truth.'

'And are you left with one such ... alternative?'

'One or two ... yes. But I am still working on them.'

'Are we talking about the second theft?' enquired Araminta. Holmes demurred.

'No ma'am, I've known the culprit from the moment I read about the case in the newspaper.'

'So you know who the villain is?'

'Irene Adler ... yes.'

'That's a relief, then Mr Holmes. So are you going to arrest her?'

'Ma'am, that's easier said than done ... catching Miss Adler is probably more difficult than trapping smoke in a bag.'

'Really?'

'But the police will do their best, they assure me.'

'In that case, there is nothing more to say, is there?' For the first time the Countess showed some irritation.

'I told you, ma'am, I am seizing this opportunity to shed some light on the first theft, since I am already ... what's the expression? *In situ.*'

'Kill two birds with one stone, eh, what?' intervened Watson with a gruff little laugh. Holmes nodded. 'Maybe it's more appropriate to talk about two stones.' Her ladyship smiled, but it was a weary smile, a smile which was not really a smile, but a device to hide her growing discomfiture. She hesitated before speaking.

'You said that you had two possible answers to the first ... f-felony?'

'The human brain, ma'am is a mystery to me. Would you believe that in the short spate of time that we were engaged in our conversation, one of the two possible alternatives has proved untenable.'

'Leaving you with just the one?' Araminta said with a moue. Holmes nodded.

'And you are sure you've got it right?'

'Ma'am, Irene Adler was certainly not involved the first time,' said Holmes. Araminta conceded the point with a nod.

'And having ascertained that no one could have had possession of the Yale keys to the secured room without first laying hands on the key you keep around your neck at all times...' He paused and bit his lips in a gesture indicating his reluctance to continue.

In spite of her obvious unease, the lady spoke. 'Yes, Mr Holmes, do go on.'

'In the light of what your ladyship has herself revealed about how light a sleeper the Earl is, there is one person I cannot eliminate as a possible suspect.'

'And who is that suspect, dare I ask?'

'Please do not dare ask.'

'Will you tell me if I ask everybody to leave?'

'No Ma'am, I couldn't. What do they say about walls and ears?'

'Really? So what are you going to do?' Holmes stayed silent for a long while, peering at the Countess inscrutably until he saw her blush.

'Probably nothing. But it depends on you. Do you understand me?

'I think I do, Mr Holmes. Is there anything I can do?'

'Oh yes, ma'am, there is. I've got a letter here addressed to Mr Charles Lloyd. Should you sign it...' Without further ado, he opened the letter he had been holding in his hand for a while. 'I'll pass this on to him. The matter will end here and the mislaid gem will have been considered found.'

The Countess was not one to temporize. With a nod, she snatched the letter from Holmes' hand, walked to her desk, and with despatch found a quilt and ink. She sat down, and with a smile in which you had to look hard to see traces of resignation, signed the document with a flourish. She then stood up and handed the signed document to Holmes, still smiling.

'Mr Holmes,' she said, 'it's been a pleasure doing business with you.'

'Sentiments I reciprocate entirely.'

When the two men got to Baker Street, there was a note which had been delivered in the same afternoon.

Dear Mr Holmes, Rest assured that we only ever rob the undeserving rich. Your admirer.

I.A.

CHAPTER ELEVEN
The Man with the Eyepatch
(1890)

I was amazed at the ire my story in last week's *Reynold's News* provoked. It has never been my intention to make Mr Holmes look
like a fool. I know, and the world knows that he has no equal in the
field of crime-solving. His reputation is well-nigh fireproof. I would be
a fool to suggest otherwise. I have nothing but respect and admiration
for my employer. Our readers might be surprised to find that I am still at
Number 221B. Mr Holmes found my incursion into print highly amus-
ing. The doctor isn't going to like it, he mumbled, as if to himself. But Dr
Watson greeted me with great effusion when I saw him next, beaming at
me happily. Why, Mrs Hudson, he said, you are a dark horse, eh, what!

'Aren't you upset with me?'

'Why, my good Mrs Hudson, why should I be, when Mr Lippincott
has offered me a more lucrative deal for my next three stories. The controversy has generated a lot of publicity.'

'That should satisfy Mrs Watson's need for fine silks, baubles and
bonnets,' I refrained from saying.

'Did you know that he had to reprint ten thousand more copies of
the last issue? They were sold out in a matter of hours?'

Maybe I should have a word with Mr Reynolds about the rate he pays
me, I thought.

Although I have no intention of drawing attention to the failures of
my two admirable employers. We are all in awe of Mr Holmes' uncanny

powers of observation and deduction, but have the readers of Dr Watson's accounts never wondered why Mr Holmes, who himself talks of the balance of probability, is never proved wrong in his deductions? I suggest this as proof of how the chronicler - and now colleague - filters away information likely to show his good friend in a less flattering light. Increasingly I have noticed that he is also tailoring his accounts to suit the demands of his editor Mr Lippincott. I own to overhearing him admitting as much to Mr Holmes. I hereby give an undertaking that I will never submit to any such demands, should Mr Reynolds demand them of me.

I will therefore narrate an exact account of the trials and tribulations of Mr Neville St Clair, a story Dr Watson rather colourfully called The Man with The Twisted Lips. I will tell it how it was, will not embellish or add one word or event, nor exclude a single important fact when I find it irksome.

Why he decided to turn a man with an eyepatch into a man with twisted lips, I'll never know. Perhaps he will give a reason one day. I have followed the case very closely. I have already revealed that I am an inveterate listener behind doors and windows. I ask questions of tradesmen and passers-by. I watch people's reactions and body movements.

I can vouchsafe for Dr Watson's rescuing Mr Isa Whitney from the opium den in Upper Swandham Lane where the bulk of the events of the story took place. The doctor did not meet Mr Holmes there fortuitously as he claims. The chivalrous act took place a whole week before Mrs Neville called at Baker Street and has no bearing on the sad adventures of Mr Neville St Clair. It is my understanding that the chronicler of Mr Holmes' exploits gets paid by the word.

One sunny morning in June, I opened the door to a refined young lady in her early thirties who introduced herself as Mrs St Clair. Mr Holmes was seated in his favourite armchair with his long legs outstretched and his head tossed back, the tips of the fingers of his two hands rubbing against each other sensuously, a picture of relaxed ease. Opposite him was Dr Watson, his eyes twinkling with admiration at some remark that his friend had just made. Anything coming from the mouth of his hero, every word, sounded like a piece of wisdom worthy of Solomon himself. I announced the visitor, and the pair sprang to life.

I was about to embark on the plucking of a goose that a Mrs Oakshot had brought to Mr Holmes the day before, for services rendered. My curiosity about the lady was aroused. I cannot resist the temptation of hanging just outside the door. I approached my ears to the panel. I had also elaborated a crafty technique of pulling the door behind me but manoeuvring to keep it imperceptibly ajar by a judicious use of my heel, so that it might afford me the means of eavesdropping. I saw my employer gallantly offering Mrs Neville an armchair. As usual, the doctor made a pretense of leaving but was coaxed into staying.

'Dr Watson is my trusted friend and collaborator. I urge you to feel free to talk in his presence as you would to myself.' The lady nodded, smiled and then wiped a tear. I saw her grow pale as she revealed the cause of her visit.

'It's my dear husband Mr Neville St Clair,' she said. 'He's disappeared.' She then told one of the most amazing stories that I have ever heard, and lord knows I have eavesdropped on many a queer tale in my time. A week ago, shortly after her husband left for work, she explained, she received a notice informing her that a parcel she had been eagerly awaiting was at the Aberdeen Shipping Company, ready for collection.

'Ah, I know the place,' said Mr Holmes who prided himself on his knowledge of our capital city. 'It's in Fresno Street, is it not?' That was when I heard about Mr Isa Whitney.

'Only last week I was called to rescue my friend Mr Isa Whitney from that infamous opium den in Upper Swandham round the corner,' I heard the doctor say with a nervous laugh and a surprising lack of discretion.

The gravity of the situation notwithstanding, Mrs St Clair was excessively voluble and self-assured, I thought.

'If you gentlemen will remember, last Monday was very hot. As I was unable to get into a cab, I was forced to walk. Imagine my shock when turning into Swandham Lane, walking beside a tall building and raising my head, I saw as clearly as I am seeing you now-'

'None other than your husband?' questioned Mr Holmes with a smile and a raised eyebrow, daring a contradiction from the lady. I caught that glint of a mixture of admiration and wonder in the doctor's eye through the door. I felt emboldened to push it open just a fraction more. The lady nodded and continued.

'The window was open and I felt like all my blood had drained out of my body as I distinctly saw how agitated his face seemed. He had his hands in front of his face,' she pursued. 'It seemed to me that somebody must have pulled him violently away from the window, and he disappeared.' I never heard her say that her husband waved at her or beckoned her in any way, as Dr Watson narrates. In the light of what was revealed afterwards, that seemed completely unlikely. St Clair had every reason to prevent his wife from seeing him, I daresay. As I said, Mr Holmes' chronicler gets paid by the word.

'And you haven't seen him since?' The lady nodded. Holmes then asked for some family background and Mrs Neville was only too happy to provide it.

She came from a well-to-do family of brewers who had lived in Lee, in Kent, for over a century. Mr St Clair had bought a nice villa and moved into it about seven years ago, from Chesterfield. He had seemed a pleasant man, educated, and with obvious means. After a short courtship they had married. He had been a doting husband and an affectionate father to their two children.

'How does he make his living?' asked Holmes.

'He is a freelance journalist. He occasionally gets a commission from a newspaper or magazine for an article. As he knows people in the city, some companies occasionally offer him lucrative employment and he works for them in some capacity which I have never understood ... as a sort of broker, I think he told me.'

The lady explained that, nonetheless, he had regular habits. He left early each morning, returning on the 5.14 from Cannon Street every afternoon. No, he had no debts. He had two hundred and twenty pounds in the bank.

'Right,' said Holmes. 'Let's go back to the events of last Monday. Let's take it from the point where you said somebody pulled him inside. Please.'

'I didn't actually see anybody pull him back, it only seemed so.'

'Yes, you explained that very clearly. Now, is there anything else you remember, that you think might be of help to us?'

'Yes. He was still wearing his dark coat, but he had neither tie nor collar.'

She was greatly distressed. With obvious pride she told of how she had then rushed up the steps of what proved to be an opium den. Undaunted she had begun to climb the stairs, but was stopped by a sinister looking Malay, who with the help of a dishevelled Dane pushed her into the streets none too gently. In Fresno Street she fortuitously saw Inspector Bradstreet and some police constables. She had urged them to come with her to the den. The Malay and the Dane were unable to stop entry this time. Mrs St Clair led them to the room on the floor where she had seen her husband. This was a large room that led to a small bedroom which looked out on the back of the wharves. There was no sign of her husband anywhere on this floor, which seemed to be solely occupied by a hideous-looking cripple with an eyepatch. The Malay explained he was his sole tenant. The inspector said that he knew the man. He was Hugh Boone, a well-known figure near the wharves who made a living by begging on Threadneedle Street. Both the Malay and the cripple maintained that nobody else had been in the room. They claimed that they had seen nobody fitting the description of the missing man. They were so convincing that the inspector had looked at Mrs St Clair dubiously, not trying too hard to hide his suspicion that she was suffering from delusions.

Ida St Clair had then suddenly perceived a deal box on a wooden crate. When she grabbed it, its lid burst open and children's bricks had come cascading down. She gave a little cry of surprise for her husband had promised that he was going to buy this very toy for the children on the Monday that he disappeared. This had rekindled the sagging enthusiasm of the law enforcers for a search. They soon discovered traces of blood on the windowsill as well as on the floor. At the same time Mrs St Clair found all the clothes of her missing husband apart from his coat. Neither the Malay, nor the dirty man with the eyepatch was able to offer any explanation for the presence of those items. It was now clear that a crime had been committed on the premises. A plausible explanation was that St Clair had been pushed through the window by person or persons unknown. Down below there was a narrow strip of land, now dry, but able to rise to four feet at high tide. Could he have saved himself by swimming away from his would-be assassins? If so, where was he? asked the distraught woman.

Shortly after, a couple of constables that Inspector Bradstreet had sent to the riverside came back with Neville's coat with no Neville in it. They had picked it at a spot not far from the den, where the tide had receded. They were amazed to find the pockets stuffed with pennies and half-pennies. At this point Bradstreet decided that Hugh Boone must have killed St Clair by first stabbing him - hence the blood - and then pushing him down the window to his death. The corpse must have been carried away by the tides, the lady said wiping a tear from her eyes.

Boone was taken in for questioning, but as no body had yet been found, he was released on bail, which the Malay, who seemed very protective of him had readily provided. Ida St Clair had no reason to doubt the man's guilt but, not convinced that her man had indeed been killed, she had approached Mr Holmes.

The doctor went to attend to his patients and Mr Holmes set out to see Bradstreet shortly afterwards. The inspector had summoned Boone to continue with his interrogation, and had invited Holmes to attend. When he came back he told Dr Watson who had rushed to Baker Street after surgery, that the most puzzling find was St Clair's coat with what was obviously Boone's takings in its pocket.

'421 pennies and 270 halfpennies were found in his pockets,' Holmes informed Watson. 'Small wonder,' he added, 'that it had not been swept away by the tide. But a human body is a different matter. There is a fierce eddy between the wharf and the house.' It seemed likely to him that the weighted coat had remained whilst the stripped body had been sucked away into the river.

'And what do you make of it all?' I heard the doctor ask him. I knew what his answer would be.

'My dear doctor, a conjecture based on anything but fact is both dangerous and misleading. There aren't enough clues to make any sensible deductions here. A loose conjecture,' he added a bit sternly, 'as I have often had cause to tell you, usually ends up by hardening. In no time it becomes accepted as fact. As such, it is often an enemy of reason.'

But as I knew, this would not stop him making one nonetheless.

'If we admit that the pennies were put in the pockets for the purpose of sinking an object-'

'Namely the poor fellow St Clair,' Doctor Watson interrupted needlessly.

'If that were the case,' asked Holmes, 'where is the wretched body?' The expression on the doctor's face showed him to be at a complete loss. I admit that like the two men I had no idea about what might have happened to the corpse.

Ida St Clair arrived at Number 221B early next morning, impatient to hear if there had been any developments. To my amazement, I heard her suggest that the police might consult one of those "people with gifts", as she put it, to help locate her Neville, dead or alive.

'If it was possible to prove that Boone had killed my husband, without a body, a conviction isn't going to be possible,' said Ida unhappily.

'Mrs St Clair,' said Holmes raising his eyebrows. 'Bradstreet is very good at exacting confessions from suspects ... not that I approve of his methods. Trust me, we will not rest until we find the body.'

Whilst the case was in the doldrums, Holmes became prey to depression, sitting all day in his armchair, his eyes closed. I watched him one morning. He was slouching in his usual manner, as if half asleep, his long lanky legs outstretched in front of him, his thumbs pressed against each other, with the other fingers not touching but facing each other like two armies waiting for an order to attack. Suddenly for no reason that I could see, he came animated and pulled himself up.

'As you know, Watson, I started making a study of the speech patterns and accents of the people of our land. Unfortunately I have not had the opportunity of completing it, but I have published a small monograph -'

'Oh I know the one, *Speech Patterns of Middle England*,' said Watson with a self-deprecating little laugh. 'I could never make head or tail of it.'

'When I visited the prisoner in his cell with Bradstreet, I discovered an interesting fact about Hugh Boone's accent, it's Chesterfield, North Chesterfield.' If Watson saw this as relevant, he took great care to hide it.

'That's a coincidence, wouldn't you say? Seeing that St Clair also came from that town?'

'A strange coincidence indeed,' agreed Watson, whereupon, Holmes, rather discourteously, I thought, wagged a finger at his companion, as a teacher would, at a pupil who had got the date 1066 wrong.

'My dear doctor, there was no need to qualify the coincidence.'

'W-w- what d' you mean Holmes?' said the doctor blinking profusely.

'All coincidences are strange. It is in their nature.' Holmes almost never makes an effort to be civil to his great admirer, but this time I couldn't help detecting that it was because the case was discomfiting him. 'Then they must be related,' I said to myself behind the door. The explanation might dwell in the link between the two men. I hoped that Mr Holmes would begin hacking at this seam but waited in vain to hear a confirmation that this was something he was considering.

The event of the next morning made a complete nonsense of all our combined conjectures so far. Ida St Clair again appeared at Number 221B, out of breath and in an excited condition. Her eyes were beaming with delight.

'My husband's alive,' she exclaimed the moment I opened the door to her. 'My dear husband's alive.' Holmes burst in although he was wearing only a gown over his night clothes.

'So he came home and is unhurt?' asked the sleuth in a neutral voice. Dr Watson, who was staying the night on account of his wife being away, followed and began spluttering and blustering, his kindly eyes beaming with pleasure.

'I don't know about that,' said our lady visitor. 'He sent me this. I received it late yesterday. It bears a Gravesend postmark, dated yesterday.' She handed over to my employer an envelope. He held it in his hands for a while before lifting the opened flap, and extracted from it a gold signet ring and a note. He looked questioningly at Ida St Clair who nodded.

'Yes, Mr Holmes, that's his signet ring. I gave it to him when we were wed. The note is in his writing.' Wordlessly he handed it over to the doctor who straightened his throat and read: *My dearest, I am alive and unhurt, and hope to have you in my arms in the near future, once this little complication is cleared. Trust me. All my love, Neville.*

The good doctor, normally a quiet taciturn man began jumping about quite comically, muttering a few indistinguishable words, whereupon Holmes looked at him with disapproval.

'My dear Watson, it is of course quite appropriate to celebrate the happiness of our friends but it may be a little premature here.' As Watson was staring at him with his mouth open, he said it again. 'It may be a little premature.'

'What do you mean, Mr Holmes?' asked Ida a little sharply, adding defiantly, 'this must have been definitely sent by my husband with a trusted intermediary.'

'Well, my dear lady, the signet could have been snatched from his finger.'

'But it was not,' I said to myself. 'It is worth a good twenty guineas. If there was villainy involved, the miscreants would not have parted with such a catch just to mislead the poor woman into believing that her husband was alive. There was no sensible reason for them to do that.

'However,' said Holmes after a short period of reflection, 'that seems unlikely for reasons which I shall enumerate.' Imagine my delight when he repeated almost word for word what I had just been formulating in my head.

'But there is also the note,' he said. 'Can you confirm that it is his handwriting?' Ida St Clair nodded.

'I will give instructions to Bradstreet to take in Boone, give him a good grilling and force him to reveal what they he and his accomplices have done to St Clair. That man must hold the key to our mystery.'

I was disappointed that Mr Holmes had not thought fit to explore the Chesterfield connection. He knew that Boone and St Clair both came from there. I decided that I would. I therefore despatched my young friend Teddy, a boy from Bartola's dead husband's family, to Chesterfield. He is uniquely clever even if he is only thirteen. He knows no fear, and can fend for himself.

'Go to North Chesterfield,' I instructed him. 'Enquire about the St Clairs. There can't be too many of them around. Try to find out as much as you can about a Mr Neville St Clair, who is now 34, He has worked as a journalist at one time. Ask if anybody knew a Hugh Boone.' I gave him four pounds for expenses. The moment Teddy came back from his mission, he visited me in Baker Street, and told me what he had uncovered. Neville St Clair had a twin brother who had lost an eye as a child. He left home many years ago to become a ship's cook. No one had heard from him in the last seven years. I then got Teddy to go to the public libraries to discover what articles Neville St Clair had written for the newspapers. I was surprised to hear that he had done a piece about begging in London. He mentioned that he had researched the subject, although he did not give details. These informations seemed highly relevant to the case, but I did not think my employer would have been grateful to me for upstaging him. For once, I half wished that he would open the glass case with the white powder. I might have been able to impart the knowledge to him in his drugged state and protect his pride.

After a sleepless night, I thought that I would take a leaf out of the book of the master himself. I disguised myself as a Gypsy fortune teller and wended my way to Lee one afternoon to find the distraught wife. When I found her, I told her that I could help her in finding her missing husband if he was alive, otherwise, his murderer.

'Your husband had a brother, didn't he?' I ventured. She stared at me for a bit, her face screwed up in an obvious attempt at recalling.

'I had forgotten, yes, he did.'

'Hugh St Clair, he was called, right?' I said. She stared at me for a short while, then nodded.

'Oh yes, I remember now, they were twins. He lost an eye as a child. Mr St Clair mentioned this once many years ago. I had clean forgotten it.'

'That's the one.'

'Cross my palm with silver, dear lady, and take this information to the police.'

Ida came to Baker Street and without mentioning the mystic visit revealed that Neville had a twin brother. Holmes jumped at this intelligence.

'Did you have a good look at Boone, Mrs St Clair?' he asked.

'Oh no Mr Holmes, sir, he was so fearsome. With his eyepatch and grimy face I felt his one good eye on me all the time I was in that house. No sir, I was too scared to look.'

Unfortunately young Teddy had not thought of asking for details regarding the loss of the eye. When Ida was imparting the information to the sleuth, he questioned her about the accident. Which eye? How old was he when the accident happened? Was his brother responsible? So many things we need to look into, he mumbled. You can talk, I said to myself, but you never stirred from London. I had to despatch young Teddy to Chesterfield. I heard him tell Watson that there were many unanswered questions. He suggested that the arrival of the letter with the signet and the note had added more complications to the case. Watson seemed more confused than ever. Holmes explained.

'It is only a conjecture at the moment, doctor, but imagine that the villains forced St Clair to write the letter with a knife at his throat, take off his signet, kill their victim, for whatever motive. Perhaps it was the young Neville who had been responsible for his brother's losing an eye. Hence the eyepatch. He then put the letter in the post a week after the murder. Just to bamboozle us. He was not interested in the value of the signet you see. Vengeance took precedence over all other considerations. How does that strike you?' Watson nodded his agreement, full of admiration. I must confess that I found the reasoning quite dazzling. Still, a conjecture is nothing but a conjecture until proof is added to the mix. I found that all my instincts were against it.

Mr Holmes, however, was a man who dealt with certainties. Doubt was something he did not usually indulge in.

'Watson,' he said shaking his head wearily, 'I must admit that I am stuck. If I do not pass on the information at my disposal to the police, I might become guilty of enabling a villain to escape justice.'

'And if you try to do your civic duty you run the risk of getting an innocent man sent to the gallows.' said Watson nodding gravely. 'So what shall we do?' That was one of the rare occasions that I have heard Holmes seek advice.

'Well, Holmes, remember that in England. We have the fairest judicial system in the world. No jury will hang an innocent man, eh what?'

106

Holmes looked at his friend pursing his lips. He must have allowed himself to be swayed by the doctor, for he ended up passing on the information to Bradstreet. We heard later that Boone had been arrested and that bail had been refused this time.

However when Holmes and Watson came back on the afternoon of the arrest, they were very upset. They paced across the length and breadth of the room and it took all my talent for eavesdropping to discover that something awful had happened to the suspect. The police explained that whilst under interrogation, Boone had fallen down the stairs while trying to escape, hurting his head quite badly. He had to have medical care.

'The brutes,' said Holmes.

'What do you mean, Holmes? This isn't the Continent. Our police aren't in the habit of beating up suspects. You know that my dear fellow.'

'Yes,' said Holmes tersely. 'And no innocent man is ever hanged.'

Boone seemed to have lost his mind, and kept asking not only where but *who* he was. A doctor pronounced that the knock on the head had provoked an attack of amnesia which may be only temporary, but he could give no guarantee. It was assumed that until Boone regained his memory, nothing much could be done. To my chagrin, Holmes gave in to his cocaine addiction. Watson reluctantly had to attend to his practice, which he had somewhat neglected lately.

I wish there was a way to pass on to Mr Holmes the information about Neville St Clair's article on the beggars of London. Whilst under the influence of the nefarious powder, I found him dribbling and tossing restlessly on his armchair as I came in.

'Is that you, Miss Adler?' I heard him mumble. I said nothing, but took a few steps towards him. I sat myself down beside him.'

'That idiotic king thought you weren't good enough for him.' I knew that this was the ideal occasion.

'Mr Holmes,' I said in what I thought was a hypnotic voice. 'Neville St Clair wrote articles about begging in London in the Evening Tribune. You might find it worth looking into.'

Next day, we heard that the trial was going ahead, the dazed condition of the accused notwithstanding. So much for Watson's belief in the

English justice system. Boone was being tried for murder of the first degree after the police was able to produce a signed confession. Further, Bradstreet had found the rotting corpse of what had been manifestly a long dead tramp, in Epping Forest. He had convinced the powers that be that it was Neville's. The man with the eyepatch had no idea what it was all about and stared at everybody eerily with his unique organ of vision, unable to answer any question. Under cross-examination, the accused answered, Yes, your honour, or No, your honour. His defence counsel, many had observed, was a complete nincompoop. In less than a day, the jury found him guilty as charged. It was the custom to get on with the hanging without undue delay.

CHAPTER TWELVE

The Avengers

(1886)

By the terms of the sale we are not allowed to reveal the name of the buyer of *The Eye*. He was an American and had been Mr Edison's assistant for a number of years. He had started his own telegraph company which he later sold for an astronomical sum to start a motorcar factory. We were astounded at how much he offered, but asked for ten percent more on principle, and got it. Shared equally, our dividends would have enabled us to live in comfort for the rest of our days, but we all abhorred the idea of a life without risk and danger. In other words, we were not ready to settle down. We all opted for the acquisition of a common property, which, for practical purposes, would be in Lord Clarihoe's name. Naturally we all trusted him with our lives and knew that when the time came Algernon would deal with the shares most equitably. As he comes from a reputed family, when he comes forward as a potential buyer, no one would raise an eyebrow. Everybody in the *Club* had a say in what to buy. Unanimity was a *sine qua non*. We began by consulting the foremost house and land agents in London, Higham, Higham & Higham of Regent Street. When Elias Higham sent word that there was a property in Hertfordshire, and described it as comprising of fifty acres of prime woodland with a natural lake, stables and paddocks, croquet lawns and similar amenities, a recently built stone mansion on three floors with fifteen bedrooms, three libraries, four dining rooms, six salons and many other mouth-watering features, we thought we needed to have a look.

We had all, however, already made up our minds. The property changed hands without a hitch, and our ill-gotten wealth made us land owners. As we were deeply attached to London, we had no plans to relocate wholesale to *Le Cabanon*, Armande's name choice for the estate. We planned to spend a lot of time in Hertfordshire, especially during the summer months.

We all fell in love with our property at first sight. It was the closest thing to the Garden of Eden on earth. As the house was of recent construction, it had all the modern conveniences. The rooms were well insulated, the windows did not rattle and closed perfectly. After minor repairs it became eminently habitable. Although it came with all the furnishings, we meant to give it our own cachet. The first thing we did was to get rid of most of the existing furniture and fittings and bring in our own.

Whenever I slept there, every morning I went for a long walk before breakfast, which I made myself. I don't suppose that I need to mention that as equalisers we would never have personal maids or butlers, but there were gamekeepers, carpenters, gardeners. We were all able to clean for ourselves. Cooking was a communal event, although we hired some kitchen hands. Armande proudly announced that she was to act as head chef, the French having unilaterally awarded themselves the certificate for Best Cooks In The World. Algernon began by buying horses. In the beginning only he and Ivan Vissarionovich, who had ridden bareback with his Cossack friends, showed any interest in those equines. However, I soon began to develop a curiosity about riding. With the Russian as my mentor, I became addicted to horsemanship after my first lesson. I soon became a very competent rider. The same thing with guns. I abhorred them at first, but could not resist their fascination. Once more it was Ivan who taught me their finer points and in a matter of weeks, I was shooting as well as him. That was *his* opinion. The others followed in my footsteps with varying degrees of enthusiasm and success. When the hunting season arrived, we often went deer hunting in Ashridge Forest. Wonders will never cease, I again took to this like duck to water. I am not given to boasting but I never guessed that I was so gifted in so many areas. I wryly reflected that had I achieved the modest success that I had craved for on the stage, I would never have discovered my potential in so many diverse fields.

We did not expect to do much socialising, as none of us were that way inclined. We were self-sufficient. We never asked anybody round. Few of the people we encountered seemed of any interest to us. We politely discouraged all intercourse with them. Still, with our staff, we inevitably got to hear the gossip, and some strange tales about our neighbours came our way. We were not interested in who was courting who, or what one lady thought of another.

One day Bartola and the gardeners were having a cup of tea in the kitchen when I came in. I immediately noticed that they all had glum faces.

'What's the matter?' I asked chirpily.

'Another Romany girl has disappeared,' said Robert the tiler.

'What do you mean, *another*?' I asked.

'Must be the seventh since last year,' Philip the carpenter answered. I was stunned. It was not something I had heard of. A harrowing tale unfolded when I questioned them. I was obviously aware of the Romany camps in the surroundings. I had been fascinated by their colourful caravans punctuating the drab landscape. I revelled in the sound of laughing children, fiddling and dancing, crowing roosters, barking dogs and neighing horses filling the atmosphere.

The Romany folks earned a precarious living by horse-trading and doing odd jobs such as selling rags and metal oddments or sharpening knives, sometimes fortune-telling. They rarely worked for others. Most people looked down upon them. Many were openly hostile to them. Whenever anything untoward happened, fingers were immediately pointed at them. The moment a new horse appeared in one of their camps, tongues started wagging, to the effect that some esquire in Berkshire must have carelessly left his stable door unlocked. Stories about Romanies stealing children were common currency, but you had to wonder why they would do that when they had so many hungry little mouths to feed already. Still, on the whole they kept themselves to themselves, only fighting each other and never interfering with others. Now, suddenly I hear that one of their children had gone missing and that this was not the first time.

'Have the family gone to the police?' I asked and did not understand the sour hilarity this provoked. They explained that Romanies avoided the police like cats, dogs.

'Surely in a serious matter like child abduction there's only one thing to do,' I exclaimed indignantly.

'The police have the habit of arresting any Romany outside their natural patch, on sight. The poor fellows get verbal abuse, beaten up or worse.'

'But that's not right,' I said. It was at this point that someone mentioned Lord Stonehead. We knew from his huge manor that he was a powerful and rich landowner. The collective opinion of the local craftsmen working for us was that he was a rake, a ruthless and lawless individual, not someone to be trifled with. He was surely involved in this outrage.

'Ma'am,' said Robert quietly, 'can I advise you to forget about it. Them's, not our people.' I would be surprised to learn later that his wife Yolanda was of Romany stock.

'And in any case,' said Robert, 'he is not someone who answers to the police.'

'No,' I shouted. 'In this country we are equal before the law.' The men laughed again and Bartola would have joined them if she had not seen the look of dismay on my face.

That night, we were three in the *Le Cabanon*, Bartola, Artémise and myself. After dinner, I raised the issue of the missing Gypsy child and asked for suggestions. After a short discussion it was decided that we would all go to the Hertfordshire constabulary and make an official complaint. We now had a hansom cab permanently on site and John the carpenter who doubled up as our cocher drove us to St Albans.

The policemen on duty received us with courtesy bordering on obsequiousness. The moment I opened my mouth, I realised that I seemed to be always taking the lead and remembered that we were supposed to be a club of equals, but it was too late.

There was a balding constable at the desk, and he signalled to us to come in and take a seat.

'Constable Balding at your service,' he said addressing me. 'Yes, your ladyship?' I kept quiet and deferred to Bartola.

'A little girl has gone missing,' she said. 'You must find her.'

'Your child, ma'am?' Balding asked.

'No, officer, a Romany child!'

'A Romany child!' What does it mean?' exclaimed the officer, as if we were speaking a foreign language.

'It seems that this is the seventh child to go missing this year.'

'Seventh?'

'Yes,' I snapped, 'the one that comes after the sixth.' That seemed to have done the trick.

'And what do you expect the constabulary to do, your ladyship?'

'Find the child, man,' I said emphatically.

'You said a Romany child, not a child of yours,' he said moving his eyes across the three of us. We shook our heads.

'No Romany has come forward to report a missing child ma'am,' he said with a shrug.

'Romanies who approach your station get thrown in the cell,' said Artémise.

'We have locked up any Romany for reporting a missing child,' protested the copper. 'Only for theft or drunkenness.' He wiped the sweat on his forehead, coughed before speaking. 'If the parent of the child comes to lodge an official complaint, we might look into it.'

'What do you mean, might,' thundered Bartola.

'We hear that Lord Stonehead might know something about it? I chipped in. Balding blanched and began to stammer.

'I meantersay Lord Stonehead ... You don't trifle with 'is Lordship. E's got a temper 'e 'as, your ladyship. And 'e's got power, 'e's a friend of the Prince of Wales.'

'But if he's done something unlawful-' I began. Constable Balding was unable to contemplate that eventuality. He was in all states as he spoke.

'B-b-ut Lord Stonehead cannot... no... 'e cannot break the law, we cannot question 'is lawdship... it's not done... why did you come 'ere... not your child. Tell the Gypsy scoundrel to come make a complaint, hisself,' he conceded finally.

When we saw how scared the man was the moment we mentioned Stonehead, we knew that we were whistling against the wind and left. We needed to work out a strategy and got Robert to take us to the Romany camp in Wheathampstead. We were initially received with obvious hostility, but when we spoke of our concern for the missing girl, their suspicions gradually disappeared.

We were given seats in a rather spectacularly decorated caravan, with crimson red lions and green roosters painted on the outside. Inside there were embroidered silks, weavings, shiny brass jugs, varnished fiddles and porcelain plates. There was a pervasive smoky smell around the camp, but inside there was an aroma of attar. Marius introduced himself as the father of Wilhemina, the missing girl. He was a dignified well-shaven suntanned man with a shiny face, coal black hair and a pencil moustache. He explained (in clear and perfect English) that the little girl had been playing with her friends not far from the camp, when a ball went flying into the bush. She put her wings on and went after it. Next thing a horse was seen and heard riding away, and then there was no sign of her. Her playmates were sure that she had been kidnapped by the horseman, but no one had seen her on the horse. Nor had anybody seen the rider.

'But we do not need nobody to tell us that it was that b-bastard Lord Stonehead. That's what 'e does. Steal children, and then...' Marius could not continue as he was choked with tears of helplessness and anger. When he calmed down, he told us about the six other children, boys as well as girls, who had disappeared in the last twelve months, all under similar circumstances. He explained that the first time a father had gone to the constabulary, they accused him of murdering his own child. They said they would lock him up if he came back. From that day, Romany people decided that going to the police was a waste of time.

'They are convinced we are the scum of the earth, that one of our children going missing means one less problem for society. No, my friends, there is only one thing to do, and we are considering doing it. We're moving outa here.'

'But Marius, do you think that we will find peace elsewhere? Our people have always been persecuted. Our people will always be oppressed,' a wizened old woman with all her front teeth missing said tearfully. We felt powerless in the knowledge that Romany people were indeed considered subhumans not worth helping by police or anybody else. That's when we, the *Club,* as equalisers, feel we are needed most. We would have to find a solution.

Robert brought Yolanda to talk to us next day. Before she was wed, she worked as a maid at Stonehead Manor. She had no doubt in her mind that the evil Lord was responsible for all the crimes taking place in the area.

' 'E's a lecher, 'e is,' she said. 'No young girl is safe with 'im and 'is friends.'

'Young girls? How young?' we asked.

'Very young. Mebbe five or six.'

'Have you seen them with your own eyes?' Bartola asked. Yolanda hesitated.

'Those as I 'ave seen wi' me own eyes, woz fourteen or fifteen, but we *'eard* little 'uns many a time.'

'What did you hear?'

'At first they giggled and laughed. Then we 'eard 'em scream and shout No! No! Please, sir, don't.'

'We never saw them none, but Agnes, she's a light sleeper. She says she 'as 'eard commotion of nights, when bundles of drugged children 'ave been quietly smuggled in and kept locked in the cellar. She says she 'as sometimes 'eard them whimper. No one believed 'er. They say she's wrong in the 'ead, she 'ears voices and sees things.'

'Would it be possible to talk to Agnes?' asked Ivan Vissarionovich.

'Don't think so, she's too scared to leave the castle. Her mind's gone now anyroad.'

'So no one has *seen* any children?' we asked.

'Agnes says she's seen them digging graves in the moonlight, and burying dead children.'

'Did she say where?' Yolanda was overcome by terror at this point and began trembling, unable to talk. We asked again. She nodded. 'You know the little river that flows by the side of the ridge. There's a big oak which was struck by lightning many years ago. It lies on the ground. Mushrooms grow on it. We seen 'em every year. Agnes said she saw Lord Stonehead and his guests dig graves there one moonlit night after an orgy. They carried things and buried them there.' She stopped and wiped a tear. 'She swore on our Lord's wounds that them woz little 'uns.'

'But I've seen wi' me own eyes, as clear as I see you now, Lord Stonehead and 'is friends chasing half-dressed screaming young wenches across the woods. When they catch them they carry them inside,' she went on. 'It were a game like, they played. I think they woz 'arlots ... young like ... in the morning they was paid and taken back to London.'

'Anything else?'

'When the orgy is over, 'e and 'is friends lock theirselves in the big room, and indulge.'

'Indulge?'

'They eat opium. They just lie there for two three days on end, 'ardly eat or drink nuffin'... and they...'

'They what?'

'Do unnatural things wiv' each other.'

'Anything else?'

'Ask my Robert, 'e knows. They sometimes light a big fire in the woods ... on the river bank ... where ... you know ... them graves ... and they dance round it and sing in Latin ... They worship Satan, that's what my Robert says.'

Bartola and Armande were deeply shocked, but Algernon agreed with me that a lot was probably fantasy. Clarihoe said that he had friends who gave raucous parties where nothing worse than a little hanky panky with young London whores and Nancy Boys, with a bit of opium eating thrown in for good measure. Lighting a fire, dancing and hollering around it was not uncommon. That did not mean that his friends were Satan worshippers.

'But what about the graves?' Artémise wanted to know, whereupon Algie promptly reassured everybody that he was not denying their existence. He was just urging caution.

'We need to probe this matter very carefully of course,' he concluded.

We were determined to watch Stonehead closely. What better way than to give a party to celebrate Madame la Comtesse de la Marne's fortieth birthday. Lord Clarihoe sent out the invitations in his own name, not only to Stonehead, but to the other six families whose seats were closest to *Le Cabanon*.

Lord Clarihoe of Colburn Abbey has the honour to invite you to the birthday celebration of his dear friends Monsieur le Comte et Madame la Comtesse de la Marne at Le Cabanon on Saturday the sixth of May.

The aim of the exercise was to give us the opportunity of developing a closer rapport with his sinister lordship. The illustrious couple, known to their intimates as Armande and Anatole were a great success. I was introduced to Stonehead as Lavinia the widow of Wexford Aloysius Sadler III, a man who owned tin mines in South America. Bartola was my cousin la Contessa della Boccablanca. Ivan was naturally a Romanov (not entirely untrue), Artémise a celebrated artist, friend of Van Gogh, travelling incognito. Coleridge was the younger brother of the Baganda of Buganda.

Everybody came, dressed in their finest, their jewels sparkling and tinkling like little bells. We had made sure that wines and spirits would flow to everybody's satisfaction. Armande had personally ordered the finest savouries, patisseries, cheeses, caviar, and *amuse-gueules*. We had further hired a team of Gypsy fiddlers and musicians for the evening.

Lord Stonehead invited me for a polka and as we danced, I told him about Wexford Sadler who had made his fortune in the gold rush, and about my own Italian ancestor Il Conte Bruschetta della Mascarponi.

He wasted no time flirting with me with a singular lack of subtlety and I responded in a way which suggested that as I was a widow, I was not averse to the attention of suitable men. I implied that what happened to my poor husband had left me less than devastated.

'You did nothing to force the hands of destiny though did you?' This was put to me as a sort of challenge. I smiled enigmatically.

'I think that living within the rigid confines of the law is a burden to those of us who are able to think for ourselves,' he said. I beamed at him. 'You mean that you have done reprehensible things, milord? I don't believe it.'

'Reprehensible? By whose laws? Not mine, I assure you.'

'You mean you have ... eh ... shot people?' He laughed at my naivety. 'Who hasn't, eh?' he said finally.

'Tell me, Milord-'

'Oh, stuff that milord nonsense, why don't you call me Peregrine ... like the hawk,' he said.

'Of course Peregrine like the hawk, and I beg you to call me...' I stopped suddenly, for I had a complete blank regarding the name we had chosen for me and by which I had been introduced.

'No, I think we do not know each other sufficiently for such intimacies - yet.' Perversely, the moment I had opted out, the name came back to me. Lavinia! I found that unintentionally I had created a mystique that would serve me well. I peered at him, giving him the impression that I was attracted to his person, but I was watching his withering, implacable, burning eyes and deciding how much of what we had heard could be true. I arrived at the conclusion that most of it could well be. I saw greed for money and power in those mirrors of the soul. Contempt for the human condition. I saw cruelty and heartlessness. I was convinced that here was indeed a man who was capable of tearing a child from limb to limb. I saw voracious sexual appetites in the way Stonehead leered at me, although he tried to hide this by his banter. The *Club* might well be relentless and piti-less in our pursuit of our natural enemies, but first we have to make sure that we get our facts right. We will never stop working on it.

Coleridge was surprised that so many aristocratic ladies seemed to be lusting after him. I saw him disappear into the gazebo in the early hours with a buxom young thing. He winked at me when they came back a good hour later. I saw Clarihoe exchange cards with an effete young man in blue silk. I lost trace of Ivan, but he was all smiles next day. I think Armande and Anatole were beginning to conflate their assumed identi-ties with reality. I saw them at least once embracing passionately behind a pillar. Good luck to them.

In the interest of fairness, I found myself questioning my judge-ment of Stonehead again and again. He had expressed enough words to condemn himself, but did I have any valid proof? Eyewitness accounts? Could all his rash words have been nothing but *braggadocio*? When I had unwisely implied a hand in Wexford Sandler III's demise, he gave me a congratulatory nod. Men like being outrageous in the mistaken belief that women fall for it. Was that belief really mistaken? If not, why did that man and his words occupy my thoughts so much?

Before the month was out, we were asked to Stonehead Manor for a spectacular soirée, at which, Bertie himself would attend, but incognito. I had, of course, heard stories of scandal relating to the Prince of Wales, but I must say that I saw no great interest in the man. When he arrived, he had a mask covering his eyes but his face and his characteristic jowls were visible for everyone to see. Besides he acted in a loud regal manner, ordering and commanding. There could not have been one person in the crowd who was left with any doubt about the identity of the masked guest of honour. I had a hunch that Peregrine had warned him off me, for His Royal Highness returned my bow with a smile and turned away self-consciously, leaving me with the conviction that given half the chance he would throw himself at my feet and swear that unless he had me before sunrise, he would renounce his royal heritage. Stories circulated freely to the effect that he was much given to excesses of the sort.

His Highness spoke French to Armande. She told us later how atrocious his accent was. To our relief he scarcely looked in my direction. He did stare at Bartola, but disappeared with some of Peregrine's friends soon after. I am already calling him Peregrine in my thoughts. Why? I spent the whole evening dancing with him. This time, convinced that like a ripe plum I was ready to fall in his hands, he made little effort to hide his outrageous views and his misanthropy. Yes, he was proud to declare that ninety-nine percent of humanity were filth and if he had his way he would exterminate them.

'Painlessly of course?'

'No, Lavinia, what's wrong with a slow painful death for those scum?'

'You frighten me, Peregrine.'

'I don't think it's easy to do that,' he said holding me tighter. 'Be mine tonight dearest,' he whispered.

'I will give myself to you, but only when I am good and ready. Please don't insist.' The idea of giving myself to him was a repulsive one. Should he attempt to molest me, like the romantic heroines of the popular serials, I'd throw myself from a window. Or give him a resounding slap.

He explained to me at great length how much he disliked the staid hunting traditions of the country. He much preferred hunting on horseback, like the tribesmen of Central Asia. He was a past master at using his gun in the saddle. 'I will take you partridge hunting in Nuthampstead next September. Write it in your diary. I must have you then.'

'Only if you bag twenty braces,' I whispered, controlling my urge to be sick.

'You drive a hard bargain, but no challenge is too big for Peregrine Stonehead when the prize is so tantalizing.'

I accepted that for the sake of our plan to work, I might have to submit myself to that blackguard. The night before the hunt, I lay awake shuddering at the thought. How would I react if he should fraudulently arrange to show me the twenty braces? How my attitude to the man changed and with such speed, I will never understand. The dim figure arising in the mist of insomnia began shedding many of his negative attributes, and I found myself beginning to question my harsh evaluation of the man. He had been nothing but courteous and kind to me, to the *Club*. All those accusations were unsubstantiated. The Gypsies may be our friends, but they are a disorderly lot. They are horse thieves and it was well-known that they stole other people's children. My goodness me, was he attractive! Those piercing eyes that seem to see right through you, can create physical discomfort in one. No, I cannot be falling for that miscreant. I am a clear-thinking woman inured to the ways of the world, am I not? But when I am in the mood I am in now, he can do what he likes with me. As a rule I have complete control over my senses. I could happily contemplate living like a nun, but when I am unchained, I lose all control.

My friends in the *Club* recognised the excitable state that I was in on the morning of the hunt, but they no doubt thought that I was fired by my sole determination to bring the villain to book. The hunting expedition proved a failure for him, as he was only able to bag three braces, providing me with a ready-made excuse for keeping him at bay. However, by now my desire for him had assumed unmanageable proportions and saying that I felt sorry for him, I gave myself to him that night.

I stayed at the Manor for three days, convincing myself that my aim was to investigate the terrain around the fallen oak on the bank of the rivulet, although I had become more or less convinced that all those tales of horror were nothing but malicious gossip. When my *soi-disant* lover announced that he needed to go to London for a day, I claimed that I wanted to stay at the manor and wait for his return. Twirling his whiskers he begged me to. I would have the freedom of the woods, I told myself. I would be able to check for myself and dispel all doubts about those accusations. I would then put my relationship with him on a clear footing. Yes, I had finally met a man I could be besotted with.

I had no difficulty in locating the place by the rivulet and it was now a matter of time before we got incontrovertible evidence pointing to the fact that Peregrine was just a boastful wag. He was arrogant, but definitely not the sort to harm anybody, let alone children. What had happened between the two of us was more than just physical. It was so endearing how, once he had met me, he paid attention to nobody else. I almost made up my mind to inform the *Club* that I had looked everywhere and could not locate that fallen oak. There were no buried children. I sat on the oak and started shivering although it was not cold. The place looked forlorn and I was filled by an infinite sadness. Why was I feeing tearful? I thought I heard the cry of a baby, but it was only a stray cat. No, my instincts informed me that Stonehead could not be a child murderer. I was not going to stab him in the back. I left the area and made for the house.

When I came back to *Le Cabanon*, I had not made up my mind about what to tell my companions, but as no one asked I said nothing. A headache gave me the perfect excuse to turn in early. I was woken up before sunrise the next day by a racket. I rushed downstairs where I was greeted by a crowd of glum Romanies being comforted by Algernon and the others. I did not immediately see a shivering little girl of about seven or eight with blood-stained clothes. Yolanda, Armande and Bartola were comforting her with a glass of hot milk. A small group of Romany men and women were standing around speechless, their eyes glazed. I have often wondered about how trivial things can get them all excited, but tragedies leave them calm and dignified. The girl eyed the beverage greedily but rocked by her tears she was unable to drink any of it.

'Tell the ladies and the gentlemen what happened last night, Violca,' Yolanda prompted her. It was clear that the little thing was in no position to comply. Finally Yolanda decided to tell us herself: Little Violca had gone hawthorn berry picking with her friends, but had not heard when the others said it was time to go. She had just espied a juicy bunch, and had become absorbed in her quest. When she came down, her friends, thinking that she was following behind, had disappeared from view. Suddenly a man had grabbed her, put a sack over her head and carried her away. When her head was uncovered, she found herself in a cellar with her hands tied behind her back, lying on the ground. She was crying, had wet herself and a huge man with droopy mustaches told her to stop snivelling if she did not want a thrashing, which helped not a bit. Then two gentlemen came in and talked to her nicely.

'Would you like some sweets, sweetheart?' one of them said. When she kept quiet, he slapped her and his ring tore into her cheek. The sight of her blood trickling down gave her a fright and she began screaming. The men then forced a drink down her, one pinching her nose to make her swallow. Then the man with the droopy moustache gave some money to her kidnapper.

'Well done Arthur, you deserve a reward for you trouble. We leave the article in your hands, we'll send for her later,' she heard him say. When they left, Violca became violently sick and vomited but Arthur was too drunk to notice. She was terrified and cold. She thought that she was going to die. Suddenly she became aware that her jailer had fallen asleep. As the rope round her wrists was not tied too tightly, she managed to wrestle her hands free, crept towards the door, pushed it open and was relieved to find herself in the grounds of the manor. She had no idea where she was or how to escape. She wandered round randomly until she saw a hedge. Luckily she was able to go through it, albeit at the cost of a few scratches. How she reached her camp she did not know.

'But us folks 'ave a knack for finding our way,' Yolanda said. Whatever positive attributes I might have been ready to confer onto that monster rapidly dissolved in the avalanche of evidence which was now pouring down on us. Little Violca, now calmed down, agreed to be washed and her wounds dressed. We arranged for the visitors to sleep in *Le Cabanon* after promising that we would decide on a course of action with despatch. I had entirely dismissed my short-lived infatuation with the murderer as an unexplainable aberration.

It did not take long to elaborate a watertight plan and before dawn a small party armed with the appropriate tools sneaked out and made its way to the castle. Fortunately it was full moon. When we arrived at our destination, we forced our way in through the hedge, located the fallen oak and began digging. It did not take us too long to find what we were looking for. We put one tiny skull and a couple of bones looking to be from arms of little children in a bag, and made our way back with heavy hearts.

Next day, we made our way to St Albans where Constable Balding said he was expecting us. We were surprised and asked him how he knew.

He realised that he had given the game away, and stupidly revealed that the guilty man had sent word to him.

' 'Ave you come to report a stolen child?'

'On the contrary,' Lord Clarihoe said with a little laugh. 'We have found one.'

'Really, your lordship? Surely you 'aven't come to complain that you 'ave actually found a girl. So what are you complaining about then? You should rejoice.'

'We now have concrete evidence that criminal activities have been taking place at Stonehead Castle. We've dug out some bones.' At this point one of ours handed over the bones to the constable.

'A small ape,' said the officer on seeing the skull. Then he took the bones and demurred. 'Looks like a dog's leg.'

'Look, my good man,' said Ivan Vissarionovitch angrily, 'are you an expert pathologist?'

'Inform the foreign gentleman that it's not the English way ... eh ... we don't gain nothing by losing our rag, do we sir,' said the constable

addressing Lord Clarihoe. In a more conciliatory tone he added, 'I ain't
no medical expert, as the foreign gentlemen said, so I will take possession of them bones, give you a receipt and send them to Scotland Yard
for tests. We can only take action after the results come.'

We knew that we would never get any justice when big and powerful
men were involved, but the *Club* never accepts defeat. We would convene
later and find a solution. It did not take us long to decide that if we
wanted justice, we'd have to hand it down ourselves. Having been on a
few hunts with Stonehead, a workable plan spontaneously sprouted in
my head like field mushrooms on an autumn morning following a thunderous night. I also had a personal account to settle with the malefactor.

Our spies informed us that a hunt was organised for the following
Saturday. By now I had acquired a thorough knowledge of the geography
of Ashridge Forest. We knew we could depend on our Romany friends.
They may appear to us to be loud and undisciplined, but their loyalty
was unflinching. Yolanda, who had impressed by her common sense, was
going to arrange for a party of her fellows to spread themselves around
the forest, ostensibly for mushroom picking. Few Anglo-Saxons want
anything to do with fungi, thinking them to be all poisonous, but the
travellers know all there is to know about naturally growing food naturally, like fungi, berries, roots, nuts, samphires, leaves, and are therefore
very keen on them. There is a variety called the *porshinu* (Yolanda told
me) which is as tasty as meat. This can be found abundantly in autumn.
Ivan identified it as the cep, much valued in his native Russia. It has a
brown head and can be as big as the palm of one hand. Her team was
actively looking for those delicacies, and at the same time watching the
hunt with their hawks' eyes. They were going to communicate with her
by means of bird calls. I put my gear on, got on *Caravaggio* and discreetly
made my way to Ashridge.

Since Peregrine insisted on showing his mastery and his superiority,
he would usually lead by a good hundred yards, the others lagging behind
to humour him. A path to the left of the Bridgewater monument led to
a copse where stags could sometimes be seen searching for water which
was abundant in the area owing to depressions in the land which served
as natural pools.

Yolanda's brother Djordi and some men had already worked on a diseased oak in preparation. They were in position at a short distance between the monument and the water meadows. As the hunt progressed across the forest, their lordships were irritated by the Gypsy ragamuffins. Not only was the sight of them contemptible, but they believed their presence was not conducive to a good hunt. They caused unnecessary noise and frightened the game. The hunters glared at them, and when there were little ones close enough they lashed at them with their whips. The little fellows took evasive actions with little effort, and then, to much hilarity, wiggled their little bottoms at their lordships in defiance.

Yolanda was by my side on a path leading towards the water meadows, and translated each whistle and bird call to me. The hunt was now approaching the Bridgewater Monument. Stonehead was now ten yards in front with only his hound *Blackamoor* keeping up with him. He was speeding, and his fellow huntsmen were out of sight. Peregrine was now exactly where we wanted him, cut off from his companions and approaching the final path. At this point, Yolanda became greatly excited. Provided we get the timing right, miss, she whispered to me. At exactly the same moment, I heard the galloping child murderer and caught a glimpse of him coming towards us through the trees. Suddenly my companion emitted a squeak that I did not recognise from any creature I knew. I heard a prolonged and mournful screech and at the same time a thunderous crash, followed shortly after by a muffled sound. It was a big tree tearing away from its base and toppling over, hitting the ground, attempting to rise but unable to do so, giving up finally. The little ones would tell us later that, as the rest of the party drew near, their horses panicked at the sound of the crash and at least two cavaliers were unhorsed. The loud noise coincided with the approach of horse and rider to my little device. Neither saw or anticipated the rope that I had fixed tightly to two birches on opposite sides of the lane about two feet above the ground. Peregrine directed his mount right onto it. He immediately toppled over, head first, then rolled over landing on his back, his gun flying away, with the poor horse another regretted victim.

His lordship gives a shriek of pain as he touches the ground, probably with a broken back. I spring towards his gun, grab it and rush towards him. He opens his eyes wide with horror and fright. I put my right foot on his chest, and point his own gun at him.

'Stonehead,' I say to him, 'I am going to execute you for the murder of countless little children, make a prayer.' He mumbles something, probably a curse. I pull the trigger aiming for his head which bursts open, splattering blood and brains all around. With amazing calm I place the gun by his side, push his body with my feet to start it rolling, and position it over the weapon, in order to facilitate the wrong conclusion that he had fallen over his gun and accidentally shot himself.

Next, I detach the rope from the two birches, for if the coroner is to pronounce a verdict of accidental death, we do not want to leave clues behind undermining that plausible hypothesis. I then make my way out of Ashridge unseen by anybody but our allies.

There was great upheaval in the area following the incident, and great rejoicing in the Romany camps. A team of experts from the police and the health department came to the scene of the death, questioned the Gypsy children who told them what Yolanda had taught them. They pronounced a verdict of accidental death provoked by the horse of his lordship panicking on hearing the fall of a diseased oak whose time had arrived. His gun had set itself off as a result.

I was pleased that our former dalliance and my momentary weakness towards the depraved man notwithstanding, the only feeling I had when it was all over and done with, was one of unalloyed exhilaration. I was greatly relieved that a criminal who thought himself above the law had met his just deserts. The children of the area would henceforth live in safety.

The following nights, as I lay on my bed trying to get some sleep, I kept questioning my judgement over the man. How could I, who prided myself on my clearheadedness, even after I got to meet the man, allow myself to be blinded to the extent of blaming the victims for spreading gossip about an innocent man? I felt soiled. That night I dreamt of Mam and she told me that to cleanse myself I needed to go to Lourdes and atone for my sins before resuming normal life. Normal life to us in the *Club*, that is. I always listened to my mother when she was alive and do not see why her death would make any difference. I wonder if Algernon would like to accompany me.

CHAPTER THIRTEEN
Neville St Clair
(1890)

When I made him breakfast, I found that there was no sign of Mr. Holmes. It was so unlike him to throw his hands up in the air and give up, but when I found a copy of the Evening Tribune on his desk carrying St Clair's article, I knew that there was only one explanation to his disappearance: he had gone to Chesterfield.

He turned up late next day. Boone was due for hanging at dawn in the morning. He sent word to Watson by Charlie, the retired jockey whose hansom cab was usually parked at the corner from number 221B, to come to Baker Street with despatch, and the good doctor duly arrived at the stroke of midnight.

'It's the wrong eye, Watson, I tell you it's the wrong eye.' The good doctor looked at him in wonderment, little doubting that I knew exactly what that was all about.

In great haste they proceeded to South Kensington where Mycroft had his lodgings. Together the Holmes brothers and Dr Watson made for the Home Minister's residence.

The Home Minister was not amused to be woken up in the middle of the night. Holmes did his best to convince him that he was hanging an innocent man.

'But how can that be? The fellow has been judged by his peers and found guilty of for murder.'

'For murdering himself, sir,' said Holmes. 'He didn't murder anybody. He happens to be the very person he's supposed to have killed.'

'Why didn't he say so?' asked the Minister. Nobody answered.

Reluctantly the Home Minister jumped in the cab and they all made their way to Newgate. The proximity of death had given Boone a severe jolt and had driven away his amnesia. He was screaming when the Home Minister and party arrived at Newgate just as he was being led to the gallows in the yard.

'I am Neville St Clair, I am Neville St Clair. I never killed anybody! Ask my Malay friend.'

The guards laughed their heads off at the man who seemed to be claiming that he was the very man he had murdered. Holmes explained to the still half-asleep minister that indeed the prisoner about to be hanged was none other than the man he was supposed to have killed, that the real Hugh had lost his right eye, and was alive and well in Australia, whereas the man about to be hanged had a patch over his left one.

'If anybody had bothered to look, they'd have found a good eye under that patch.' No one was in a hurry to check.

With great difficulty the detective explained the facts. Neville, having researched his article too earnestly by posing as a beggar for a few days, had been greatly impressed by how much more he could earn by begging. His brokerage business undergoing a slump, he had thought he could make good his shortfalls by practising what he had found to be a lucrative trade, albeit temporarily. He knew that he could not carry out this fraught enterprise under his own identity as he had to safeguard family honour. Remembering what an impressive figure his twin brother cut with the eyepatch, he thought that this, with some grime should be enough of a disguise. He needed a base, and his Malay friend The Tenku who he had known for years, and who operated a legal if dubious business kindly obliged by allowing him use of his den.

Holmes himself revealed the good left eye by removing the patch before the minister gave the order to rescind the execution. He suspected that the latter had arrived at this decision, not because he understood that the condemned man was blameless but because, still half-asleep, he understood nothing at all.

Neville was released to his wife, to whom he tearfully explained that he kept wanting to make a clean breast of how he had been earning a living, but that his courage failed him at the last minute. When she saw him on that fateful Monday, he was in a state of shock. His first thought was how to stop her finding out about his double life. He would naturally not feel able to return to begging after this great ordeal. Having gained a certain notoriety, he would surely be able to operate successfully as a broker now.

'Whatever you say, sweetheart,' Ida said. In any case Mr Beeston, who never let a golden opportunity slip by had commissioned him to write a ten thousand word account (at sixpence a word) of his travails.

That night the abstemious Holmes was making an exception and had opened a bottle of Armagnac to share with Watson. On a sudden impulse, he decided to invite me to join in. Alcohol produces an extraordinary effect upon him. I had never seen him in such a jovial mood. To my considerable amusement, he alarmed the good doctor by suggesting that as he did not have any case pending, and as he happened to be a master of disguises, he might as well stake a claim to the vacated beat of St Clair. Later, as he was handing over the glass to me, he said, 'A toast to Mrs Hudson, without whose help I would not have been able to get to Newgate on time.' I must have stared at him. He must surely have known all along what part I had played in establishing the Chesterfield connection. Had I not drawn his attention to the article on begging? Still, he was only prepared to give me credit my contribution in more mundane matters.

'When I came back from Chesterfield, had you not forced that curried mutton upon me, I'd have passed out before getting anywhere.'

CHAPTER FOURTEEN

Bartola's Niece

(1886)

None of us doubted that Bartola had never poisoned her husband. If any one was minded to question our assumption, there would have been no better proof than the fact that all the dead man's relatives were devoted to her. Teddy, her brother-in-law's clever son most of all. She visited them regularly and there existed the most harmonious rapport between them. Having seen me put my thoughts on paper and make myself a comfortable nest egg, she has been playing with the notion of writing her own account of the tragic case, so I will leave that seam unexploited. However Bartola herself has urged me to write the story of her goddaughter and niece Clara, Teddy's older sister. She has generously provided me with the background facts.

Clara was eighteen at the time the events I am about to describe took place. She was thrilled to bits about a position she had been offered at Harrods of Knightsbridge. She was a pretty, sweet, naive thing and the apple of her parents' eyes. She lived with them, poor crofters, in the apple growing region of Kent. They could barely scratch a living, and, were it not for Bartola (who had inherited her husband's property), she would not have been able to go to Orpington Ladies Day School, where she was a moderately hardworking pupil. Although the landowners, the Harrowmore family, were reputed to be proud and overbearing, their own Priscilla Harrowmore, who was of Clara's age, had chosen her as her best friend. It was at Priscilla's seventeenth birthday party, or 'Coming

Out Party' as polite society called it, that she met Piers Crickster, the nineteen-year-old son of Ranulph Crickster of the Mayfair House and Land Agents. As a girlish prank, the landowner's daughter had introduced her friend to the young man as her cousin from a cattle farming dynasty and Clara had rather enjoyed being paid attention to under that guise. It took only a few days for Piers to write his first love letter to the young crofter's daughter. At first Clara laughed it off, but Priscilla, playing Cupid, encouraged the romance and when the second letter arrived, Clara felt weak at the knees as she read it. She had not been able to resist the wiles of the handsome young swain.

The *Club* became involved when an anguished Bartola returned from Kent one day and tearfully told us that her darling little Clara, who was only a toddler yesterday, was in the family way. She was devastated if only because the position Harrod's had offered her when she left college was in the balance. The poor thing had succumbed to the entreaties of the hot-blooded Piers, but as he had promised to marry her, she had not thought that her situation was all that dire. However, next time we saw her, Bartola read to us a long letter that Piers had written to Clara, accusing her of having misled him into believing that she was an heiress, when in fact she was a pauper. "*I did not fall in love with you because I thought your father was rich. I would have married you even if you were a pauper but I cannot abide the lies you told me. A good marriage cannot prosper on lies. In any case, how am I to know that the baby you claim to be carrying is mine, seeing how readily you gave yourself to me?*" Clara had urged her aunt to do something, for if she could not marry him, she said, she would throw herself from the cliffs. ("*Zia Bartola, can you tell me how to get to the Dover cliffs?*")

'The *Club* must do something,' our friend urged. Naturally we readily concurred. We sat down one evening and planned a course of action.

The first thing we did was to ask the careless and credulous young lady to come visit us in Water Lane. We were there in full force, from the Bishop to Vissarionovich. We were able to question her fully. She saw us as no more than dear friends of her aunt. She had no idea of the more swashbuckling, not to say sinister, aspects of our lives. As an extra precaution we never revealed our true names to her. We indicated that we were going to help her, but gave her not the slightest whiff of our plans.

The most important intelligence we obtained was how the young fellow spent his day. The coachman who fortuitously happened to be Clara's own Uncle Albert took Piers in the hansom cab from their house in Orpington every morning. He passed through Crystal Palace and Streatham Common before heading towards the Thames. He crossed Battersea Bridge, before reaching Soho Square where he worked in the office of the bankers Harshmallow and Sons, friends of Sir Ranulph. He usually ate lunch at the *Bocca d'Oro* a small but chic Italian restaurant in Dean Street, spending whatever time was left of his lunch break in Soho Square. Sometimes, the love-struck Clara travelled upwards of two hours by tram and Shillibeer omnibus, spending all the pocket money that Bartola gave her, to meet him to spend fifteen minutes in his illustrious company. Twice a week, on Tuesdays and Fridays, the Square was host to stallholders selling exotic products, snake oil, fake jewellery, trinkets, carved statuettes, balms, ribald postcards and things of a similar nature. The young fellow loved spending time there, losing to Three Card tricksters, having his future told by Gypsy clairvoyants, watching practitioners of fire-eating or knife-throwing, listening to accordionists or staring at jugglers.

It had been estimated that our campaign would last three weeks and would involve a modest expenditure. To this effect, a generous budget was allocated to the project by Frunk. The first shot of the campaign was to be fired on the following Tuesday. We all had a part to play. The overture would involve Anatole, Ivan Vissarionovich and the Bishop, disguised as fairground tricksters, and yours truly in the character of a fat Gypsy fortuneteller. Slim practitioners are not thought credible. The others were all to be present in some capacity.

Before noon we were already in position in Soho Square. Much padded and gaudily apparelled, I wore big circular earrings, multicoloured beads round my neck, and a bright green skirt reaching down to my ankles. I had a vermilion scarf over my head, and exulted in my grotesque appearance. I sat cross-legged on a piece of sail cloth, waiting for our quarry. It was funny how, although I had one client in mind and made no effort to inveigle innocent passers-by, people kept stopping to have their palms read. In the meantime, my three friends had set up their stall on a soapbox, offering three half-crowns for a sixpenny bet on a three card trick. The Bishop had learnt the technique from a reformed reprobate so he could earn some money for his church at charity events. He proved very adept at hoodwinking the naive punters who allowed themselves to be tempted by an easy win. As our purpose was not to defraud, we had set enough money aside and we were only too happy to let the risk takers win every now and then.

At half past noon, Piers appeared. He was easy to spot as Clara had described him to us perfectly: slim and not too tall, a small elongated head with shiny dark brown hair, thin twirly moustache, grey laughing eyes, immaculately dressed in light grey, and walking with a very slight stoop. Artémise and Lord Clarihoe, dressed as casual workers, jostled him, manoeuvring him towards my beat.

'There's a young man with rich promises for you,' I said in my most beguiling voice. 'You can see happiness in those eyes. Come to me dear sir, this Gypsy 'ag 'ere will tell you fings wot will warm the cockles of yer 'eart.' He looked at me, still undecided. After all the care we had put in perfecting our schemes, we simply could not let the occasion slip.

'Sir, this Gypsy 'ag ain't no fike.' He had turned his back on me so I pressed on. 'She can tell yer fings about yesself ... your name begins with a ... let me see.' At this point I closed my eyes and he took two steps away from me, but I insisted. 'A P sir ... funny, it ain't Peter ... or Patrick... what can it be?' He stopped, turned round, his interest suddenly awakened. 'Yes, Piers, sir. Come Mr Piers.' Perplexed, he took small tentative steps towards me. 'You'll be surprised what the Gypsy 'ag can already see for you. Great wonderful fings, Mister Piers.' He was now hooked. A small crowd gathered around us, and he offered me his hand.

'Mr Piers, if only you knew how blest you are, sir! It must be because you are cushioned in a good woman's love, I can feel it.' The crowd showered their goodwill on this undeserving scoundrel, as if they could have a share in his good fortune.

'Mr Piers, this Gypsy 'ag 'ere does not trust no stars sir, because she can see all she needs in the aura surrounding you. Can you see his aura?'I asked my audience. No one reacted. 'In Gypsy lore,' I explained, 'it is said that one person in sixty-six can. Then those with the gift can sharpen it.'

Bartola, in the guise of a passer-by opened her mouth in a very obvious manner.

'Madam,' I said opening my eyes wide. 'You can, I know you can.'

'Yes,' she admitted shyly, nodding with obvious enthusiasm.

'Tell me what you see, ma'am.' She hesitated, and in a stammer explained that she could see like a pale bluish haze all around Piers.

'Is that all?'

'No, the haze keeps changing from blue to flame colour.'

'From blue to flame colour ... absolutely. Indeed madam, you are blessed with the gift ... but Mister Piers sir, since you've already got all the love any man would need, I'll tell you more. Mammon, the god of wealth is smiling on you sir. All that you touch will turn into gold.' I could see that he was now eating out of the palm of my hands.

'Put my words to the test Mister Piers. Look at them cardsharps over there. Even they, with all their trickery can't defeat you on this lucky day. Just go my good sir.' He made to go but I stopped him.

'No Mister Piers, nothing will work out for you unless you cross my palm with silver.' Grudgingly he put a silver threepenny bit in my hand and made directly for the stall where my three companions were ready for him. He went away to his office two pounds the richer. This episode was designed to gain his trust. My gentle readers will have understood that.

Friday was the other day when the Square hosted a fair and we did a repeat performance. This time, seeing that Piers Crickster had acknowledged my *bona fide* he came directly to me without any prompting and I went a step further.

'Ah, Mister Piers,' I said welcoming him, 'I wonder if your good luck is still following you around.' He smiled, and a winning smile it was too. I could see why that foolish girl got her head turned.

'Yes, Gyppo hag, that's what I want you to tell me.' I took hold of his hand and put on a dubious scowl on my face. When he saw this he frowned, and looked at me questioningly.

'I think it's best if I keep my mouth shut this time,' I said.

'No, Gyppo hag, you can't, I don't pay you for keeping your lips tight, I insist that you tell me forthright.'

134

'Why, young sir, since you insist. When it comes to money I can't see no change, you've still got the touch, the aura's still there.' This intelligence was greeted by a broad smile lighting up his face.

'That's alright then, what else do I want?' I think he meant to go away at this juncture, so I had to stop him.

'Whilst the peerless love of that young woman is still there for you, yes, you will prosper, but I see signs that maybe it is frittering away.'

'Really?'

'Yes, now this is what I see, but let me not spoil your day. You don't want to hear it.'

'I do, out with it, don't waste my time, hag.'

'Well, since you ask, it works out like this Mister Piers. If you're unable to keep the love of that wonderful woman who is so devoted to you ... name beginning with C ... then your life will take an unexpected turn, for the worse, I am afraid.'

'In what way?'

'Fortunately when it comes to money I don't see your luck changing all that much at the moment, but if you lose her love, and I can see that 'appening, you will also suffer in other fields ... for example your 'ealth... aye, your 'ealth sir,. Now hold on, what do I see here? Oh sir, I see an attack of some sort. Maybe even a fatal assault or accident ... no, a series of accidents leading to your death possibly.'

'Poppycock,' said Piers with a mocking laugh, but for all this, I couldn't help noticing that he was rattled.

'I think you are an old foolish woman. You're talking a lot of balderdash. I've never been healthier in my whole life.' I shrugged.

'But you've still got your winning streak, you can check that easily enough. Better do it today, for it might be gone next time.' He went away to the three card tricksters.

'Just beware of robbers and cutthroats,' I said.

'I might as well go and get some money from those saps,' he said. He directed his steps towards my companions and their marked cards. He came back shortly after and, with a sneer, waved a handful of sterling notes which he had won at me. We had to put his belief in our forecasts on a firm footing.

Next time we saw him, I told him that his luck was changing direction.

'Just be on the lookout for those mishaps and assaults I warned you about.' I told him as he turned away, to try and win some more money, but we made sure he lost a fair bit of money to our tricksters.

We knew from what Clara had told us that often he had to be on the road very early, when it was still dark. Our next instalment was planned with this in mind. We had mounted a two-pronged attack. As he was travelling through the fresh-fallen snows on Streatham Common on a cold dark morning before sunrise, the Gypsy hag, now transformed into a masked slim Irene suddenly emerged in front of his cab, manoeuvred *Caravaggio* into an impressive capriole which caused panic in his own timid Altai. At the same time I brandished my unloaded Sharps Carbine menacingly.

'If you do as I say, no harm will be done to you sir,' I said in a voice which struck me as more intimidating for its calmness. Lord Clarihoe also masked, who had descended from his own mount opened the door, grabbed Piers by the scruff and pulled him out. The young villain cowered, raising his hands above his head in a sign of abject surrender, whimpering. We noticed that he had wet his trousers. Addressing him by name, I said to the coachman that we meant him no harm if he promised not to do anything rash. He nodded quietly. Algernon asked the young man to hand over all his money, his gold watch, then told him that it was a disgusting habit to wet one's trousers like this.

'Take it out this instant!' he ordered. Shivering with cold and fear, Piers carried out the instruction, and we left them there on Streatham Common. We expected that Piers and his coachman would turn back and make for the comfort of his Orpington nest. I felt sorry for Uncle Albert who would certainly be ordered to hand over his dry trousers to enable the miserable puppy to change his soiled garment. Concurrently, we had carried out our burglary. On entering his part of the house later, he would have been greeted by the sight of all his possessions scattered all over the place, with his prized gun collection gone, courtesy Coleridge and Bartola.

When we saw him in Soho square the following Tuesday, he had the look of a floored pugilist.

'Are you a witch, woman?' he asked me with disdain. 'Only a witch could have known.'

'No sir, I foretell the future, is all.'

'Can you read the past as well?'

'Yes, sir, that I can. I can see that you have been the subject of a grave assault. No, hang on, can it be possible? I can see you have been the victim of two very serious calamities.'

'Is there going to be any more?'

'Afraid so... I can see no end to this stroke of bad luck dogging you, now that the love of the good woman seems lost to you. Don't blame me, sir, I can also see that you have brought this upon yourself.'

'What do you mean? '

'I don't know everything, Mr Piers, but it appears that her love was offered to you on a plate. You took some morsels and then you spat in it.'

'You don't know what you're babbling on about, old woman. I can just snap my fingers and she will come running back to me, I tell you!' He turned round with a sneer and went towards the Bishop who was fast recouping our investment.

Clara's belly was swelling visibly by now and it took all of Bartola's power to persuade her father not to throw her out. In the meantime, we were having great fun seeing our fiendish plan working towards fruition. The young man was obviously turning into a wreck, which is where we wanted him. We had a last arrow in our quiver.

The *Bocca d'Oro* was often in need of waiting staff. At the start of our campaign Armande had started working there as part of our scheme. It was therefore not too difficult for her to slip a little something in his parmesan. Bartola had carefully worked out quantities so that, whilst it would make him ill, it would not cause lasting damage. We had all the trouble in the world stopping ourselves from choking with laughter as we watched Piers coming out of the restaurant after a copious lunch, and begin doing his St Vitus dance around the Square when the spasms took hold of him. If there was a risk that the tribulations of the young betrayer causing the upsurge of pity in our hardened breasts, all we had to do was to remind ourselves of the state sweet dear young Clara was in and imagine the life of a young unmarried mother in this unforgiving society we lived in.

It was the following Saturday that the young pregnant girl turned up at Water Lane, her face glowing with the flush of victory. As we expected, the contrite Piers had come knocking at their door, arms loaded with flowers for Mum, a bottle of whisky for Dad and *patisserie* and *bonbons* for the young ones. For Clara herself, he had brought a ring.

'So when are we to expect wedding bells?' Armande asked, where-upon the young girl scowled.

'Wedding bells? Did you think that I would want to marry him after he had shown what a cad he was? Never. All I wanted was for him to recognise his paternity and accept his responsibility. I am well able to look after my little baby without his help. You will be pleased to learn that Miss Sommerville at Harrods has promised to keep my job open until after the delivery. You see, she confided to me that her own Amelia was born out of wedlock.'

CHAPTER FIFTEEN

A Mysterious Abduction

(An Unpublished Story)

(1884)

I was surprised one day while putting away some of Mr Holmes' papers, to come across an envelope containing a manuscript in Dr Watson's characteristic sixteenth-inch characters in jet black ink. I knew that I ran no risk of being caught, as the pair of them were in Devon. In any case, my employer's advice to me had always been that if I wanted to be aware of what was happening in the world around me, I should not be too coy about eavesdropping on people's conversation "provided you do it cannily." A piece of paper lying on the floor, is meant to be read, "look at both sides." He knew I often stood behind his door when a client came in with a case for him and he never showed disapproval when he caught me at it. So, I felt easy about having a closer look. I had of course been very interested in whatever he was doing. I pulled out the six or seven sheets, and a small note dropped out. It bore the Beeston heading, and a few hastily scribbled lines:

Dear Dr W.,

I admire this installment a lot, but do not feel able to use it at the present, as I think it shows our admirable Police Force in an unfavourable light. I can see no way to amend it and still do justice to a very reasonable tale.

Yrs. J.B.

I went back to the manuscript. It was entitled *A Mysterious Abduction*. To my surprise, it was something we were associated with. Because the doctor has a tendency to ramble on and talk about things whose connection with the main thrust of the tale is at best tenuous, I have taken the liberty of reworking it, keeping the essential facts.

It began when my employer's older brother arrived at Number 221B one morning. Mycroft is something of a mystery, even to Dr Watson. He seems to have an important but ill-defined role in some ministry, adviser to the cabinet, trouble-shooter or something akin to that. He is also reputedly at least as sharp an operator as his younger brother. I own to doubting that.

'Mycroft, come in illustrious brother mine, do come in. So the Prime Minister is sometimes able to manage without you, eh!'

'Yes, Runt, although perhaps what you mean is that I can manage without him sometimes, eh, what!'

Watson, unmarried then, was still living in the flat. They sat down, and Holmes gave instructions to Mrs Turner to prepare some Lapsang Souchong tea, for which Mr Mycroft had a preference. I have a notion that he saw service in India or perhaps Burma.

'I don't know what the world is coming to, Runt, it is positively scandalous.'

'O Wiser One,' Sherlock Holmes pointed out with a straight face, 'somebody, my admiration for is second to none, taught me that a pronoun is meaningless, unless the noun to which it refers had been previously defined. What, may I ask, does the "it" refer to when it occurs in the sentence, *it* is positively scandalous.'

'Very droll,' conceded Mycroft with a little bow.

'Pray pardon, my little jest and continue.'

'Right. Would you believe that there are villains abroad who would not only abduct private honest citizens, but do not stop at kidnapping officers of Her Majesty's Constabulary.' He raised his head slightly to study the effect that this revelation had produced on his younger sibling. If it had, it was concealed to the point of suggesting that the latter might not even have heard the indignant statement.

'Did I hear right?' asked Dr Watson. 'Police officers have been interfered with?'

'A mixed bag of ruffians of both sexes forced their way into the Vassal Street Police Station. Well, it's in Vassal Crescent actually, overpowered two officers and took them away. Some neighbours saw them being dragged towards a hansom cab and that was the last they were heard of.

'An interesting case, I daresay,' mumbled Sherlock peering at his fingers thoughtfully, as if deciding whether or not to link them together.

'Don't just sit there counting your fingers, man, the country wants you, nay, demands that you do something, that you find those worthy men without delay and apprehend the rascals.'

'Has there been any ransom note? Did they indicate what their grievances might be?'

'If there were, Sherlock, I would have mentioned them by now, wouldn't you say?'

'You're absolutely right. By the way, are you well? You did not give me the chance to enquire.' At this point Mrs Turner appeared with the tea and scones.

'My dear Mycroft, let us partake of this excellent offering that Mrs Turner is laying in front of us, after which I shall immediately set to work.'

***

Holmes beckoned the lad Charlie who was round the corner. He and the doctor climbed aboard and made their way to the police station just off Vassal Street. There are but few dwellings there and the station itself is but a modest little converted house on two floors with an empty terrain on either side. Directly opposite there is another field with no construction of any sort. The nearest edifice is a small block of three terraced houses when you look about twenty yards to the right and almost symmetrically another similar block on the left.

Holmes instructed Charlie to stop outside the middle of the terraced house on the left, whereupon, a door opened as if by magic. A woman with her front teeth missing emerged and smiled at the men in a welcoming manner.

'You've come to seek our 'elp, haven't you, sirs?'

'Yes, my good woman,' said Watson, 'that we 'ave ... eh, I mean that we have.'

'Come in, your worships, come in, it's a bit of a mess.'

The two sleuths made their way inside and sat on the rickety chairs which were offered to them. Yes, urged Holmes, now tell us all.

'It's as I told the uniformed men,' said the woman giving no intimation that she meant to add anything to that.

As she had left the door open, neighbours from the other blocks came in uninvited and indicated that they were determined not to miss a single word of the conversation now ready to break. Suddenly they began to speak all at once. Dr Watson explained to them in his most urbane manner that the only way any progress could be made, was if people did not interrupt each other, and allowed one person to speak at a time. The woman with the missing teeth - not by any means the only woman in that state - suddenly became more voluble. She explained that she had been preparing to go to bed after having done the cleaning and kneading the dough for tomorrow's bread, when she heard a hansom cab pulling into Vassal Crescent, closely followed by another. As there was moonlight, she thought she would try to see what was happening. She saw two men and two women get off the cab and enter the station. Two or three more people took position outside. There were comings and goings, and about fifteen minutes later, she saw the two officers, Boneheath and Deepship, being held by their scruffs, frogmarched to the cab which then drove away towards Kennington. There was unanimity about that, although the controversy about whether they were moaning with pain or mumbling or who of the policeman was being held by his right hand and who by the left gave rise to heated arguments which might have become physical had not the good doctor made more timely interventions. Clearly all this did not amount to much, but Holmes took his magnifying glass and went on his knees to study the marks on the road. If he had gleaned an idea or two, he kept them very much to himself.

That night he played his violin for more than an hour in an attempt to resist the lure of the white powder but eventually he gave up trying, and spent the whole night in a daze, reclining on his armchair, his long legs outstretched in front of him. Mrs Turner discreetly kept the coal fire going and spread a thick Hudson Bay blanket over him. The morning found him glum and irritable, and he snapped at both Watson and Mrs Turner. He said not a word the whole morning, and when he finally decided to break his silence, what he had to say was far from encouraging. 'No, Watson, I haven't got the slightest idea about that case.'

Fortunately, shortly after lunch, of which he partook but parsimoniously although Mrs Turner had prepared her best kedgeree, Mycroft turned up. He was in excellent humour.

'Runt, you've done it again. I just heard the good news about our two law enforcers, thank you. I told them my little brother never failed.'

'What do you mean?' asked Sherlock.

'I can't say more,' admitted Mycroft. 'I couldn't even finish lunch when I heard that the men had reappeared, and thought I'd come directly and thank you.'

'But I didn't do a thing, Mycroft, I spent half a day at Vassal Crescent and not a single valid idea sprouted in my dull brain. I was flummoxed, hadn't got the slightest lead. I've really contributed nothing.'

'What a man, what a man, eh what!' said Mycroft, refusing to dampen his enthusiasm. 'He does not lift a finger and yet solves a mystery.'

Mycroft finally left, without clarifying one whit the circumstances under which the two men had been rescued. However, it transpired soon enough, that the men had simply reappeared at their station. The Chief Constable demanded an explanation. At first the kidnapped constables seemed too dazed to speak. It dawned upon him that the men were actually *refusing* to speak. Pressed relentlessly they explained that what the neighbours described as a small team of men and women pushing them in a hansom cab was wrong. It was not a cab, but a craft which had come down from the skies. The people dragging them inside were Martians.

No grilling would make them change their account, so Mycroft brought in Sherlock once more.

Watson suggested that he talked to his friend Bertie Wells who had confided to him that he was thinking of writing a novel on the theme of alien visitations. The sceptic Holmes demurred, saying that his views would bring little to his investigation. Still, he said, if the doctor had the time, the sea air might do him some good. Watson did not have the time, but he made it.

'Did Wells give any credence to the tale of the kidnapped policemen,' he asked Watson when he came back from Southsea.

'He quoted Shakespeare,' Watson said merrily.

'Really? Which lines?' asked Holmes.

' "There are more things in heaven and earth Horatio, than can be dealt with in man's philosophy." '

'Next time you see him, inform him that the exact quote is: "There are more things in heaven and earth Horatio, than are dreamt of in your philosophy." '

Mr Wells' refusal to rule out the visit from outer space had left Holmes thoughtful. He revisited the Vassal Street area with the doctor. The residents, having read the account in the press, readily changed their stories. Indeed it was as the two men had said. What the constables were led into was nothing like a hansom cab. They had not realised it then. It bore all the hallmarks of having come down from the skies. It had landed in the field, not in the street as they had thought at first. He questioned them closely about the spacecraft, but everybody repeated what the newspaper had said: a round thing like two massive saucers, one on top of the other.

'How big?' There was so much contradiction that he decided to ignore the answers.

'You saw the people from space then, did you? Were they green little men?' No, they chorused. Holmes singled out one lady and asked her to describe them.

'Well, he was huge ... like a giant ... he leaned forwards as he walked. And in the moonlight he appeared black.'

'Yes,' the others agreed. 'He wasn't green but black.'

'He? Was there only one man?'

'No, I only really saw one clearly because it was so dark, but the others were the same.'

It took no more than half an hour for Holmes to dismiss the story of the perpetrators coming from outer space, although he did not entirely dismiss Mr Wells' beliefs.

'I knew we'd find nothing,' Watson mused aloud.

'On the contrary,' said Holmes, but as his companion knew, he would not elaborate.

When Mycroft called again, he suggested that he wanted to interrogate Boneheath and Deepship again, but he wanted nobody but Dr Watson present. The interview took place in the Vassal Crescent Station itself. The four men were seated facing each other.

'Boneheath and Deepship, I will tell you straight away that my investigations have revealed that the story you told us about your disappearance is balderdash. If you stick to it, I am going to recommend that you be committed to Bedlam, when you will lose your job and your pension.' On hearing this all the blood from the two men's faces drained away. For a whole minute they said nothing, but looked at each other meaningfully. Then after exchanging a nod with each other, they both spoke.

'We gave our words, sirs.'

'You gave your word? Whom to?'

'Them wot took us,' said Boneheath.

Holmes re-iterated his threat of committal and the two men finally agreed to reveal all.

They were sitting at their desk that evening when their abductors rushed in and took them away by force. 'Ruffians?'

'No, Mr 'Olmes, they were like you-'

'Like me? What do you mean?'

'Begging your pardon sir, I meant very respectable like. The gentlemen were dressed like lords and the ladies wore fine silk and 'ats.'

'And carried parasols.'

'So there were men and women? How many?'

'Was it eight, Sylvester?'

'Eight or ... eh, maybe nine, Ebenezer, three women and five ... eh ... six men.'

They were blindfolded, pushed into the hansom cab and taken to some place about a thirty minute drive away.

'Did you have a notion that you might have crossed the Thames?' No, they did not think so, but couldn't swear to it.

'Was it a direct journey, or might they have gone round a bit to mislead you?' One of them said that he had not given that any thought and had no idea, but the other demurred. 'Yes, I thought we might have been going in a circumbendibus.'

'Tell us what happened next.'

They were forcibly taken down a cellar where they were tied to a chair and their blindfolds removed.

'Yes, and after that?'

'We was fed.'

'Dry bread and water,' asked Watson. The two men looked at each other and then replied at the same time.

'No, sir ... sirs ... champagne and caviar.'

On hearing this, Dr Watson flew into a rage.

'Gentlemen, it ill behoves you to indulge in irony at this serious juncture.'

Holmes smiled and shook his head at his friend. 'No, Watson, I don't think our fellows are being facetious, or are lying.' Turning to them, he asked if there was one woman among the three, who was tall and slim and had jet black hair.

Watson as well as the two men stared at him incredulously, and then the pair nodded. Yes there was indeed one lady such as Mr Holmes had described. 'I thought so,' said Holmes. 'Please proceed.'

'That was it, they fed us ... as we said, with champagne and caviar, and then after four days they took us back.'

'Did they tell you why they went to all that trouble?' The two men pursed their lips and shook their head.

'So why did you come up with that story about green little men?'

'No one would 'ave believed us, if we had told the truth,' they said.

'You thought that making up little green men would be more credible, eh, what?' said Watson with a laugh.

'I want the full story now, my good men,' said Holmes sternly. 'Stop playing games.'

Boneheath and Deepship looked at each other, shook their heads, shrugged, and agreed to make a clean breast of it: They told the story that we knew already, about Coleridge's Somali friend Abdi's family who had suffered gross abuse from the locals.

'So, how did you handle this situation?'

'Well, Mr 'Olmes, sir, badly.'

'Yes sir, badly,' the other one echoed. 'We woz rude to the man, sir.'

'Very rude ... very rude indeed.'

'We've seen the light now, sir.'

'Oh yes, we would deal with something like this differently now.'

'If we 'ave a job to go to after the enquiry.'

Holmes wanted to know what made them see the light.

'We saw the light by ourselves,' the two men said at the same time.

'Honest to god, we did.' Holmes asked them to elaborate. It was Deepship who volunteered the explanation.

'Well sir, when we arrived in our destination, we woz taken into the cellar-'

'Fed on caviare and champagne,' Holmes added absently.

'One gentleman speaking with a funny accent reminded us of our role as law enforcers and asked us to reflect upon our conduct until we saw the light. So we talked it over between ourselves when they left us. We asked ourselves questions. Were we carrying our duties to the best of our ability? Like good Christians? Should our dark friends be treated different under the law?

'And lots more questions like that.'

'And we realised that we had strayed from the path of righteousness.'

'By yourselves, without any prompting?' enquired Dr Watson, and men nodded.

'Our captors promised that we would be released once we had seen the errors of our ways.'

'And repented sincerely.'

'And you have?'

'Forsooth we 'ave, sirs.'

'With a little prompting from your abductors?'

'None, sir, they said we was to do this by ourselves. Only that we would be kept prisoner until we had regained the path of righteousness. Wouldn't 'ave been be freed until we 'ad.'

'After three days, when we wuz tested, and judged to have seen the light.'

'We wuz released.'

'Then they blindfolded us again, saying it was for our own protection this time, and took us back.' Holmes told them that he needed to think things over, and left with the doctor.

That night, he played the violin for over an hour, after which he snorted some white powder, went into a daze and never uttered a single word the next day. On the morrow, however, he asked Watson to join him in his study.

'You had understood, Watson, that this affair bears the stamp of that woman, Irene Adler. What a woman, eh!'

'How did you know that?'

'Tell me, Watson, who else would feed their prisoners on champagne and caviar?' After a short silence, he added, 'Nothing about her surprises me. She can carry out robberies - mind you, never any violence in them. Always carried out after faultless planning, using her brains. Admirable!'

'What do you mean, Holmes, admirable? She's just a thief.'

'If she was just a thief, as you put it Watson, I'd have put an end to her activities a long time ago, but that woman needs to be left in peace.'

'And what will your advice be about those two scoundrels?'

'That they be left in peace.'

'But... b-b.'

'Watson, wouldn't you say that after their ordeal, they have emerged finer officers?'

'Perhaps,' conceded the doctor.

'Remember, Watson, if they do anything reprehensible, the *Club des As*... Oh yes, I've suspected them for a while... have you not seen the file that I am building about them? Anyway, the *Club* knows where they live, and something tells me that they will not require too much persuasion to do a repeat action if they feel it is called for. I imagine they still have plenty of champagne and caviar left after that little action of theirs on Messrs Scarlatti & Windmill, Suppliers of Quality Comestibles to Her Majesty.'

'And what will you tell the Home Office?'

'I will ask your friend Mr Wells to go talk to them.'

No wonder neither Mr Lippincott in America nor Mr Beeston would touch a story like this, but Mr Reynolds looked at it and winked at me conspiratorially.

'Policemen kidnapped by Martians. Full Account!'

CHAPTER SIXTEEN

Moriarty, Holmes and Irene

(1888)

I have often feared that my unconventional life might have earned for myself the mortal enmity of two men who prided themselves on their superior intellect and somehow put me in danger: one, a man I had much respect for even if he considered himself as an adversary of mine, Sherlock Holmes. The other, a thoroughly repugnant individual, Professor Moriarty. I am not privy to whether they are aware of the details of my various ventures, many of which were technically of dubious legality, but, in my estimate, never unjustifiable. Strangely enough I have encountered both men, although neither would have been aware of this.

The subjects of our conversation in our soirées in Water Lane were manifold, but not a single one of them passed without some reference to the criminal activity of known criminals: cutthroats, thieves, bankers or lawyers. I doubt whether anybody's name figured more frequently than that of the unspeakable Moriarty. He had lived like a respectable Professor of Mathematics for many years. His students talked not only of his unique insight into the properties and patterns of numbers and his inspirational lectures, but also of how he loved to flaunt his misanthropy. However, once Holmes had pierced his mystery, having deduced that no one on a professor's salary could afford to buy Greuze's famous painting *La Jeune Fille à l'Agneau* which he was known to possess, the police and public became wise to his activities, although he was too shrewd to leave any incriminating evidence of his felonies. His speciality was leaving false clues to make monkeys of Scotland Yard. He often sent messages to the newspapers, claiming responsibility for such and such malfeasance, but when questioned he denied any part and produced seemingly watertight alibis, laughing openly at the police. His stock explanation for the provenance of those messages, was that they were sent by his enemies in the academic world, bent on eliminating him, as he was on the verge of proving Fermat's Theorem, a prize all mathematicians were aiming for.

It was an open secret that he was an overlord of smaller criminal clans to which he afforded protection and expertise for a share in their takings. He had no qualms about shooting his enemies - or innocents who stumbled in his path - with his famous air-rifle, made for him by the infamous blind genius Klaus Von Herder. To all intents and purposes, it looked like a harmless cane, but could discharge lethal bullets silently.

The first time I saw Holmes at Baker's Gallery, I kept out of his way, as I had my own agenda that day. When I saw him in court when he came to testify in the Lord Clarihoe case, I was able to study him more closely, his physical bearing, his walk, his piercing eyes, his speech patterns, the way he moved his head and his hands. As for Moriarty, although he lived openly as a free citizen, I will only be bestowed the dubious honour of meeting him later, and am about to recount the circumstances shortly. Neither gentleman had ever met me, although alarmingly my name was gaining a notorious currency that I had wished to avoid. When I left the safety of my Water Lane lodgings, I usually adopted a different persona, often that of an elderly dodderer, so as not to attract attention to myself. Strangely, for someone who men of the world have found irresistible, I had no wish to dazzle anybody with my so-called beauty. It is only skin deep, Mam never stopped telling me.

Only my close associates in the *Club* know me for who I am. They are people who I would trust with my life under any circumstances.

One evening, we had been talking about a story in the day's newspapers about some atrocity Moriarty was supposed to have committed, when Frunk's suddenly eyes became glazed. 'Count Tamasj Erymöri,' he ejaculated.

'What are you talking about, man?' asked Coleridge, whereupon Frunk took out a notebook and printed TAMASJ ERYMÖRI on it and passed it round.

'James Moriarty!' I exclaimed. 'Is that relevant?' Frunk explained that when he was working at the Bank of Helvetia, a regular customer was Count Tamasj Erymöri, who said that he was a Magyar nobleman.

'I remember once referring to him as a Hungarian, and he rather aggressively told me that no sir, he was a Magyar.' said Anatole.

The Magyar Count used to make huge deposits and withdrawals. Frunk said that on at least one occasion he deposited half a million Swiss francs into his account at Helvetia only days after a similar sum had been stolen from the Zürcher Privatbank AG.

'I see,' said Bartola suddenly. She had just worked out that Tamasj Erymöri was an anagram of James Moriarty.

We thought that Frunk's was an interesting piece of news, although none of us had any idea how it could have been of use to us. We did not give the professor any undue thought until a week later one bizarre story hit the headlines: The *Refuge International Pour Personnes Handicappées*, in the Swiss canton of Valais which had just been completed after a watch-maker who had no family had left his fortune to a foundation with the express instructions that the legacy be used for this purpose, had been deliberately set on fire. The reverberations of things happening beyond our shores do not usually make themselves felt here, but this one did, and for a very simple reason. The papers had published an article purporting to have been sent by the abominable professor in which he expounded his reasons for carrying out this criminal act, although he used the word cerebral. I will give a summary of the contents of that article:

The world has limited resources, and these must be used with judicious-ness. Malthus has warned us that as food production cannot keep up with population growth, thinking people must not allow themselves to be swayed by sentimental considerations. The handicapped, mentally as well as physi-cally, the invalids and the aged, have no contribution to make to humanity. They use up resources which could be channelled to worthier causes. He favoured the painless elimination of all babies born with any defects. He and like-minded men of superior intellect had aired their views but no notice had been taken of them. He had thought out his plan of action carefully and had arrived at the conclusion that he needed to jolt the public into thinking about the problem.

We were unanimous in our condemnation of the man and his nefarious ideology. The paper sent their man to interview him. Whilst he did not deny that his views about the waste of resources were not dissimilar to those expressed in the article, he claimed that he never advocated arson or any form of violence in their furtherance. He maintained that the article was written by malicious rivals, suggesting that the attack might have been planned with his downfall in mind.

We chose to believe that he was guilty and decided to act. We spent a whole week planning our action. Anatole was despatched to Geneva where he was to meet old colleagues at the Helvetia, gathering information for our coup. I was to meet him a week later as the plan involved the two of us.

Anatole was very sanguine when he came to meet me at Geneva Railway Station. The Count had given prior notice to the bank about a massive withdrawal of half a million Swiss francs. Strangely, it was well-known that, although he was an entrenched criminal mastermind, he thought the rest of the world was timid and lacked imagination. He was convinced that with his air-rifle, no one in his right mind would dare trifle with him. Frunk's former colleague, to whom he had promised a handsome cut, had passed relevant information to him. We had scoured the markets and shops of the city in search of just the right valises. We ended up buying a medium-sized black case and a smaller one in blue leather. We filled the smaller one with old newspaper and put it inside the black one. I disguised myself as an elderly lady, wearing a lace veil of the type worn by recently widowed dowagers, who could hardly walk, even with a cane. My nephew Frunk was there to be my guide.

There we were, pitting our wits against one of the sharpest minds in Europe. On the appointed day, the two of us sat in the passenger room at the railway station in Geneva, waiting for Erymöri. Five minutes before the train was due to leave we beheld him. He exceeded almost everybody in height by a whole head, and was walking towards the platform where the train to Paris was waiting. He walked in large strides, head held high, his back ramrod straight, carrying a small blue leather bag in one hand, swinging a cane in the other. Of course we knew that it wasn't really a cane.

As there was no time to waste, we barely gave him thirty-seconds before following him into the train. We had luck on our side. He walked in an otherwise empty first class compartment, choosing a corner seat.

'*Prenez mon bras ma tante*,' said Frunk. Quivering like an aspen leaf - something I had learnt when I had to play Lady Furze at the Alhambra - I wrapped my hand round Anatole's forearm and leaned on him. Dutifully he helped me get into the carriage. I took five minutes before regaining my breath. Moriarty did not acknowledge our presence. He sat scowling in his corner, obviously frustrated at having to share his compartment. When we bade him a good day, he gave a curt nod and turned his head away, indicating that he desired no intercourse with us.

We noticed that he had chained and locked his blue valise to the metallic frame of the luggage rack above our heads but of course we had come prepared. He closed his eyes and appeared to snore but we knew that he was only pretending. I caught him casting an oblique glance at his loot at irregular intervals. We were biding our time. He would no doubt need to stretch his oversize legs over the ten hour journey. My veil gave me the opportunity of watching our quarry undetected. I noticed his face twitch at the same time as he moved his legs nervously, indicating to me that he was probably in need of using the facilities. With his small size, Frunk looked even less threatening than his poor grief-stricken, wobbly aunt, but I imagine that a man of Moriarty's criminal bent must see enemies everywhere, making it unlikely that he would dare leave the two of us in the compartment whilst he went to ease himself. How Frunk did it, I will never know, or perhaps I do know: by dint of the concurrence of our ideologies, we in the *Club* have gradually been developing something akin to telepathic powers. Anyway, I tried to communicate to him that he should go for a walk in the corridor, and was delighted when he took the cue. '*Ma tante, mes jambes sont ankylosées, je vais les secouer un peu,*' he said suddenly. In my trembling voice, I answered, '*C'est ça mon garçon, vas-y.*' Anatole left. Our target immediately reacted. He stood up, seized his cane, cast an involuntary look at his valise, and rushed out. I had to act quickly. Frunk had positioned himself between the closet and the compartment to make it a little more difficult for the man to get back in if my manoeuvre took longer than planned.

Inured in the art of manipulating locks with hairpins as I was, it took me next to no time to detach the case from its lock, even less to remove the identical one we had in our black bag and engineer the switch over. I heard steps and feared that I might not have completed the operation in time, but Anatole clumsily began to tie his shoelaces, blocking the narrow passage. When Moriarty re-entered, I was seated in my corner, snoring rather inelegantly. I saw him cast a glance at the bag to reassure himself that nothing untoward had happened. The rest of the journey went on without an incident, and we got down in Paris. To my surprise, Moriarty helped me down the train and bade me a '*Bonne continuation madame*'.

The whole word knows that the *Refuge* project so dear to the heart of the old watchmaker was revived, but no one but our clique knows who the anonymous donors were. A week later, Moriarty sent the following message to The *Reynolds' News* office: *Miss Irene Adler has earned for herself the eternal enmity of some very angry (and powerful) people who will not rest until appropriate retribution is visited upon her. I will find her, and I will deal with her,* he threatened. I would be a fool if I did not take him at his word, which is why we have doubled our vigilance.

When I was smitten with pneumonia, our friends at Water Lane watched over me like an obsessive-compulsive mother her sick only child. Armande who never did things by halves kept vigil over me every night, sleeping in a couch she had moved into my bedroom. The others never failed to pop in most days to sit with me and keep me entertained. Coleridge had never lost his great voice sang *arias* to me. The Bishop would list the many inconsistencies inherent in the Bible. Algernon would hold my hands and tell me how he wished that he was not a Uranian. Most mornings, as I was dopey with medication, Armande reluctantly left me on my own for no more than one hour, to attend to mundane chores like going to the post office which had recently opened in Stockwell. She naturally made sure I was comfortable first. It was on one such morning that the arch-villain chose to burst in on me. He must have planned his coup and was waiting for Armande to leave for. Here I was, utterly helpless, needing no chain to keep me tied to my bed, completely drained of all energy. He tiptoed in, brandishing his lethal cane negligently.

'I hope, *chère madame*, that you have recovered from your tragic loss.' I had no idea what he was referring to. 'I haven't yet recovered from mine.' I tried to speak, but no voice would come out - which was not as bad as it sounds, as I had no idea what to say. He took a chair and dragged it towards my bed, turned the back rest. With a smile and a curtsy he sat himself with his arms around it. He placed his infamous air-rifle tantalisingly close to my head, but even if I could grab it, I had no strength in me to do anything with it. He made as if to seize my hand but stopped halfway seeming to change his mind.

'First, let me assure you that I am full of admiration for your exploit. Who wouldn't? Let me tell you that the admiration comes wrapped in layers of vengeful anger. I have never, did you hear, never, been bested in my life. To be bested by a woman is absolutely intolerable to me.' I managed to open my eyes and looked at him imploringly, hoping that he would consider it beneath him to attack a sick woman. He must have understood, for he smiled and nodded. I was suddenly seized by a bout of coughing and he gently raised my head and tapped me gently on the back. When I had stopped, he said to listen carefully. Weak and sleepy as I was, I made the effort.

'Irene,' he began. 'A lovely name for a lovely woman, I daresay. If my life wasn't so complicated, I'd whisk you away and marry you, and keep you locked in a castle. You see, so many good people depend on me for advice and support, it would be impossible. My time's not my own. That's out of question. Don't go to sleep, hear me out.' I made a superhuman effort to stay awake.

'Since I am unable to marry you, I have a proposition for you.' He's going to ask me to team up with him in his criminal ventures, I thought. He must have read my mind.

'Rest assured, I am not going to ask you to join us. I believe that you were lucky last time in the train. You and I think alike, so I have no use for you. Have you ever thought of the future?' I must admit that I tend to live for the present and rarely worry about tomorrow. Or the hereafter for that matter. I must have frowned.

'I see you have no idea what I am talking about. I mean neither of us is immortal, although we're working on this. But I must admit to being less than sanguine about my hope of the project bearing fruit in our lifetime.' He gave me time to allow this profundity to sink in, then smiled and nodded to himself, obviously pleased at having arrived at this extraordinary conclusion.

'When you and I go - curses! - who is going to take our place?' Why should anybody take our place, I was wondering.

'We cannot leave the world in the hands of a mediocre bunch of criminals. Not that I think of myself as one, I hasten to add.' I never thought of myself as a criminal either. I still don't think shooting Stonehead was a crime in the eyes of the Lord.

'Think of what I am saying,' he said, nodding earnestly. As far as I was concerned, he had said nothing yet. Suddenly it hit me. I tried hard to hide this discovery from him, but I did not need to, for he was ready to spell it out.

'Yes, Irene, think of it. A child with us as its generators.' I did not much care for the word generators in this context. After a little silence, I was propelled into full wakefulness with his next pronouncement.

'You see, I have come prepared. I abstained for a fortnight so my emission would be plentiful *and* of high quality. I have come to put my plan into action. You must understand that the child will have to live with you. I will of course provide for it. I am sanguine about the female sex, which, thanks to your good self, I no longer believe is the weaker one. I will inform you of when I plan to visit of course.' Provide for *it*, he had said. I stared at him, too confused and shocked to say anything. Not that my weak condition would have helped. Finally I managed to form a whole sentence in my head.

'But professor, I am not consenting ... I am not cons-' I was unable to finish due to a coughing spell.

'That's the whole point, can't you see? I seek no consent,' he said with a little laugh. 'Move over now, there's a dear.'

'But that's rape,' I said with a vigour which surprised me. He gave out a big indecent laugh.

'Rape grape,' he said. 'What's rape? I've done worse! You've done much worse. Make some space, woman.' Menacingly he picked his air-rifle, but he only used it to lift up my blanket playfully, before placing it against the backrest. He bent over in an attempt to get hold of my body. How was I going to resist this brute in the state I was in?

'You might as well accept the inevitability of the situation and enjoy it. Close your eyes and think of England, they advise.' He said. 'There's no one to help you.' *Where's Armande?*

'But there is,' a voice I had heard before said. I recognised it as that of Sherlock Holmes'. How he had come in I had no idea. Moriarty made an attempt to reach for his cane but I got it first and threw it with all my vigour to Holmes who caught it in mid-air. Approaching the bed, he raised the weapon and pointed it at his enemy's head. How I got the strength, I will never know.

'Holmes,' said Moriarty unfazed. 'What a surprise! You're the last person I was expecting. You're not planning to spoil my little party, are you?'

'I am planning to rid this blessed planet of ours of the vermin that you are, Moriarty, and I am going to use your own weapon to shoot you like a dog. Miss Adler here will testify that it was in self-defence.' *Would I?*

'Tut tut, my dear fellow, you have a weapon and I have none, where's your sporting spirit, eh, what?' To my disappointment, Holmes seemed to be taking the bait. *When I had the villainous Stonehead at my mercy, I never gave a second thought to sportsmanship.*

'Holmes,' said Moriarty, assuming a tone of familiarity. 'Think on it, when did the three brainiest people in this country last gather in a single room? Instead of killing each other, we should celebrate the occasion.

Let us have a duel of wits. First put that cane down.' To my amazement, Holmes did his bidding. It was as if the professor had hypnotised him. Moriarty breathed a sigh of relief. He was now obviously in command. He was controlling the only man who had the wherewithals to outwit him, like a yo-yo. When the man from Baker Street burst in, I had thought that was the end of my ordeal, and of that abominable criminal.

I was saved, but now he was putty in the hands of his old enemy. It was sad to see the man I probably admired above all men reduced to this limpness.

'I see,' said Moriarty with a wink. 'You too want your wicked ways with the lady. You do, admit it, eh, what? I never believed those rumours about you and Dr Watson. Now this is what I propose.' To my surprise, Holmes nodded in anticipation, like Moses on being told by God that He had an errand for him.

'Let Irene be the arbiter. Let her set us a puzzle. The one who solves it first is the winner. Gets the prize.' I was horrified when I saw that Holmes seemed agreeable to this scandalous proposition. Nothing blurs a man's judgement or contaminates his sense of decency more than the defence of his male pride. In other circumstances, I might not have been averse to sharing my bed with the genius detective, but I am not an object, a lottery win, and I deeply resented this man's game.

'You better hurry, dearest,' said Moriarty. 'Or we'll just toss a coin.' I was too upset to think. To my utter disgust the two men started bantering.

'Do I take it, Holmsy, that you'd also like dear Irene to bear your child?'

'Only to stop her having yours, you criminal villain,' laughed the detective.

'I'll own that your child will be quite handsome, but not half as brainy!' said the criminal mastermind. I concentrated really hard, in an attempt to find an insoluble puzzle. To my delight I found a perfect one.

'You have two jugs,' I began. 'One has a capacity of two gallons, and the other four. You have no other implement. You have water coming out of a tap. How could you by using nothing else, collect exactly one -' I had not finished when both men shouted in unison. 'That's impossible.' I laughed triumphantly. 'You both lost.' The two men who had so far been quite courteous snarled at me. How did I dare contradict them.

'Let me assure you, dear lady, as a mathematician, I ought to know, no combination of even numbers can ever produce an odd number.'

'Absolutely.' Holmes added. I smiled wanly, for I was exhausted. I took a deep breath.

'If you fill both containers to the brim, you will get six gallons.'

'Of course,' they both chorused, 'but you said one-'

'You did not let me finish. I was going to say *one half dozen* gallons. So I won.' I was not surprised that neither of the two men were ready to concede, and they began squabbling. I was too tired to listen. When the words coming out of the pair began sounding like nightmare gibberish, I must have dozed off.

A while later, I heard the door slam, and Armande walked in.

'Are they gone?' I asked her.

'Are who gone?'

'Holmes and Moriarty,' I whispered. Armande frowned.

'They were here, you know, both of them.' Armande burst out laughing.

'What did they want?'

'You won't believe me.'

'No,' admitted my friend. 'I probably won't.'

'They only wanted me to father my child.'

'I told you to go eeasy on that sedatif, *ma chèrie*, it contens opiumme, and it gives you, *comment dit-on?oui*, des allucinations.'

CHAPTER SEVENTEEN
The King of Bohemia
(1889)

I have tried to convey a picture of our life and activities and do not propose to rewrite the history of the *Club des As* at length here, although I might come back to that later, in the unlikely event that I find myself in financial straits. This might happen sooner than I think, for I had rented an expensive flat in Regent's Wood - not that I neglected my friends in Water Lane. I visit them regularly. I do, however, feel the need to correct the many misconceptions about my encounter with Mr Sherlock Holmes, a man I have always had great admiration for. I have heard whispers to the effect that this is mutual. Dr Watson, his sincere friend, gave a modified account of the events in his *A Scandal in Bohemia* - modified to the extent that ... nevermind. Here is my version.

My good friend Lord Clarihoe was always excellent company. He had money to burn, of course, but since in our case crime pays, we were acquiring more money than we knew what to do with. Algernon manifestly valued my company and often insisted on my accompanying him on his peregrinations to the fashionable resorts of Europe. It did not take me long to develop a taste for this.

About two years ago, we went to Davos together, and met this one-eyed giant of a man who introduced himself to us as Count Von Kramm of Bohemia. I was immediately bowled over by him. He was built like a horse, had a sculptured face with the nose of a Greek statue and his eyes twinkled with humour. He revealed to us, and to everybody else he met, that he was travelling incognito, but was really Prince Sigsmund, the hereditary King of Bohemia. His one-eyedness, as evidenced by an extravagant eyepatch was nothing but a disguise to throw his many enemies off the scent. Rest, assured, he had two good eyes. The waiters readily greeted him by the appellation that he thrived in: "Your Majesty," to which he would shake his head and wag an admonishing finger half-heartedly before putting it over his lips in a farcical attempt at shushing them. I do not, as a rule, value the acquaintance of the aristocracy above that of folks of my own standing. I certainly had no wish to get entangled with royalty, but I soon arrived at the conclusion that physically he and I were made for each other.

Unfortunately, I discovered that he was shallow, indiscreet, vain, and boring in the extreme. I reviewed my original opinion of his fetching eyes. It was arrogance and malice that they were filled with, and not good-humoured sense of fun. He told me that he possessed the greatest collection of erotica in Europe, and that he had mastered most of the techniques therein. I can vouchsafe for this, but although we spent much time in bed, we hardly ever talked. When I tried to address this, I found that he knew no literature, had no interest in art or music. All he was able to talk about was his royal circle, his prowesses in the alcove and how much money he had lost in the casinos of Switzerland.

Although I never questioned him, it was he who revealed to me a large number of fairly trivial facts, thinking that I would be impressed because much of what he told me were state secrets. I learnt about the indiscretions of his aunt Princess Béatrice who seduced him when he was sixteen and whose ambition was to bed all the grooms in the palace. He told me about the alcoholic Duke of Pullenberg and *his* fondness for grooms and gardeners. He revealed the layouts of the secret tunnels leading out of the castle in case of insurrection and where their entrances were. And a great deal more. He went as far as to tell me the detailed plans for the defence of Bohemia in case of an attack by the forces of East Westphalia, their traditional enemy. This was to prove my undoing.

Thanks to Dr Watson's account, the whole world knows of how he approached Sherlock Holmes to solve the problem of Irene Adler. At the *Club*, we had followed the amazing work of that great mind, and when Sigsmund approached him, we thought that with his unique intellect the man from Baker Street would pierce the real aim of his visit and give him short shrift. Sadly, we were disappointed when we learned that he had swallowed the king's line, hook and sinker. It is well-known of course that even the great brains of the nation can be dazzled by low calibre individuals with royal connections.

According to Dr Watson, the future King Sigsmund arrived wearing a mask. He had a great fondness for melodrama and indeed told me once that if his position had not been an impediment to this, he would have loved to tread the planks. He intimated to Holmes that he was after a photograph of the two of us taken on the top of the recently constructed Eiffel Tower, because he lived in fear of being blackmailed by me. He further lied about my threatening to stop him marrying his Princess Clotilde, claiming that I had sent some incriminating evidence to her.

Mr Holmes is by far the best when it comes to making deductions from facts. I have no doubt that if he was ever involved in the enquiries concerning the *Club*'s exploits, he would have caused serious prejudice to our existence. That man takes one look at the dirt on your shoe and tells you where you have been in the last forty-eight hours. The way you walk informs him about how you make your living. He spots some ash on a crime scene and deduces in which shop in Bond Street the killer bought his tobacco. However, that same Mr Holmes, when it comes to the reading of human relationships, can be as clueless as a newborn babe. He saw no cause to doubt that big royal clod, and naturally, a man of his self-acknowledged infallibility would never revisit an opinion once acquired. So he set about trying to get me in a tight corner to filch the aforesaid photograph, little knowing that he was an accessory to a heinous crime in the making.

I take my hat off to Holmes for nearly outwitting me, even though unbeknown to him, I was expecting his intervention.

What the great detective did not know, was that Sigsmund was clearing the decks so his secret service could carry out his plans to get me killed.

Although when he told me he meant to get wed to the Princess Euphemia Eriksdotter of Scandinavia (*Why Dr Watson thought fit to change her name to Clotilde, in his account of the tale, I do not know*), I said that they had my good wishes and blessing, but mean-spirited as he was, he refused to believe me. With his inflated ego, he was convinced that marrying him, or becoming his mistress was the thing dearest to my heart. In reality, my dearest wish was to put an end to an unsatisfactory relationship.

He had often boasted to me that the secret service of his country was by far the most efficient in Europe. I think he meant ruthless. He laughingly told me how they hunted and killed enemies of the state with cold efficiency. I had paid little attention to this, knowing that he was an inveterate embellisher of realities. However, shortly after he had met Euphemia, one afternoon he and I were having tea in Mayfair. I suddenly felt uneasy when I caught him peering at me in a strange way.

'Will you be a good girl and keep your mouth shut,' he said suddenly. I had no idea what he was talking about, and must have frowned.

'I mean you asked so many questions and I told you so many crucial secrets.'

'Ha! I'll probably sell them to the highest bidder,' I laughed, but he winced. An ugly expression took possession of his face, which made me suddenly remember that the part of his brain which normally lodged his sense of humour had expelled it and leased itself to a lump of paranoia.

'Sigsmund, *liebchen*,' I told him to put him out of his misery, 'rest assured. I am myself getting married-'

'But you can't, I won't permit it,' he shouted imperiously. 'You can't! You belong to me!'

'Majesty,' I said with a sneer, 'I have never belonged to anybody, least of all you. For your information I intend to marry someone and not sell myself to him as his slave.' I could see from his eyes that this news, far from giving him comfort, had exacerbated the situation. I knew it in my bones. He had already decided to have me eliminated, to make sure that since he was not going to have me, nobody else should. However, I instantly knew how to counteract his schemes. I would make use of that photograph of the two of us taken on the Eiffel Tower as a bargaining chip.

'*Liebchen*,' I said, 'I hope you are not thinking what I am thinking you are thinking, because it will only end in disaster for you.'

'Me planning to get you disappeared?' he made a hollow laugh. 'Why I wasn't even considering such a thing. Why would I? Nobody knows about us. I mean I have always travelled incognito.' Then he suddenly became gloomy, and I knew he was thinking about that photograph.

'Irene, *liebchen*,' he said with a glint in his eye, 'I'll give you five thou- sand gold sovereigns for that photograph. Only then will I be safe.' It meant nothing to me, I would have given it to him for free, had he asked. I may be a killer, but am no blackmailer.

'But I was joking,' I said. 'I would never dream of harming you, we had some good times together.' I meant it. I had nothing to gain by disgracing him.

'If I could only believe you,' he sighed. He peered at me intently. 'My Secret Service experts think that ... ach ... but trust me, I'll never sanction anything likely to cause you harm.' I looked at him obliquely but that's not what I read on his face and in his eyes. Instead I read: If I can't have you, I'll make sure nobody else will.'

I had to produce my trump card.

'*Liebchen*,' I said, 'I am not in the least worried about you or your Secret Service, I know you are a man of your word,' (Did I heck?). 'But you know me, my middle name is Prudence-'

'All this time we've been together I've never known that. Prudence eh!' he interrupted, confirming my suspicion about the seismic cataclysm that occurred in his brains.

'I found an expert at the Daguerreotype process who was able to pro- duce two perfect facsimiles of the photograph. I have lodged them with my lawyers, with instruction to send one of them to your sworn enemy, King Otto of East Westphalia. The other one to your little princess in case something happens to me.' I am not convinced that he believed me.

How did I know that when he left me he was making his way to Baker Street? Must be those *antennes* that Armande kept talking about.

Sadly, Mr Holmes readily believed that I was out to do damage to a nation friendly to our own and was resolved to stop me. I alerted my friends from the *Club*. As expected, they served me well. By a strange quirk of fate, Lord Bickeringstone, dear Algernon's obnoxious father had given him an ultimatum: get yourself a wife to stop tongues wagging or face the consequences. Naturally he did not wish to lose his inheritance. When he revealed that he aimed to find himself a nominal wife, all the three women of the *Club* volunteered for the honour. We drew lots and I won (I cheated).

Having been apprised of Sherlock Holmes unwise involvement with the disreputable Sigsmund, the Club took immediate contingency measures. One of our men, disguised as a delivery man was hanging outside Number 221B, heard the detective instruct a cabby to come pick him up at nine in the morning to take him to St John's Wood. His plans began to emerge. We were ready for him. It was the Bishop who came up with the idea and the plan to cozen the great detective into becoming a witness to the nuptials. We know from the doctor's account that Mr Holmes boasted about what he thought of as his exploit, when in reality he was hoodwinked by us, and never realised it. Frunk was not only a genius at timing, but had no peer when it comes to communication. He had elaborated a system of coloured kerchiefs to enable exchanges between us. He had equipped himself with binoculars and a good vantage point on the top floor of Briony Lodge. Armande disguised as an old beggar was to be found squatting in a strategic corner opposite. To cut a long story short, the moment the great Sherlock Holmes was sighted, we were able to trace his every single movement to within ten yards and pass on the intelligence to each other.

Holmes had disguised himself as an unemployed groom and was seen exchanging pleasantries with some ostlers by our team, among whom was Hugh Probert playing the part of a cabman. For someone the whole world knows is such a stickler for details, it was disappointing, possibly even inexcusable for him to claim to be a starving man looking for work one moment, and then the next buying drinks for his new friends. Hugh played his part with great aplomb. No wonder he was able, in all innocence, to destroy the career of an emerging actress so thoroughly. He now fed him what can only be called misinformations when the "groom" approached him. Oh yes, he told the inquisitive fellow, Miss Adler has an army of admirers, almost everyone on this street, but there is only one she receives in the lodge. That was the lucky Mr Edwards Norton, our friend, better known as Lord Clarihoe. Hidden messages having been successfully transmitted, Algernon suddenly made an appearance, ostentatiously producing his watch, a bit like the rabbit in Alice in Wonderland. Shaking his head impatiently he indicated how late he was. Next he came inside. We drank some coffee and ate this delightful new French fluffy bread Augustin the baker in the Edgware Road calls *croissant*, regaling me with fantasies like how many children would ensue from our *mariage en blanc*. I will own to not thinking much of his tact. Even if I did not dream of a romantic attachment, the idea of having a child of my own was very close to my heart. But I digress.

Half an hour later, Algie left, and this did not fail to be noticed by our vigilant hounds. My "affianced" made much of the panic he thought was required, and commandeered a hansom. Loudly he instructed the cabman to take him, first to Gross & Hankey's in Regent Street, and thence to St Monica's in Edgware Road. Do it in twenty minutes, my good man, and you will earn yourself a sovereign. The Bishop did not need to be told twice, he was always a fiend for speed. Mr Holmes spun on himself rather comically as he could not decide whether to follow Algie or to keep a close eye on Briony Lodge. I decided to release him from his misery. I had already dressed myself as immaculately as I could, for, fake marriage though this was, I wanted to look my radiant best on this day. I emerged in apparent panic and Frunk moved his caleche towards me. Take me to St Monica's church, my good man, I said in a loud and haughty voice, and if you do it in twenty minutes there's half a crown for you. Sherlock Holmes knew what to do now. He summoned the next cab on the line, and Ivan Vissarionovich obligingly moved forward. Sherlock asked the Russian to follow me, promising him a whole shilling if he made the journey to St Monica's in eighteen minutes, something which, to a Russian who had raced bare-back riding Cossacks and survived six duels, was no great challenge.

In St Monica's, Algie enlisted the bemused Mr Holmes' service as a witness, and the Reverend Clarence de Vere Streaughteren (pronounced Stratton), a one-time lover of my fiancé, performed the ceremony. I gave our worthy witness a whole sovereign for his trouble. Then, to his amazement, freshly wed though we were, we went our separate ways.

I hoped that I would now have some respite from the eagle-eyed sleuth, and was therefore caught off balance. I was coming back home after coffee with Bartola in Kensignton next day, and my landau was already slowing down as we turned into Serpentine Avenue when I spotted a doddering man of the cloth. I blush to admit that I was completely taken in by Holmes' second disguise in as many days. He was accompanied by Dr Watson whom I did not know then, as well as by his paid team of performers. Armande had often said that it was surprising that someone with my *antennes* could take so many things at their face value.

I am aware of the rampant poverty in London, and have always sympathised with folks wanting to earn a penny whenever they could. So when one of the rowdies rushed towards the door of the cab to open it for me, I thought nothing of it. Nor did my feelers pick any signals when two others joined in, jostling the first fellow rather aggressively. To my alarm, blows began to fly. The old reverend raised his hands to appeal for calm, at which he appeared to receive a lethal knock. He collapsed on the ground. His fragile head hit the hard surface of the road and his face became covered in blood. This immediately brought to mind Hugh Probert's Lear in his death scene, although I never had the privilege of seeing it since "twas ere my time." I asked if the man was badly hurt and someone said that he was dead. I panicked. The miscreants had all escaped, but other passers-by had assembled. Someone suggested that the wounded man be taken to hospital and his neighbour tut tutted. 'He would be dead by the time they got to the hospital door.' There was only one thing to do, and I did it. Take the poor fellow inside the house, I said. Some volunteers readily acceded to my request. How, with my theatrical experience I could be fooled by the red paint, I cannot explain. I asked Clara (Bartola's niece), who was spending a few days with me, to give the old priest some cognac, which seemed to revive him a bit. That was when he signified that he could not breathe. I opened the window to let more air in.

This was no doubt the signal previously convened, for Watson to throw in the smoke bomb. I admit that I was still in a confused state and unable to think clearly. Of course I played right into his hands. As he no doubt expected, my immediate reaction was to rescue the photograph which I had hidden in a recess behind a sliding panel just above the right bell-pull. I had no fears about this dear old heroic clergyman piercing my secret. When he cried that it was a false alarm, in a flash I saw through his stratagem and came to my senses. I did well to hide this, replaced the cabinet back and left. Almost immediately my nemesis left too. I watched him through the widow as he walked towards Watson with whom he exchanged a little laugh. Unbeknownst to him, I went back into the lodge.

Next day, when Holmes came back to the lodge with the king, they made for the recess. All they found was a carefully written undertaking that I would never do anything to endanger either his kingdom or his person, a photograph, not the one they were seeking but another one of myself in my glory years, dedicated to the preposterous Sigsmund, a little revenge, to remind him of what he would be missing. I also wrote this note for Mr Holmes:

My dear Mr Holmes,

Only if you knew the magnitude of the regard and admiration that I have for your resourcefulness and your perspicacity, could you appreciate the peerless quality of the bliss that I have been enveloped with in coming out as the victor in our battle of wits.

I.A.

I was well aware that the danger to which I had been exposed by my association with that wretched monarch was not going away. I knew that he would redouble his effort to hunt me down. Of course I was not going to let him. My dear friends at the *Club* suggested that I moved away from London and changed my appearance. Or perhaps put out the news of my demise. This was something I did, but was not sure if anybody was convinced. Naturally I left Regent's Wood and sought sanctuary in Water Lane once more.

One evening Algernon arrived at Water Lane in a sweat. The poor man was speechless. All he could do was to brandish a sheet of paper inviting me to read it. It bore the heading of Count Tamasj Erymöri. There was only one line of writing: *Your lordship, If you value your friend, give her the enclosed. J.M / C.T.E.* If there was one thing I did not wish to see added to my troubles it was the untimely intervention of that diabolical man in my life.

'Where is it?' I asked Algernon.

'Where is what?'

'The letter, Algie,' I said with undisguised impatience.

'But you have it, I, eh... I.' Then suddenly he smiled.

'I am shaken, dearest, that man reaching me at the *Patroclus* fairly shook me. You are in mortal danger.' He explained that the porter at the club had handed the packet to him. Worth had asked about its provenance, and the man had said, 'Give this to Clarihoe, he'll find out who my boss is soon enough.'

'Yes, yes, Algie, but where is *my* letter?' Algernon shook his head, smiling apologetically. 'Excuse me, dearest, I am losing my head over this, I am so worried for you.' He finally produced a sealed envelope from his inside pocket and handed it over to me. I tore it and read:

My dearest Irene,

You must allow me to call you by your name. I am writing to inform you that some parties connected to a certain royal family have approached me with the offer of a considerable sum of money if I arrange your permanent elimination, or lead them to you for that purpose.

Now, although you have caused me considerable grief, and I have sworn to exact my own revenge, I cannot permit others interfering with my own plans for your quietus. I am writing to you, not as a friend, as you might have thought, but as your sworn enemy. Keep yourself safe from the above-mentioned parties until such times as I am ready to act. I know you are a friend of Clarihoe. We will find you through him when we are ready.

Let me assure you, however, that my unmitigated enmity for you does not preclude an overwhelming admiration for your spectacular action on the train. How I wish we could work together!

Count T.E.

At first I made light of my predicament, but one night, an irresistible idea sprouted in my brain. Nowhere would I be safer than under the protection of my old enemy Sherlock Holmes - not that I ever considered him as such. Even adversary would be the wrong word. If I managed to bamboozle him the first time, I would not have to worry about the rest. He had had a good look at me in Briony Lodge, so I had better watch my step. He himself is a dab hand at disguise so I might need all my make-up skills if I am to pass muster. It would be easy, and in view of my partiality for gourmet food, fun too, to augment my girth by acquiring two stones. Then another two stones, as in pebbles, put in my mouth might just give my face a puffed up appearance. Maybe not. A little shade under my eyes would age me by ten years. With his claim to infallibility, I knew that if he had failed to detect the strategy the first time, he would never revisit his opinion, especially as he only looks properly at the fair sex in the exercise of his detective function. I heard that his housekeeper Mrs Turner had left and moved back to Yorkshire. My mind is made up. I am going to apply for her post. I would need to re-invent my history ... perhaps pull out a sister, a previous employer ... a lord no less ... Washwell, there's a good name. Lord Washwell. How about a niece? A nephew might be better. And I would need to be consistent and tell everybody the same story. Imagine the thrill of sharing my life with such a brilliant mind, albeit in an unromantic capacity. Not that I would much mind a bit of romance. Obviously I cannot apply in my own name. Mam was a Hudson, wasn't she?

CHAPTER EIGHTEEN

How Holmes Proved Fermat's Theorem

(1892)

I t did not come as a surprise to me when one evening Holmes asked me to join him in the sitting room for a nightcap. When we were both seated, he looked at me with those inscrutable eyes of his and, without preamble, said: 'Mrs Hudson, or shall I call you Miss Adler? I will own to not immediately seeing through your subterfuge when you came seeking a housekeeper's job. So yes, you did fool me - at first. Trust me, it did not take me very long to discover the truth, but by then I was too fascinated by the oddness of it all that I pretended ignorance. I even know why you had recourse to ... eh ... I was going to say such lowly tricks. You might have come clean and said you needed my protection.' He stopped suddenly, and by the wrinkles creasing his forehead, I knew that he was deep in thought. He looked up at me. With the ghost of a smile he nodded gravely. 'No, I doubt whether I would have offered you hospitality,' he said frankly. 'Your solution was the perfect one, I'll grant you - which does not surprise me. You are a lady of unique mental powers.' He remained quiet for a while. Having done justice to the cocoa and biscuit, I began to feel uneasy.

'Is that all, Mr Holmes?' He stared at me as if I were a complete stranger and suddenly exploded.

'No, I told you all this because you are in mortal danger.'

'Really,' I said with a laugh. 'You can't be serious. I have always thrived on danger, but thanks for your concern.'

'That fatuous King of Bohemia was a fool, he and his secret agents are amateurs, no, Miss Adler, it's much worse. Your enemy ... our common enemy is much more ... shall I say deadly?'

'You don't mean Professor Moriarty?'

'He paid me a visit not long ago. What presumption! You had gone to see your sick sister that night, you said. Let me tell you that two weeks after you arrived here, I had you followed and discovered that you go regularly to Water Lane to visit your infamous friends. I know you don't have a sister. I know that you are a sort of godmother to a young lad called Teddy, and that some of the things you wrote for Mr Reynolds are made up. I suppose you wanted to make your cover watertight.' Strangely this did not surprise me either. He peered through me to let the information sink in, I suppose.

'What did Moriarty want?'

'First, you may not know the extent of the man's villainy. Let me put you in the picture. The man can be called the Napoleon of crime. He is the brains behind a good many of the crimes in this city, and nearly all that remains unsolved. He is a mathematician of genius proportions, a philosopher, an abstract thinker specialising in evil. He has a brain of the first order and is expected to be the first man to solve Fermat's Last Theorem. You know ... eh ... that the equation x to the power of n plus y to the power of n equals z to the power of n cannot be solved for real whole numbers.'

'I have no idea what you are talking about,' I said. My employer had a ready answer, for he had a yellowed piece of paper in his hand and passed it over to me. I seized it, looked at it, read it, and it still made no sense to me. Clearly Mr Holmes thought it was very important. If only I knew to what length he had gone to lay hands on it, he said. He further explained that as I could no doubt guess from the quality of the paper, this was a good few years old. It had come from one of the professor's old note books. He had just been appointed to the Chair of Theoretical Mathematics at University College. Full of hope and ambition, he had expected to beat the rest of the Mathematical world to that biggest of prizes. Clearly his capital idea had not worked. I bit my lips and shook my head to show that I was still lost.

'Yes, I am sorry. I am no mathematician myself, but as a scientist I have been intrigued by the problem and have dabbled. Sorry, I am getting sidetracked. Now where was I?' Holmes said, taking a handkerchief out of his pocket and wiping his brow.

'Oh yes, he has a multitude of accomplices, minor villains who will do his bidding. He sits motionless like a spider in the center of its web, but that web has a thousand radiations, and he knows well every quiver of each of them. He is protected and feels he is beyond the law, for you see, he only does the planning. When a crime is committed, he is usually miles away. His alibis are water-tight. His agents are numerous, organised and disciplined. Is there a crime to be done, a paper to be abstracted, we will say, a house to be rifled, a man to be removed, the word is passed to the professor. He decides how best the matter is organised and executed and is amply rewarded by the perpetrators. If one of his agents is caught, money is found for his bail or his defence. But the central power which uses the agent is never caught, never so much as formally suspected. As you know, I too have got my men, and together we have mounted an operation to which I have devoted my whole energy and resources in the hope of exposing his operations and breaking them up.'

He then explained how he had been working on this for over a year. In the beginning, he and his team met with a brick wall, for the enemy was unexpectedly resourceful, but they never gave up.

'And now,' he said, 'the work is almost done. Obviously Moriarty has his ears to the ground and is aware of the threat I pose to him. So he only came to warn me off. He's getting desperate. Did I tell you already?' he stopped, clearly his impeccable memory failing him just a little bit at this point. 'Something I found most alarming - did I - no, I didn't. The reason I am mentioning this to you, is that he said that the ludicrous Sigsmund of Bohemia had realised that you had not died. A clever strategy that was...but he ignored your whereabouts. He talked to one of Moriarty's men and has offered two thousand guineas towards your elimination.'

He must have seen the shocked expression on my face. 'Yes,' he said, 'I thought you'd like to take cognizance of that fact.'

'So, Mr Holmes, what is your advice?'

'Advice?' he sounded shocked. 'Miss Adler, I am a detective, I solve crimes. I do not function as an adviser. I just thought that you should be made aware of the facts in my possession.' I gave him a look in which my disappointment in him was clear. He pursed his lips, nodded, then he smiled and seemed to relax.

'But I will give you an account of what went on when he visited, to enable you to get a better idea of what is in store for us. You and me. I will try to repeat his very words.' I crossed my legs and nodded. Holmes relayed the following:

'Moriarty smiled a smile that did not hide its sinister undertone,' Holmes began. 'He said to me: "I am telling you all this Holmes, because otherwise the duel ahead won't be challenging, since I have all the trumps, but it will be more profitable for both of us if you saw reason and desisted. You crossed my path on the fourth of January. On the twenty-third you incommoded me; I was seriously inconvenienced by you in February. At the end of March I was absolutely hampered in my plans. Now, at the close of April, I find myself placed in such a position through your continual persecution that I am in positive danger of losing my liberty. The situation is becoming an impossible one." '

'Have you any suggestion to make?' Holmes had asked

'You must drop it, Mr. Holmes,' said he. 'You really must, you know.'

'After Monday,' Holmes said, 'when I will have completed my mission and handed over all the evidence to the police.' Moriarty demurred and shook his head.

'I am quite sure that a man of your intelligence will see that there can be but one outcome to this affair. You must stop your harassment forthwith or face the consequences. You have worked things in such a fashion that we have only one resource left. It has been intellectually stimulating to see the way in which you have grappled with this affair, and I say, unaffectedly, that it would be a grief to me to be forced to take any extreme measure. You smile, sir, but I assure you that it really would.'

'Danger is part of my trade,' Holmes had remarked.

'Danger is one thing, Holmes, but willful stupidity is another. You think you know what a mighty organisation we are, but you still are in the dark about its full extent. Let me tell you one thing: we hold all the trumps, and I'll tell you how. You have some old-fashioned ideas about fair play, and that's a millstone round your neck. We set ourselves an aim, and the only consideration is how to achieve it. So, my dear fellow, you see that you cannot win. The dice is loaded in our favour. Fairness, chivalry, sportsmanship? Poppycock!'

'I am afraid that in the pleasure of this conversation I am neglecting business of importance which awaits me elsewhere,' said Holmes, whereupon his adversary also rose looked at him, and shook his head sadly.

'Well, well,' said he, at last. 'It seems a pity, but I have done what I could. I know every move of your game. You can do nothing before Monday. It has been a duel between you and me. You hope to place me in the dock. I tell you that I will never stand in the dock. You hope to beat me. I tell you that you will never beat me. If you are clever enough to bring destruction upon me, rest assured that I shall do as much to you.'

'You have paid me several compliments, Moriarty,' said Holmes. 'Let me pay you one in return when I say that if I were assured of the former eventuality I would, in the interests of the public, cheerfully accept the latter.' This declaration of Holmes filled me with admiration for the man. Not that I had ever doubted that he was the sort who was ready to lay down his life for a cause he believed in.

'I can promise you the one, but not the other,' Moriarty had hissed, reminding the detective of a snake coiling up before an attack, but as he left, he turned round, and said, 'If only you and I could join forces, Holmes, we could hold the whole world.'

'At this point' Holmes said to me, 'he paused, looked at me straight in the eyes, and in a whisper, said, "Holmes, how much is your Mrs Hudson worth to you? Would you take half of two thousand guineas to let her go? I understand that she cocked a snoop at you. Men like us don't forgive slights easily, do we?" He left without waiting for an answer.'

'That was my singular interview with Professor Moriarty,' Holmes told me, admitting that he had not immediately appreciated the last insinuation.

It was in the following week that my employer encountered a series of misadventures at least once every day, all of them potentially fatal to him,..

It made me smile to find him so shaken when he came to me, like a child running to his mother for protection. On Monday he came into the house pale as a ghost, shaking, I made him a cup of tea and he told me how, on his way to Oxford Street, as he was passing the corner which leads from Bentinck Street on to Welbeck Street, had he not sprang for the footpath, he would surely have been trampled to death by a two-horse van which was obviously aiming to do just that. He had not the slightest doubt in his mind that it was something Moriarty had a hand in.

Next day as he walked down Vere Street, he instinctively raised his head when he heard a rustle and saw two men on the roof of one of the houses. At that very moment they dropped a couple of bricks which missed him by a hair's breadth and were shattered to fragments at his feet. He called the police and explained what he had seen. They examined the place and concluded that as there were slates and bricks piled up on the roof, it seemed that some repairs were being prepared and that it was the wind which had toppled over those bricks. We crime detectors, Inspector Emley told him with a smile, are always imagining wrongdoing even when there is none. It goes with the job.

That was unfortunately not the end of Mr Holmes' troubles. Less than twenty-four hours after the brick incident, he was attacked by a ruffian with a bludgeon. He had been on his guard, was able to knock him down and hand him over to the police.

'But I can tell you with utmost confidence, Mrs Hudson, that no possible connection will ever be traced between the gentleman upon whose front teeth I have barked my knuckles, and the mathematical genius, who is, I dare say, working out problems upon a blackboard some ten miles away.'

Although he had claimed that he never gave advice, I was not surprised when he did. 'As Moriarty has an army of henchmen ready to carry out his dastardly orders, you and I must not baulk at enlisting as much help as we can muster. I know that you have some very resourceful friends.' He hinted that should I seek shelter in Water Lane. Naturally I would never dream of leaving him all alone in Baker Street to face the villainous professor.

'Until now I have refrained from alarming the doctor, but we need all the help we can get. He's the only man I can trust one hundred percent, so I might well...' He never finished the sentence.

I'll own to having some uncharitable thoughts concerning the amiable doctor. He is a good sincere man, fearless and devoted to his friend, but he reminds me of the story of the man who was befriended by a bear. Watching over his human friend dozing under a tree with peerless devotion, when he saw a bee land on his face, he thought he would do his friend a favour by hitting it with a big stone. Clearly here Sherlock Holmes was allowing loyalty precedence over common sense. I kept this uncharitable thought to myself.

I now know that Holmes went to visit Watson to confide in him his fears, but refused his generous hospitality, as he did not wish to endanger his life. I know that he was also concerned about leaving me unprotected at Number 221B.

Much of what happened later, has been chronicled by Dr Watson in his touching account of Holmes' final moment. He clearly had no idea of what part I played. For instance, he never mentioned my being kidnapped. He was probably unaware of this for a long time. I will come to that later.

In his account Watson describes how he accompanied Holmes to Newhaven, Brussels and Strasbourg.

He left his practice in the hands of his neighbour and was ready to travel at one day's notice. Holmes had given him a list of precise instructions and made him understand that he was to stick to them scrupulously.

'You are now playing a double-handed game with me against the cleverest rogue and the most powerful syndicate of criminals in Europe,' he quoted Holmes as saying. He then gave the doctor instructions about what to do with the luggage, and to make sure that he got to Victoria in time for the departure of the Continental Express. He had (unnecessarily) arranged for Mycroft to be part of the show, by convincing his brother to play the part of a coachman. He has always been in thrall to sensationalism. He would have been a big success putting on those melodramas the public are always clamouring for. Why, Holmes would have been a resounding success at anything.

Watson had been told that the second first class carriage from the front would be reserved for them. With his army training, the doctor was used to obeying orders and he naturally followed Holmes's injunctions to the letter. When he arrived at Victoria, he was pleased that so far all had gone well. His luggage was waiting for him and he had no difficulty in finding the carriage which Holmes had indicated, the less so as it was the only one in the train which was marked "ENGAGED".

The doctor began to fret when only seven minutes from departure there was no sign of his friend. He searched in vain among the groups of travellers and leave-takers for the distinctive figure of his friend, but found no sign of him. To quote from Dr Watson's account again:

> '*I spent a few minutes in assisting a venerable Italian priest, who was endeavouring to make a porter understand, in his broken English, that his luggage was to be booked through to Paris. Then, having taken another look round, I returned to my carriage, where I found that the porter, in spite of the ticket, had given me the decrepit Italian priest as a travelling companion. It was useless for me to explain to him that his presence was an intrusion, for my Italian was even more limited than his English, so I shrugged my shoulders resignedly, and continued to look out anxiously for my friend. A chill of fear had come over me, as I thought that his absence might mean that some blow had fallen during the night. Already the doors had all been shut and the whistle blown, when—*

> '*My dear Watson,' said a voice, 'you have not even condescended to say Good morning.'*

The excellent doctor still did not understand, and he gamely admits this.

> '*I turned in uncontrollable astonishment, the aged ecclesiastic had turned his face towards me. For an instant the wrinkles were smoothed away, the nose drew away from the chin, the lower lip ceased to protrude and the mouth to mumble, the dull eyes regained their fire, the drooping figure expanded.*

The next the whole frame collapsed again, and Holmes had gone as quickly as he had come.'

'Good heavens!' I cried, 'how you startled me!'

'Every precaution is still necessary,' Holmes whispered. 'I have reason to think that they are hot upon our trail. Ah, there is Moriarty himself.'

The train had already begun to move as Holmes spoke. I quote Watson again:

'Glancing back, I saw a tall man pushing his way furiously through the crowd, and waving his hand as if he desired to have the train stopped. It was too late, however, for we were rapidly gathering momentum, and an instant later had shot clear of the station.'

I have my reason to doubt that it was Moriarty, although the possibility cannot be entirely discarded. Back to the accredited chronicler:

'With all our precautions, you see that we have cut it rather fine,' said Holmes, laughing. He rose, and throwing off the black cassock and hat which had formed his disguise, he packed them away in a handbag.

'Have you seen the morning paper, Watson?'

'No.'

'You haven't seen about Baker Street, then?'

'Baker Street?'

'They set fire to our rooms last night, but no great harm was done.

'Good heavens, Holmes! This is intolerable.'

'They must have lost my track completely after their bludgeon-man was arrested. Otherwise they could not have imagined that I had returned to my rooms. They have evidently taken the precaution of watching you, however, and that is what has brought Moriarty to Victoria. You could not have made any slip in coming?'

'I did exactly what you advised.'

Moriarty having missed the train, Holmes said, 'I know how the minds of criminals work, this train stops at Canterbury. There is always at least a quarter of an hour's delay at the boat. He will catch us there.'

Dr Watson wondered why Holmes did not get him arrested on his arrival.

'We should get the big fish, but the smaller would dart right and left out of the net. On Monday we should have them all. No, an arrest is inadmissible.'

They decided to make a cross-country journey to Newhaven, and so over to Dieppe. The detective expected that Moriarty would get on to Paris, mark down our luggage, and wait for two days at the depot, whilst they would arrange for the final lap to Switzerland, via Luxembourg and Basel. So they got down at Canterbury and waited a whole hour for their train to Newhaven.

I was still looking rather ruefully after the rapidly disappearing luggage-van which contained my wardrobe, when Holmes pulled my sleeve and pointed up the line.

They made their way to Brussels that night and spent two days there, moving on upon the third day as far as Strasbourg.

It's time to explain my own involvement in this drama. A week earlier, when Holmes was obliged to leave London for just one day, and, having the house to myself, I had the shock of my life when the villainous

Moriarty burst in like a starving fox in a chicken coop. He is a powerful man and had no difficulty in overpowering me and giving me an injection. When I woke up, I knew not how long afterwards, I found myself tied to a bed and through the window I perceived a mountainous landscape, with snow on the caps. A persistent rumble revealed itself to be coming from a cataract. I am not much given to screaming, so I lay there making conjectures about what might have happened, and where I might have landed. The only sure thing was that I had been kidnapped by Moriarty and was being kept prisoner in this lodge, possibly in Switzerland, as a sort of trade off. Perhaps he was going to hand me over to Sigsmund, or use me to lure his nemesis to his death. I had never felt so helpless in all my life. How I had hoped that I would have been able to join forces with my esteemed employer to defeat the hateful man! Now I was a millstone round his neck.

I found out later that Moriarty had a double agenda. He had been quoted as saying that effectively he operated like a man with two brains, being able to handle two unrelated issues at the same time, like a virtuoso pianist her two hands. He was negotiating with the King *and* planning to use me to get at Holmes. With his organisational skills, he had planned everything to perfection. His army of spies had kept him informed of Holmes' impending absence, and to one such as he, no doors remained unopened for long if he wished it otherwise. It transpired that he had a team of fake undertakers bring in a coffin in a hired hearse. Having drugged me, they forced me inside it and in blissful ignorance, I was doing a Cook's tour of the Continent. He had naturally seen to it that I had enough oxygen, by dint of cleverly drilled holes. He had left instructions to Holmes about how to save me if, as he expected, chivalry got the better of caution. '*Sigsmund wants Miss Adler alive, but will still pay if she dies.*' he had written. '*My spies will be watching every single step you take and will report to me on a twice-daily basis.*' He had rightly read the mind of Sherlock Holmes - an easy enough feat. To such a man, doing nothing was not an option. He would have come to my rescue even if he thought that the chances were a million to one against.

My gaolers were two surly Swiss men in their forties, Otto and Raoul. They fed me and took me to the closet, locking me in when I needed to use the facilities. They were curt but courteous. There was no escape. Even if that possibility existed, I would not have wanted to leave Holmes to face his fate on his own. Whilst in there, I studied the lie of the land. I identified the outlines of the Eiger, Mönch and Jungfrau, and knew now that I was in Meiringen or Interlaken. Yes, the Reichenbach Falls. At other times, I was kept tied to the bed.

After three days (might have been four), Moriarty himself showed up. He greeted me with outward friendliness and bonhomie.

'I have great news for you at last. Holmes and Watson have finally arrived and, following my instructions, have put up at the *Englischer Hof*. I am expecting the King's right hand man later in the afternoon, so, as you shall see, the scene is set for the last round.'

I was speechless and just stared at him stupidly. He pretended to leave, but arriving at the door, he tut tutted. 'My mind's going, I have a little treat for you.' Then, just like theatrical villains, he clapped his hands and my surly gaolers came in. He spoke German to them and I gathered that he was sending them to fetch something or someone called Clocko. Strangely I had already experienced the sensation of being in Moriarty's claws when I was delirious with fever. I felt that this made it easier to handle the situation now, under these very real circumstances. What or who the hell is Clocko, I wondered, but it did not take me long to discover.

The two men were sweating profusely as they dragged in a massive contraption in cast iron almost reaching to the ceiling, which looked like the inside of a giant clock, painted red and green. From its top came a cord over of a pulley.

'My own design. I got my esteemed German friend Klaus von Helder, you know, the man who made my treasured air-rifle here,' he said tapping on his notorious weapon. 'I got him to make it for me. Clocko I call it. You never know when a little persuasion might be called for in my line of work.' I assumed a complete lack of interest in Clocko, feeling in my bones that it was not going to do me much good. Moriarty clicked his fingers imperiously and Otto came forward and gave him a key to wind the machine up. Moriarty inserted the winder in a hole and turned it round a few times, the end of the rope coming down gradually until the spring seemed as tight as it could be. He then expertly made a noose and Raoul came forward, bent down with a smile, lowered his neck and Moriarty inserted his head into it. At this point, the rope was hanging freely and there was no pressure on the Swiss man's neck. To my horror, two minutes later, as the clockwork unwounded, the rope got raised by a few inches. The enormity of what was in store hit me in the face suddenly.

'I think you will agree with me, Miss Adler, that to a non-swimmer five feet six high, a depth of five feet six and a half of water is as lethal as seven hundred, right?' He did not let me answer and went on. 'With Clocko here,' he said, looking at the gadget like it was a much-loved child, 'the moment your feet loses contact with the ground, the hanging process begins. I can assure you that it is an insalubrious experience. After I witnessed the first trial I could hardly touch my food - a side to my nature you wouldn't know. I would not inflict it on my worst enemy unless I had a good reason to. Imagine the mixture of the mental agony, the excruciating inhuman pain as your neck gets stretched and you begin choking. You become blue, your eyes pop out, you feel you are going to explode. Which, regrettably, is the point of it all. Tsk!' So was his plan to hang me? Moriarty was obviously a man who loved the sound of his own voice, for he had not finished.

'I will set it up so that every five minutes the noose will go up by one inch. You are a clever woman, work out for yourself how long it would take for the victim's feet to lose contact the ground.' I didn't mean to but the answer stared me in the eyes right away: much less than one would have thought. Then he spoke to the guard rather sharply.

'Bring a chair for the lady, Raoul, where are your manners?' His eyes were glowing and his face was flushed.

'Now, the two of you, go get the *Arbalète*.'

Arbalète? It was at this point that I noticed that there were markings on the floor. The two underlings came back with a crossbow, mounted on a strong cast iron frame, about half the size of Clocko, painted red and green like Clocko. I guessed these to be markings destined for the use of this new instrument of death. He read my mind.

'Yes, another little masterpiece from Von Helder's workshop. Notice this eyepiece here and admit how impressed you are. It is calibrated for pinpointing to near perfect accuracy where the arrow will hit.' Otto helped Raoul and they fixed the weapon on the markings, punctiliously moving it until they thought that they had got it right. I noticed the arrow was pointing towards Clocko. With obvious relish the Professor made some adjustments and using another key he primed the *Arbalète*.

'A woman with an inquisitive mind such as yours must be wondering how these two little babies will work. In tandem, of course. As you had indubitably surmised. I will set them both so that the moment the victim's feet are seen to be clearly off the floor, the *Arbalète* will shoot its arrow directly into your heart. The precision is faultless. Von Helder said if one misses, the other won't and that got me so angry, I nearly slapped him. Do you know why?' I did, but chose not to answer.

'Because Moriarty does not even begin to entertain the possibility of one of his contraptions not working. That's Moriarty in a nutshell.'

To my horror, I was then forcibly fastened and fixed under Clocko, facing the *Arbalète*, arms legs and torso secured to the chair. I found that I could not move even one-tenth of one inch either way. It was mighty uncomfortable. I watched helplessly as the noose was slipped over my neck.

'I have sent word to the chivalrous Holmes, explaining that your life depends entirely on him. I expect him here in twenty-three minutes. Oh, I don't think we want the asinine Dr Watson here. You agree with me that he is unlikely to be of any succour to either of you. We don't want any witnesses ... so I have arranged a little subterfuge. You will laugh when I tell you.' He had a message delivered to the doctor when he was half way to the "Lodge on the Ledge" (as I would find Moriarty's chalet was called), to the effect that his professional services were urgently required by a pregnant fellow countrywoman at the *Englischer Hof*.

Clocko had been inexorably doing its nefarious stretching. The rope had become taut, but as yet the pressure on my neck was bearable. I heard the two Swiss guards search Holmes who seemed to have just arrived, and confirm that he had come unarmed. The moment he walked into the room, I heard the cog turn and felt the noose tightening, but I controlled myself. One look at me completely unsettled him. I saw the colour leave his face to be replaced by the darkest of looks. He clenched his fists and bit his lips, but he obviously knew that it was not meet for him to show his rage. Moriarty was like an excited child, and could not hide his jubilation at our plight.

'By far the happiest day of my life,' he chuckled. Needlessly he embarked upon an exposition of what was happening.

'In eleven minutes exactly,' he said, looking at his watch, 'this game is coming to an end. You obviously want to save Miss Adler and at the same time you want me, right? You can't have both. I may be wrong but I have formed the opinion that you are a man of honour. Just give me your word that you will hand over to me that incriminating sheet of paper without which no case can stand against me. Promise that never again will you meddle with my affairs, and I will release Miss Adler. You can both go back to London. Sigsmund can go to hell.' The pressure on my neck was now becoming uncomfortable. Suddenly I felt the cog turn and the rope tighten viciously round my neck. This seemed to me to be happening to another woman. From this point lucidity and confusion started playing a game of see-saw.

'I don't know if I am a man of honour, Moriarty, but I know that you are not.'

'Absolutely right,' laughed the professor. 'Honour is a hollow concept, believe me. But what is your point?

'Right, if I give you the undertaking *and* the document, what's to stop you going ahead with your dastardly plan anyway?'

Moriarty seemed lost for words. He kept quiet for a while, peered at me, then at Holmes. I was now a child on father's shoulder, walking in the Highland mists. Although these were happy memories, I willed them away and forced reality to take over.

'You know Holmes,' I clearly heard Moriarty say, 'I could surprise you and act honourably. I was not born a villain. Circumstances made me one. When I was young, all I wanted was to become the best mathematician in the world, discover new theorems, solve unproved conjectures. I knew that I had the ability. I never dreamt of riches, but when I realised that my lifetime ambition of proving Fermat's Last Theorem was going to be an impossibility, I suffered a mental shock. You could say I became deranged.' Holmes had been listening with some interest to the outpourings of the madman.

'So you got nowhere with Fermat?' said Holmes in a sympathetic tone, but Moriarty exploded with rage on hearing this. His face turned crimson and he shook his fist at his enemy.

'How dare you say that? I proved everything except one piffling case. Those envious academics would deride me if I explained what I had done.'

'And what did you succeed in proving?' Holmes asked. Moriarty looked at him in disgust but softened his gaze.

'Do you really want to know?'

'I won't understand it. Mathematics is not my forte, but I did read your paper on the Binomial Theorem.'

'Binomial theorem, tut tut. That's what my enemies call it to diminish me. It was the basis for my proof of Fermat.' He produced a sheet of paper from his inside pocket, and spoke very calmly.

'My proof for the impossibility of solving the equation. x to the power of n plus y to the power of n equals z to the power of n, where z is clearly x plus an integer Ω. Here it is.' My eyesight had become blurred so I did not see him hand over the paper to my putative saviour. 'I proved it when I was in my twenties, but for one case which has eluded me until now. I mean the special case when Ω equals 1.' In spite of the pain which had completely invaded all the parts of my body I pricked my ears in order not to miss a single syllable of what was being said.

'Over the last thirty years, not a day has gone by when I have not tried a new approach towards solving it. In vain of course. It has driven me insane. I admit it. It lies at the root of all my villainies. It is solely responsible for those atrocious things that I have committed.'

'Let me have a good look?' I heard Holmes mutter. At this point my eyesight cleared momentarily. I saw Moriarty eagerly pressing the sheet of paper into Holmes' hand, all the time keeping his eyes on me and on his satanic implements. Holmes peered at the sheet, and a broad smile appeared on his face.

'Moriarty,' he said. 'You are a ninny. You have proved the wretched theorem, man.' The professor frowned, thinking that his enemy was mocking him.

'All right, you can't do the case of z equals x plus 1, you say. But isn't that the same as y plus a number different from 1? You can prove *that*? Yes, professor, you had proved it all the time.'

Although my feet were no longer touching the floor and I was choking, I was able to see Moriarty reel back, his face flushed, but with joy this time and not anger. He was trembling with emotion, jumping up and down like a schoolboy eagerly awaiting the bell announcing the start of the school holiday. Holmes took this opportunity to knock him down with force, at the same time seizing his air-rifle. He kept it pointed at the villain but was able to aim a bullet straight at the pulley on the top of Clocko. This led to an immediate relaxation of the rope round my neck causing me to fall back on my chair. He just managed to cut down the rope tying my hands, but the *Arbalète* had been programmed to shoot its lethal arrow in our direction at that exact time. It did so without warning, and went through Holmes in the back with a thud. So powerful was its impact that it emerged through his breast. I saw a small fountain of blood spurt out of the dear man, and nearly fainted. He reeled back and fell down blood continuing to gush out of the gash. At the same moment Otto and Raoul rushed in. I grabbed the air-rifle and pointed it at them. There were too many things happening at the same time. Moriarty was going to recover, and Holmes was out of action. I had no alternative. I shot each of the two men in the leg. Then I hit Moriarty in the head with the butt of his own weapon. I lifted it up with both my hands, and pushed it down hard against the wooden floor. Twice. Holmes was bleeding profusely, but he made a superhuman effort to stand up. Unexpected Moriarty sprang up threw himself at me, grabbed the air-rifle from my hand and punched me hard on my face two or three times. He was now again in command.

'I am going to throw you down the Reichenbach Falls, Holmes. All my problems solved. Ha! Ha! Ha!' In my dazed state I could hear him cackle like a madman. He took hold of the near lifeless Sherlock Holmes and dragged him out onto the ledge. I could hardly walk but managed to drag my broken body outside by crawling on my hands and knees. Suddenly Holmes seemed to become more animated. Then, as in a dream I watched the two men grapple with each other at the top of the ledge whilst the torrents roared down below. Holmes was fighting for his life valiantly, but he had lost too much blood and clearly he was not a match for the stronger, fitter Moriarty. I should have smashed his head much harder, and a few times more. I managed to stand up and totter a few steps. I tried to shout for help, but no voice would come out of me. In any case, who was there to hear me? My eyes suddenly became more focused and I saw it happen as in a dream: as Moriarty held Holmes up by the scruff for the final push into the void, the tip of the arrow protruding through his chest went straight into the professor's eye. He recoiled in horror, screamed with pain, dropped his quarry like a hot stone, and swivelled round inexplicably. As I watched him take the plunge, I felt reinvigorated, as if I had drunk a magical potion. I am sure I heard him shout Feeermaaaat! as he plunged to his certain death. Against common sense, Sherlock, who was nearer the edge, crumpled, slipping nearer the ledge of the precipice. In the new state I was in, I found the extra strength to rush towards him and pull him up. Exhausted, we lay there waiting for a miracle.

When the miracle happened, it was in the shape of a herdsman. I arranged for my beloved friend to recover in a clinic in Interlaken. He was in a coma for weeks. When he recovered I arranged for him to convalesce in a home in the same town.

Some months later, poor Watson recounted in his touching account, how heartbroken he was when he thought that his friend had perished with his nemesis.

The reason he ignored the facts was that Holmes and I went to Australia together and travelled the length and breadth of that great country. We blamed ourselves later for not thinking of informing our friends of our sojourn down under. Holmes had an excuse, he was suffering from shock. I had none, unless it was true that I had a school girl crush on the man. I doubt it. After six months, Sherlock having recovered fully went back to London, but I stayed a bit longer, as my delightful 'husband' Algernon to whom I had finally written, had informed me of his impending visit.

Note

San Cassimally will welcome any correspondence on the book at san-cass@ blueyonder.co.uk

If you enjoyed the *Case Book of Irene Adler*, why not try the second book, *The Memoirs of Irene Adler*, also available on the Kindle Store as well as in printed form.

Made in the USA
Charleston, SC
03 July 2014